ECLIPSE DANCER

PRAISE FOR THE PEACEMAKER'S TALE SERIES

"Authentic detail, believable action and perceptive insights into connections between past and present help make these novels into significant contributions to our understanding of who we are and where we came from."

— *THE BEACON*

"Sure to keep readers turning the pages... As usual, the Gears, husband-and-wife archaeologists, have enriched and enhanced the gripping plot with plenty of anthropological, archaeological, and historical detail."

— *BOOKLIST*

"Fastidious attention to detail—in politics, military strategy, trade, dress and characterization—make for a fascinating ride."

— *PUBLISHERS WEEKLY*

ECLIPSE DANCER

THE PEACEMAKER'S TALE
BOOK EIGHT

W. MICHAEL GEAR

KATHLEEN O'NEAL GEAR

WOLFPACK
PUBLISHING
— EST 2015 —

Eclipse Dancer
Paperback Edition
Copyright © 2024 (As Revised) W. Michael Gear and
Kathleen O'Neal Gear

Wolfpack Publishing
1707 E. Diana Street
Tampa, Florida 33609

wolfpackpublishing.com

Illustrations by Ellisa Mitchel.

Paperback ISBN 978-1-63977-683-2
eBook ISBN 978-1-63977-682-5

To Jake and Shannon, our faithful muses for Gitchi

ACKNOWLEDGMENTS

There is a magical word in the Seneca language, usually stated at the beginning of the story, and by which a story may be told as a serial: *ensegaha'a*.

It has taken us around a half million words, and eight books, to convey a semblance of the richness and complexity of the Peacemaker tale. We hope you enjoy this epic tale.

NONFICTION
INTRODUCTION

The term "bury the hatchet" dates to around four
hundred years ago, just after European colonists
arrived in northeastern North America and
became acquainted with the traditions of the native
peoples, but the practice of ending violence by
burying weapons has a much older history.

Archaeologists debate the origins of the tradition, but one thing is probably certain: the elite
members of Cahokian society practiced this rite.
Cahokia, a World Heritage Site just outside of St.
Louis, Illinois, is truly one of the world's magnificent archaeological sites. Cahokia was a part of the
Mississippian moundbuilder tradition. We wrote
about this culture in *People of the River* in 1992. In
twenty years, we have learned so much more about
their astounding empire, which flourished from

around A.D. 700-1550. Peoples who belonged to this cultural tradition covered the eastern half of the United States with mound cities and were master architects, builders, astronomers, surgeons, as well as shell, stone, copper, and fabric artisans. Cahokian traders plied their wares across the North American continent. And they, like Iroquoian peoples five hundred years later, also "buried the hatchet."

At a unique hilltop site in the American Bottoms region of Illinois, the Grossman Site, archaeologists discovered a large collection of buried weapons—Pauketat, 2009. The site contains more than one hundred houses and was occupied by the Cahokian elite. Near one of the council houses, archaeologists excavated a cache of seventy buried ax heads. The largest, which had been deliberately placed on top of the cache, weighed around twenty pounds and was twenty inches long. Interestingly, the axe heads had been laid into the pit in discrete sets, as though each clan, or family, had taken turns. Usually they were placed in the pit in pairs, but one set contained twelve axe heads.

From an archaeological perspective, this is clearly a symbolic act. In our modern culture, it would be like finding a collection of buried swords with Excalibur on top. Lest you've forgotten, Excalibur was King Arthur's legendary sword.

We can only speculate about what Cahokians

might have believed, but we know that Iroquoian peoples thought that burying weapons would submerge them in the river of Great Grandmother Earth's blood that ran beneath the surface of the earth. Her blood purified the weapons, cleansing them of the hatred and despair associated with warfare.

The earliest reference to Iroquoian peoples burying weapons is found in the rich oral history of the Peacemaker tale.

We say "oral" history, because it's generally believed that North American's native cultures had no written languages. Many archaeologists have suspected for a long time that such an assumption is false, but it's been very hard to prove that the symbols we find in the archaeological record represent a written language. Wampum—more correctly called "otekoa"—may be the exception. At least a "protolanguage," a precursor, it may have been much more.

The problem arises because of definitions of what constitutes "writing." Wampum consists of a set of blackish-purple and white symbols, recorded most often with shell beads. However, the Iroquois believe that before shell wampum existed, wampum was created with black and white painted pieces of wood. The Mohawk say that the first wampum was made using different colors of eagle quills—Tehanetorens, 1999, p. 12.

Wampum could be "read" by anyone who'd been trained.

The earliest European historical records corroborate that each bead, row, or character had a definite meaning, and further state that both sides of the belt were read. Lengthy documents, for example, the minutes of meetings, the details of treaties, the Constitution of the League of the Iroquois, and much more, were recorded on belts so completely that they could still be read centuries later. In the 1700s, Moravian missionary John Heckewelder reported that wampum readers had the ability "to point out the exact place on a belt which is to answer each particular sentence, the same as we can point out a passage in a book"— Heckewelder, p. 108—and added that a great deal depended on the "*turning* of the belt," saying that "it may be as well known by it how far the speaker has advanced in his speech, as with us on taking a glance at the pages of a book or pamphlet while reading."

Knotting wampum, tying the shells in place, was considered to be a spiritual activity in which writers "talked" their messages into the shells, which sounds very much like they were recording words or phrases. And this was apparently an ancient tradition. Archaeologists have found wampum beads that date back more than two thousand years to the Adena Culture in Ohio—Slotkin and Schmitt, pp. 223-225. We wrote about Adena and Hopewell cultures in *People of the Lakes*.

The term "wampum belt" is slightly misleading. In our culture, a belt is something that encircles the waist. Depending upon how much information was being recorded, Iroquoian belts could be four or five feet long and just as wide. Prehistorically, they may have been even larger.

Because wampum belts faithfully recorded the details of treaties, they presented both the original thirteen colonies, and later the United States government, with a problem. Wampum belts were evidentiary—they had a legal status in courts. It is perhaps no surprise that Indian Agents, traders, state authorities, and anyone else who had access to purchasing wampum belts were hired by the government to acquire these belts so that they could be destroyed. The resulting loss of information can be likened to the destruction of the Mayan codices by Bishop Diego de Landa in A.D. 1562, or the destruction of the Library of Alexandria by Patriarch Theophilus around A.D. 391. The destruction of a people's history is always the first step of conquerors.

Keep in mind that human beings are storytellers. Our cultures are founded upon stories, interpreted through them, and survive because of them. Destroying a civilization doesn't require warfare or plague or starvation. Cultural midnight is always only a generation away. History has demonstrated many times that causing the death of a culture is a relatively easy process: First, destroy a people's written records. Second, destroy their language. When there's no one left who can recite the stories of the people, and no documents to tell the young about them, assimilation into the dominant culture is virtually inevitable. Why? Because when a people's words are lost, they must re-story their world from the traditions of alien nations.

Imagine, for a moment, what it must have been like for Henan Scrogg and Solon Skye, the last two people in the twentieth century able to read the original wampum of the Code of Handsome Lake, knotted by the Prophet himself in the early 1800s —Johansen and Mann, 2000, p. 328. Now imagine what it would be like today to lose the last two people who could read the Declaration of Independence and the Bill of Rights. Certainly Faithkeepers would keep both documents alive as long as possible through oral history, but the truth is that oral traditions are mutable. They change with the failing memories of the elders struggling to preserve them—especially if the young no longer care about such "fables."

The People of the Longhouse, the Haudenosaunee, managed to save some of the most critical wampum belts. They can be seen today in excellent repositories like the Iroquois Indian

Museum in Howes Cave, New York—www.iroquo-ismuseum.org—which was established by the state of New York in 1891.

We encourage you to take a trip to see these fragile, beautiful pieces of American history. Each is a story worth seeing.

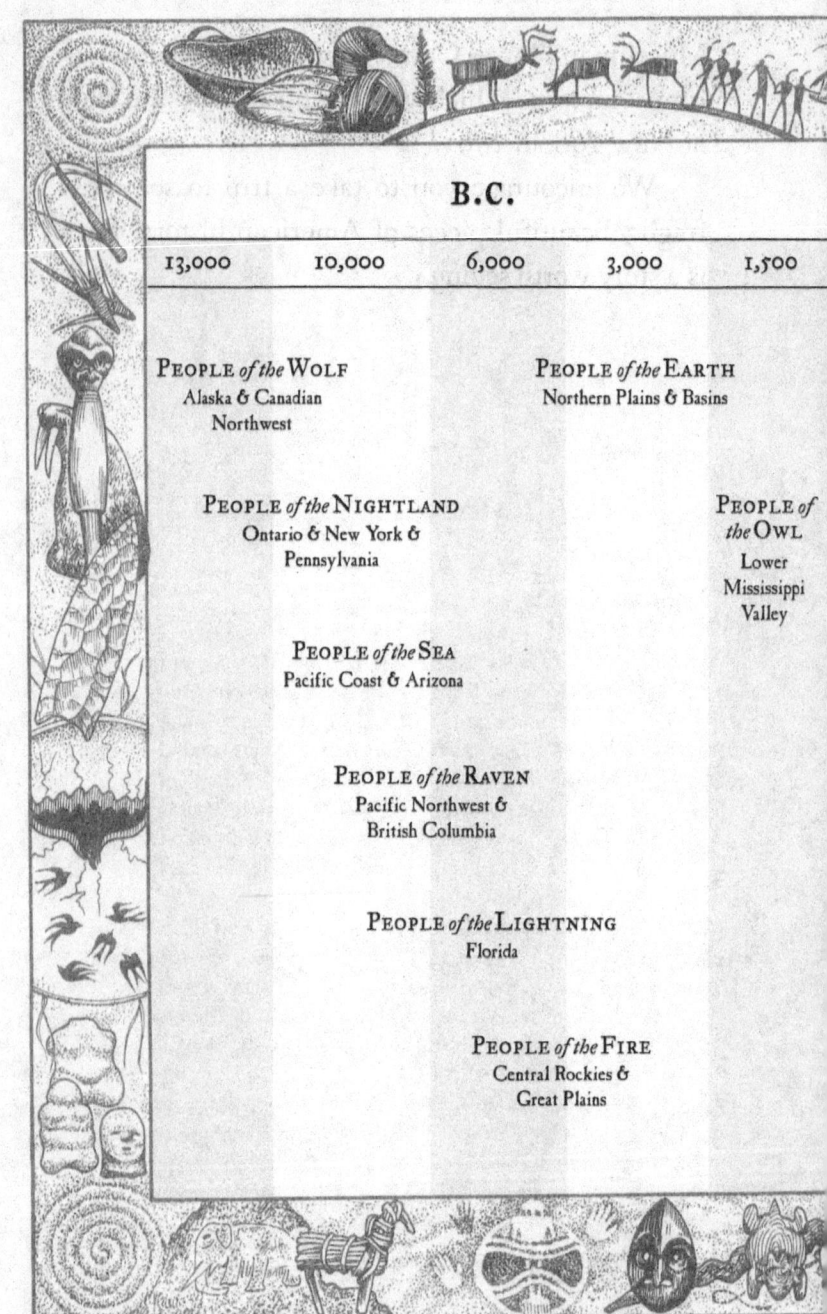

B.C.

13,000	10,000	6,000	3,000	1,500

PEOPLE *of the* **WOLF**
Alaska & Canadian
Northwest

PEOPLE *of the* **EARTH**
Northern Plains & Basins

PEOPLE *of the* **NIGHTLAND**
Ontario & New York &
Pennsylvania

PEOPLE *of
the* **OWL**
Lower
Mississippi
Valley

PEOPLE *of the* **SEA**
Pacific Coast & Arizona

PEOPLE *of the* **RAVEN**
Pacific Northwest &
British Columbia

PEOPLE *of the* **LIGHTNING**
Florida

PEOPLE *of the* **FIRE**
Central Rockies &
Great Plains

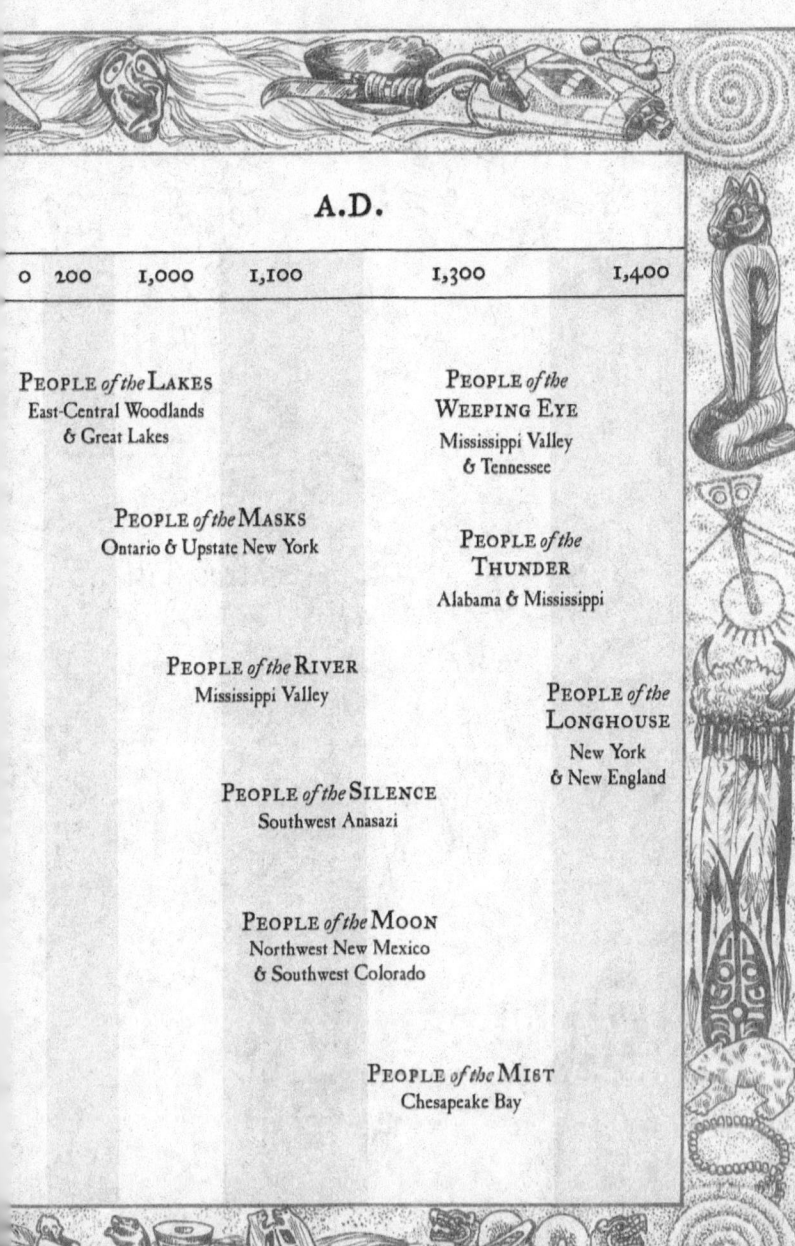

A.D.

| 0 | 200 | 1,000 | 1,100 | 1,300 | 1,400 |

PEOPLE *of the* LAKES
East-Central Woodlands
& Great Lakes

PEOPLE *of the*
WEEPING EYE
Mississippi Valley
& Tennessee

PEOPLE *of the* MASKS
Ontario & Upstate New York

PEOPLE *of the*
THUNDER
Alabama & Mississippi

PEOPLE *of the* RIVER
Mississippi Valley

PEOPLE *of the*
LONGHOUSE
New York
& New England

PEOPLE *of the* SILENCE
Southwest Anasazi

PEOPLE *of the* MOON
Northwest New Mexico
& Southwest Colorado

PEOPLE *of the* MIST
Chesapeake Bay

Skanodario Lake

Canassatego Village ○

IROQUOIA
The Lands of the
People of the
Longhouse

Atotarho Village
Yellowtail Village
Bur Oak Village
White Dog Village

Forks River

Singleleaf Village

Wild River Village

Rapid River

The Lands of the
People of the
Dawnland

Hawk Moth
Village

Forks River

Singleleaf
Village

Wild River
Village

Bog
Willow
Village

Pine
Hill
Village

Rapid River

IROQUOIA

Quill River

Quill River

ECLIPSE DANCER

1

Cloud People blanketed the night sky, turning it pitch black and ominous. The mist rising from Reed Marsh had a damp, caressing feel against Gonda's face. He adjusted his pack, checked his slung bow and quiver, and examined the shoulder-width hole they'd chopped from the frozen soil beneath the exterior palisade. The black oval was barely visible. Situated at the point farthest away from Yellowtail Village, the enemy warriors on the Yellowtail catwalks could not possibly observe their emergence from the ground. There could, however, be fifty men with bows sitting in the limbs of the nearby trees, watching for the slightest movements along the Bur Oak palisades.

Gonda turned to his volunteers. "Last chance. Anyone who wishes to back out should do so now."

Three warriors stood with him, their breaths frosting and mingling in the night air. Each carried a bow and overstuffed quiver, and wore a knee-length black shirt and high-topped black moccasins. In addition, they'd covered every bit of exposed skin with soot. In the darkness he thought Sindak and Wampa had their arms folded, but couldn't be sure. Young Papon noisily swallowed. Eighteen summers old, he had buck teeth that made him tend to slur his words. He also had a reputation for exaggeration. But Jigonsaseh insisted he was a bold fighter—and that's what Gonda needed tonight.

He whispered, "All right. High Matron Kittle has ordered the fires extinguished to help cover our movements. Our opponents probably assume it is to conserve firewood. But they may also think we're up to something."

"They do," Sindak said from Gonda's right. "This isn't normal. They know we have wounded and children to keep warm. They'll be especially on guard."

Gonda nodded, though he knew they probably couldn't see it. "I just spoke with War Chief Deru. He's ready. He'll be watching for us to emerge from the marsh at the predetermined location. Once he either sees us, or the fires erupt, he will begin his diversion. When we're in the marsh, we must take our time. We don't want to startle any of the birds perched on the reeds and cattails. Any sudden squawking or chirping and we're all dead."

Sindak waited for Gonda to continue. When he didn't, Sindak added, "Also, if you must get out of the marsh, be vigilant about the patches of snow that still cling against the western palisade wall. Not only will they crunch if you step on them, your blackened body will show up clear as day."

Gonda looked for nodding heads, but the sable darkness cloaked their bodies so completely they were just faintly darker silhouettes cast against the cobalt background.

"One last thing," Gonda said. "As soon as we're through this hole, it will be covered up. The only way we're getting back into Bur Oak Village is through the front gates, and the guards have orders not to open them for us unless we're in the clear. Understand?"

Papon slurred, "So, if we're being closely followed, they won't open the gates?"

"That's right."

Papon shifted uncomfortably. He had a wife and four children.

Gonda lowered his voice, and used a deadly tone. "And I don't want any misunderstandings. Each of us is expendable. Our only purpose is to buy the people in Bur Oak Village a chance. Anyone who is caught, wounded, or doesn't make the rendezvous *will be left behind.* Those are Matron Jigonsaseh's orders. Am I clear?"

He heard grunts of assent.

"Very well. Everyone ready?"

"Ready." Sindak's voice.

"Me, too." War Chief Wampa.

Barely audible, Papon hissed, "Yes."

Gonda got down on his knees, shrugged out of his pack and weapons, and pushed them through ahead of him as he slid into the hole on his belly. Coming up on the other side like a muskrat through an ice hole, he shouldered his load and crawled toward the marsh. The old autumn leaves that covered the ground were drenched with mist, quiet and slick. When he reached the marsh's edge, he eased aside the reeds and glided into the water. He almost gasped at the bitter cold, but stopped himself. Sindak entered the water next, followed by Wampa and Papon.

Gonda looked around. Here, it was dark, but in forty paces, the halo of firelight streaming from Yellowtail Village gave the calm water a supernatural sheen. The dark reflections of the trees stood out so clearly they might have been painted upon the marsh. Fortunately, the cattails grew thickly there, too. The stripes they cast upon the water would cloak their shapes...he hoped.

"You all know the plan," Gonda whispered.

Silence.

"Sindak comes with me. Wampa, you and Papon are the best shots in the village. You will remain in the marsh, paralleling our course, with your bows aimed at the palisade. You'll see warriors targeting us long before we do."

Wampa's head turned. Around two hundred enemy warriors stood on the catwalks, talking, joking, ripping off strips of jerky with their teeth. Their conversations drifted through the still night air. Wampa was probably wondering how the thirty arrows in her quiver, plus another thirty in Papon's, could possibly make a difference.

Gonda continued, "Wampa and Papon, don't leave the marsh unless you're forced to. Use the cattails, rushes, and trees as cover when you let fly. As soon as Sindak and I have finished our last duty —if we're able—we're going to come boiling back into the marsh, and we'll all make our way back to Bur Oak Village. Any questions?"

The only sound was the slight rustling of reeds.

"Then let's go."

Gonda bent low and began wading through the waist-deep water. Mist swirled by, scalloped here and there with the curls spun off their arm movements as they pushed aside a cattail, pointed to a floating branch, or sleeping bird, or adjusted quivers when they slipped sideways.

Cold, bitter and numbing, ate into Gonda's feet and legs. He moved around a thick stand of reeds and waded into the copper-colored portion of the marsh that shone in the firelight streaming from Yellowtail Village. Reflections of tree branches combined with those of the reeds to form a dark filigree upon the water. The effect was stunningly beautiful—perhaps more so because Gonda suspected it might be his last such sight.

Gonda studied the treetops, then pointed out the two sentries high in the branches. Placed as they were, they'd be sure to spot anyone who tried to sneak between the marsh and Yellowtail Village. If it were Negano's work, it was smartly done.

Gonda hissed, "Wampa, shoot them first."

"Understood." She touched Papon's shoulder, pointed at herself, then the man on the right. Next, she pointed to Papon, and the man on the left. He jerked his head in understanding, and the two began to wade toward their targets.

Gonda's gaze returned to the Hills' warriors on the catwalks. One man was gesturing wildly as he told some story. The others around him smiled and nodded, then laughed out loud.

"All right, Sindak." Gonda gestured to chokecherries, masking the shoreline. "I'll go first."

Gonda maneuvered through the cattails to the stand of chokecherries. Their smooth gray-brown bark shone with firelight. He ducked down behind them, waiting until Sindak caught up and crouched beside him.

Gonda looked at him. In the reflected light, patterned by cattails, Sindak's lean face might have been carved of stone, but the lines around his deeply sunken eyes had gone tight. The War Chief's gaze methodically studied the palisade, noting faces, probably saying names in his head. Was he remembering moments of laughter with these men and women? Perhaps times when he'd saved their lives? Or they, his?

Gonda asked, "The jokester and the three men beside him, who are they?"

"The jokester, on the far right, is War Chief Joondoh of Turtleback Village. He's short, so he makes up for it by being loud. The tall, thin man beside him is Oswego, one of his deputy war chiefs. The other two warriors are from Atotarho Village." A barely audible tightness entered his voice: "Lonkol and Tadu."

Gonda was watching Sindak very closely. "Tell me about them."

Sindak shrugged as though there wasn't much to tell. "Both are good warriors."

"Married?"

"Yes."

"What are their wives' names?"

Sindak shot Gonda a look that seemed to see straight through to Gonda's souls. "Osto and Tawisa." He hesitated. "Why?"

"I'm just wondering how you can kill them."

Sindak frowned. "Now is a fine time to ask."

"I thought I'd wait until you could see their faces."

"Their faces? You thought...what? That I'd crumble when I saw them?"

Gonda exhaled hard. "I suspect some of these warriors are lifelong friends, men and women who have guarded your back in a hundred battles. Some may have saved your life, and you are about to repay them by killing them." Gonda paused to study Sindak's stony features. "I'm not sure I could kill my friends and relatives."

Sindak didn't respond. He was staring at the people on the catwalk. The longer he looked, the harder the set of his mouth became.

Wind Woman's gentle daughter, Gaha, swept the surface of the pond, turning it into a sea of golden glitter, broken here and there by swaying cattails. The scent of the oak fires kindled in Yellowtail Village wafted over them.

"Jigonsaseh says you were such a beloved war chief that your people will hesitate to kill you if they see you. I, on the other hand, think the reverse is probably more likely true."

Sindak took a deep breath and nodded his understanding. "You think I will be the one to hesitate?"

"Just tell me why you volunteered to do this."

Sindak looked back at the warriors on the

palisade and his eyes glistened, as though he were straining against his better judgment. Standing silhouetted against the firelight, the warriors made perfect targets. Except for Joondoh's group, most were vigilantly watching Bur Oak Village, the marsh, and scanning the surrounding hills. "May I ask you a question, Gonda?"

"Of course."

"Do you think that you and I are here by chance?"

"Chance? What do you mean?"

"I mean that I think you and I are meant to be here. From that fateful instant twelve summers ago when Towa and I were ordered to help you and Koracoo find the missing children right up to this conversation, I don't think any of it has been chance. Do you believe in Sky Messenger's Dream?"

"If I didn't, I wouldn't be out here with my testicles so frozen they've knotted up against the bottom of my throat."

Firelight reflecting from the marsh danced over Sindak's lean, soot-coated face and seemed alive in his eyes. "Is there anything else you want to know?"

"No."

Gonda looked back at Papon and Wampa. They were almost invisible in the eddying mist.

Both stood watching and waiting, undoubtedly wondering what was taking so long.

"When we get inside the palisade, I'll go right and you go left. The crumbling remains of refugee shelters fill the space between the palisades. It's a trash heap of charred bark, old cloth, torn baskets, and rush matting. Finding quiet footing is going to be the challenge."

"I understand."

Veering around the chokecherries, Gonda got down on his belly, and slid ashore. Sindak was right behind him. They slithered around the patches of snow that dotted the dark leafbed, and headed straight for the southwestern palisade wall of Yellowtail Village. Beneath where War Chief Joondoh and his friends stood, a black gaping hole had been burned through the palisade logs—a vulnerability in the defenses, which probably explained War Chief Joondoh's presence above it.

Heart pounding, Gonda moved with the stealth of a hunting serpent. He still half-expected Sindak to warn his friends and betray their mission.

Wampa and Papon must have managed their tasks in utter silence for the sentries in the marsh had called no alarm.

When they reached the blackened hole, Gonda flattened himself against the wall as he quietly slipped his pack from his shoulders and pushed it through the gap, before he crawled through. A few heartbeats later, Sindak pushed through, glanced at Gonda, then looked up. Through the slats in the catwalk above them, they could see the men moving and hear them talking.

"Ready?" Sindak asked, lips to Gonda's ears.

Gonda gave Sindak a firm nod and bent to his business. His fingers were shaking—from cold and fear—as he untied the laces. Carefully, he removed the pots of walnut oil mixed with pitch, the bag of wood shavings, and pots of hot coals gathered from the fires of the Bur Oak longhouses.

He leaned close to Sindak, busy with his own pack, and whispered. "I think we have around six hundred heartbeats before Deru starts letting fly."

"Which means we have to hurry."

"I'll count to five hundred and meet you back here."

"Good luck!"

Gonda watched Sindak disappear among the shadows and pulled the wooden stopper from his own oil pot. Silently, he moved along beneath the catwalk, tiptoeing through ankle-deep ash, slabs of burned bark, and useless chunks of basketry.

Glancing up, he saw two men standing above him. He edged forward, moving ten paces farther down the wall to a twisted wad of half-burned reed matting.

Gonda dribbled oil on the mat, then shook out a small amount of hot coals in the middle. It would take a little while to catch, but not long. He had to move quickly. The warriors on the catwalks continued talking, laughing, completely unaware of his presence.

When he'd gone halfway around the curve in the wall, one of the warriors on the catwalk suddenly stopped talking in midsentence and leaned over. "Who's there?"

Motionless in the shadows, Gonda thought his heart was going to batter its way through his breastbone.

The man illuminated in the firelight above was a square-jawed man with long hair streaming over his shoulders.

In the midst of thick shadows, Gonda's black-clothed body should blend with the background, but mist glistened in the firelight. If it eddied around him, creating unusual swirls...

"What did you see?" the man's friend asked.

"I don't know. Something moved down there."

"Could be a wood rat. I just about jumped out of my skin last night when one knocked a pot over. They're after the moldy corn kernels scattered down there."

The warrior straightened up, sighed, and went back to his former conversation. "As I was saying, how did the Flint People expect Atotarho to act when he discovered they'd allied themselves with our enemies? They should have known he would ambush their trail home. I tell you, no one hides better than we do! No one is craftier than we are. This war is over. The world belongs to Atotarho."

His friend replied, "I'm sure the Flint People expected us to take revenge, just not so soon. That's one thing Negano did right. That ambush was perfect. You have to admit it."

"Any time you kill four hundred Flint warriors in a single attack, it's a great victory. But that's all Negano has done right. If you're as hungry as I am, you know he's an incompetent fool. Another quarter moon here, and we'll all be starving and desperate enough to slit Negano's throat and eat him to fill our bellies. I can't believe he's the new War Chief, he..."

Gonda stopped breathing. Atotarho ambushed and killed four hundred Flint warriors? Blessed gods, not Cord's war party?

Worry about it later.

Gonda silently tiptoed forward, pouring more pitch and coals into the back of each of the crowded shelters, until he rounded the northern edge of the palisade and could see the Yellowtail gates. No guards stood outside, but around twenty warriors with slung bows overlooked the entry. He could just see the tops of their shoulders and heads over the palisade.

Gonda slipped up to a pile of charred timbers the enemy had scavenged for firewood. Charred wood caught fire quicker and burned hotter. He poured the last of his oil, shavings, and all of the remaining coals at the base of the woodpile. He could already smell smoke on the breeze.

A commotion started along on the southern palisade catwalk that overlooked Bur Oak Village. Questioning voices rose, then someone shouted, "Fire!" and a staccato of feet pounded the catwalk, shaking the palisade. "There are fires all along the wall! Get water!"

Several of the warriors stationed overlooking the northeastern gates ran back to help.

Gonda's heart kicked into a gallop as he raced back, using the noise on the catwalks as cover. Flames danced in at least half the shelters he'd fired. With the commotion, no one seemed to notice him as he thrashed back toward the gap where he was supposed to meet Sindak. He pressed his back against the wall and gritted his teeth, his gaze straining to see Sindak coming around the curve in the wall.

Wait. Wait...

Gonda's gaze shot upward when what appeared to be falling stars began plunging from the darkness. War Chief Deru's diversion was right on time. Flaming arrows punctured the mist and rained down upon Yellowtail Village, lodging in the newly repaired roofs of longhouses, the piles of debris in the plaza, and piercing the bodies of anyone who stood in the plaza. Wave after wave of arrows arced through the night sky. Panicked cries erupted inside Yellowtail Village, accompanied by shouts and desperate running. Atotarho's warriors screamed orders. *Sindak, blessed gods, where are you?*

War Chief Deru's voice boomed from the Bur Oak catwalks, "Fight, you filthy worms!"

"We are attacked!" a man roared. "Get to the southern end of the village. Defend the walls!" Then, "Deru, you have the testicles of a gnat! Only a gutless coward attacks at night!"

The spitting hum of a thousand arrows launched and in flight combined with the rapid-fire *shish-thumps* of stone points impacting wood, frozen ground, and flesh. Ululating clan war cries split the darkness.

Sindak appeared like a ghost from the shadows, and Gonda said, "Come on. Hurry!" and shoved Sindak through the gap in the wall.

Gonda leaped out behind him to find Sindak staring to the north. Men were screaming. Two toppled over the palisade wall, landing hard not more than three paces from them. From the marsh, Wampa and Papon fired smoothly, one arrow after another, taking the warriors in the chests or heads. Several of the Hills warriors had rushed to the western wall to shoot into the marsh at their invisible assailants.

"I don't think we want to go running out there!" Sindak pointed toward the marsh. "Did you notice the pile of timbers stacked outside the gate?"

"I set fire to a big stack of firewood on the inside. That's enough. Let's go!" Gonda grabbed his sleeve and tried to drag him away.

"No, wait!" Sindak jerked back so hard he almost toppled Gonda. "We can use the logs to block the gates. Look!"

Gonda turned and immediately saw what Sindak had noticed. Logs, evidently discarded during makeshift repairs, lay piled near the gate. Inside, a merry blaze was roaring through Gonda's woodpile.

"Blessed gods. You're a diabolical weasel, Sindak." He slapped him on the shoulder. "Just my kind." Then he glanced up at the archers overhead. "Think we can make it?"

"We're dead men anyway. Let's try."

The warriors above had all of their attention fixed on dodging the flaming arrows that continued to drop from the sky. Sindak led the charge to the timbers at a desperate run. Gonda followed right behind him.

"It'll take both of us!" Sindak shouted. They each took an end, lifted a log, and groaned as they hauled it toward the gates. The wood was wet and heavy.

The last remaining warrior over the gate ran to

see what they were doing. "*Sindak. It's Sindak! Someone help me! It's War Chief Sindak!*"

To Gonda's amazement, the warrior hesitated long enough that they could brace their first log against the planks, and run back for another before arrows started slicing the air above and around them. Most of the arrows came from the marsh, where Wampa and Papon were covering them. They grabbed the second timber and charged for the gate again.

"*Blessed gods!*" the man on the catwalk yelled as he dove for the safety behind the palisade. Incoming arrows slammed the logs in front of him. "*I need help over here. Help!*"

Warriors rushed along the catwalks toward him, their bows drawn.

As Gonda and Sindak braced the timber, Sindak bellowed, "Run!" and they sprinted for the safety of the marsh.

We've done it! Exhilaration pumping in Gonda's veins, he leaped a rock and...

Crack!

A jolt ran through his bones. At the same time, the muscles in his right calf ripped apart. He stumbled and went down hard, the wind knocked from his lungs. He slid face-first through the wet leaves at the edge of the marsh.

For a dazed instant he wondered what had gone wrong. He struggled to breathe, to get air into his now panicked lungs. The sounds of the battle had grown oddly distant, removed. Yellow sparks of light, like disembodied fireflies, twinkled in his graying vision.

An arrow hissed past his right ear and thumped into the earth, quivering from the impact. A fierce agony burned in his leg. Gasping, he dug his fingers into the soggy leaves and tried to drag himself into the water.

"Gonda?" Sindak shouted.

Sindak charged back for him.

"No! No! Run!" Gonda ordered hoarsely.

Then Sindak was there, bending down.

"Leave me! Get out of here, you fool!"

Grabbing a fistful of Gonda's shirt, Sindak dragged Gonda's wounded body up. The world spun crazily as Sindak muscled Gonda onto his shoulder and pounded back toward the marsh.

Gonda rasped, "My leg is broken! I can't run. You have to go on without me!"

Arrows cut the air around them as Sindak splashed into the reeds. Weaving, half-stumbling beneath Gonda's weight, he struggled deeper into the darkness, sloshing through the cattail stalks.

Gonda saw Wampa and Papon ahead, using the trees as cover to shoot at the archers on the catwalk, and he shouted, "Get back to Bur Oak Village! Now!"

Wampa and Papon immediately turned and splashed back through the marsh.

"Sindak, curse you, drop me! You have to get out of here!" Instead of obeying, Sindak dragged Gonda's arm over his shoulder and hauled him out beyond the gaudy halo of firelight to where the black water was neck-deep.

"Put me down!" Gonda shouted. "Blast you! You have never been able to obey orders!"

Sindak heaved Gonda aside, and commanded, "Hold tight to my shirt, or I'll knock you senseless and drag you!"

Gonda clamped on to the man's wet shirt, and Sindak stroked hard for Bur Oak Village.

Gonda mostly managed to keep his head above water until they reached the cattail shallows. When he tried to stand, to follow Sindak out of the water to make a run for the gate, his leg went out from under him. He flipped to his side, and dragging his injured leg, pulled himself ashore, gasping in pain.

Sindak never hesitated. He grasped Gonda's arm, grunted, and lifted him, carrying Gonda behind the curve in the palisade wall, out of the shower of arrows. "Saponi! Disu! Where are you?"

Two of Sindak's warriors appeared out of the darkness where they'd been hiding, demanding, "Sindak? Is that you?"

"Yes, and Gonda's hurt!" Sindak managed

through ragged breaths. Through the pain, Gonda growled, "I swear you are the worst warrior in the world. One of these days, your problems with authority are going to get you killed."

Sindak spared only enough breath to reply, "This isn't my day to die...or yours, apparently."

When Deru launched another wave of flaming arrows, the enemy warriors on the Yellowtail catwalks ducked down. "We have to go now!" Saponi said.

Three heartbeats later, Saponi and Disú hoisted Gonda's arms over their shoulders and pelted for the gate.

Sindak covered the retreat, calling, "Deru, we're coming in! Don't shoot!"

Gonda's scrambled vision recorded images of the gate, as he was dragged through in the safety of the palisade, and unceremoniously dropped on the ground. The two guards on the gate swiftly swung it closed, but not before Gonda noticed that the mist had picked up the orange gleam from the fires. It had shimmered into a huge gauzy halo over Yellowtail Village.

Sindak, breathless, turned to Saponi and Disu. "Get back to the fight. Follow Deru's orders. I'll meet you soon."

"Yes, War Chief." The two men ran.

Sindak knelt beside Gonda. The marsh had washed most of the soot from his serious face, but his beaked nose still bore smears of black. "How's your leg?"

"It hurts!"

"Well, I know that..."

The timbre of screams rising from Yellowtail Village changed, going from pain to breathless shrieks, the screams of men on fire.

Sindak went still, listening, and his expression slackened.

Weakly, Gonda said, "Leave me. I'll be fine."

Sindak just nodded. He sprinted away, nocking an arrow as he ran.

Gonda barely had time to catch his breath before his stomach lurched, and he threw up.

2

Negano jerked from a sound sleep when screams shredded the cold mist. In one fluid move, he rolled out of his blanket with his war club in his fist, and lunged to his feet. All around him, other sleeping warriors had grabbed weapons and leaped up. Panicked conversations erupted around hundreds of campfires.

It took only a few moments before Negano's sleep-numbed mind focused on Yellowtail Village where flames roared.

"Dear gods, what happened?"

From Negano's position on the hillside, he could gaze down, horror-struck, into the village where his warriors dodged toppling longhouse walls or sections of collapsing palisade, shrieking as they ran for their lives. Several men jumped from the palisade with their clothing flaming. A few managed to drag themselves out into the meadow, where showers of arrows, shot from the Bur Oak Village catwalks, lanced their bodies.

"Grab your weapons! We have to get down there to help them!" Snatching up his bow and quiver, he shouted, "Follow me!"

Negano led the charge down the hillside, splashed across the small creek, and up the incline that led to the villages situated on the rise. He didn't know how many warriors had followed him, but could hear feet pounding behind him.

As he dashed for Yellowtail Village, he saw the logs propped against the gates, locking everyone inside. The burning palisades had effectively ringed the village with flames.

He swung around and saw perhaps three hundred warriors. When he spotted deputy war chief Nesi, he shouted, "Nesi! Form a team, knock those logs down, and get those gates open!"

Nesi and two men charged for the timbers. The gates in front of them flamed, singeing their hair. When they managed to shove aside the logs and throw the gates open, thick, blinding smoke boiled out, swallowing them.

Negano threw up his sleeve to cover his nose and mouth and squinted, trying to make out...

Five men came hobbling out, supporting one

another, coughing, their soot-coated faces streaked with tears. One man gasped, "They attacked...so quickly...there was nothing we..." He fell into an uncontrollable coughing fit. The warrior supporting him dragged him away from the extreme heat and smoke.

Negano stared through the entry into the plaza. As some of the smoke cleared, he could see a little better. There must have been debris piled everywhere. Stacks of bark, old chunks of catwalks, and useless palisade poles lay in flaming heaps right next to the longhouses. Gods! No wonder the place had gone up like a torch!

Negano shouted. "Nesi, anyone who can still walk can make it out now. Let's take care of the Bur Oak archers!"

He led his warriors around the eastern side of Yellowtail Village and straight into a volley of arrows. Men went down all around him, shrieking. Hoarse cries, groans, and coughing wavered like a haunted chorus. There had to be five hundred archers on the Bur Oak catwalks! Some were old gray-haired elders and children barely old enough to carry bows, but they shot straight.

Negano managed to let two arrows fly, before he called, *"Retreat! Go back."*

As soon as they started to run, Jigonsaseh's deep voice rang out, and the gates of Bur Oak

Village were flung open. A flood of warriors sprinted out, chasing after Negano's forces with their bows singing.

He stumbled over his dead, dying, and wounded warriors as he dashed away from the shower of arrows. Something slammed into his quiver, the impact enough to send him staggering. In shock, his mind refused to believe the number of freshly killed men and women who lay sprawled across the frozen ground. Half? Maybe half the warriors who had followed him just moments ago? Gods, that couldn't be right.

When he veered around the blazing curve of the Yellowtail palisades, out of the line of fire, he turned to look back. Counting...counting warriors. Maybe forty. Forty out of three hundred. *No, no, there must be more.* The thick smoke boiling out of Yellowtail probably concealed...

"Don't stop! They're still after us!" Nesi shouted. "Blessed gods, how many arrows did Bur Oak Village stockpile?"

Negano shouted back, "The only thing I care about is how many they still have!"

He spun to look through the wide-open gates of Yellowtail Village and into the inferno, and readied himself to lead his remaining warriors inside to get them out of the line of...

Nesi called, "Don't do it, Negano!"

"Why not?" He swung around to glare at Nesi. "It's safer inside than outside!"

"Look at it!" He flung out a muscular arm, pointing to the plaza roaring with flames. "You lead a team in there, and Deru will box the village up so that none of us gets out alive! We have to retreat and regroup!"

Negano didn't even think, he just shouted, "Grab as many of the wounded as you can. Support them back to our camp!"

As warriors scurried to obey, dragging arms over shoulders, hauling another twenty or so men and women to their feet, the Bur Oak archers rounded the curve in the wall and started letting fly again.

"Run! Hurry!"

All across the battlefield, cries erupted, the wounded he'd left behind pleading for him to save them. The screams became more panicked when he charged in the opposite direction.

Twenty terrible heartbeats later, Jigonsaseh yelled another command, and the Bur Oak archers ceased pursuing them, and turned to silence the cries of the wounded. One by one, the begging voices were cut short in mid-scream.

Negano slowed to a trot and stared at the twenty or so shocked warriors who ran behind him, breathing hard. They appeared as dazed as men who'd been struck in the heads with war clubs. Nostrils flared. The sickly sweet scent of burning human flesh and scorched hair filled the night. None of them hauled wounded. Those who had tried must have lagged behind and been cut down. *Gods, I should have never given that order...*

Negano rubbed his numb face, struggling to gain a hold on his senses as he led the way through the firelit darkness toward the creek. From his own camp, hundreds of warriors flocked down the hillside, men and women who'd finally understood what was happening and grabbed their weapons to come help.

"Go back!" he ordered. "There's nothing more we can do tonight!"

Warriors stared wide-eyed as he tramped past. They gaped first at him, then at Yellowtail Village, then at the warriors who followed him as he splashed across the creek. Many called questions:

"What happened?"

"Night attack," he answered. "The enemy set their own village on fire with our warriors inside."

A man called, "Gods, who made it out alive? Where's my brother?"

Someone else yelled, "Where's my wife? She was assigned to guard the Yellowtail palisade!"

Negano felt physically ill. He should never have used Yellowtail...

"Stop it," Nesi said as he trotted up beside him.

Negano turned. The square-jawed giant wore a threatening expression. His facial scars twitched.

"Stop what?"

"Stop second-guessing yourself. You did the right thing sending those warriors into Yellowtail Village."

"But Nesi—"

"Listen to me!" He stabbed his war club at Negano's chest. "Joondoh was in charge of the Yellowtail Village defense. He missed something. I don't know what, but this would have never happened if he'd been paying attention. You know it as well as I."

"Maybe, but—"

"It was Joondoh's fault. Do you *understand?*" Nesi's eyes glanced suggestively up the slope toward the crest of the ridge where Atotarho's camp nestled.

The chief stood before his fire, propped on his walking stick. Silhouetted in front of the flames, his hunched form was black as coal. Because of the way the mist eddied and shifted, Atotarho appeared to be standing in the midst of the blaze with flames shooting up all around him. Even from here, Negano could sense the old man's rage: it shivxsered the air.

"I understand, Nesi."

Negano had to concentrate. He needed an explanation. It hadn't occurred to him that as soon

as he set foot in camp, Chief Atotarho would be
waiting for him.

"Good," Nesi said. "Now, before you have to
face him, stop and let me pull this accursed arrow
out of your quiver. A finger's width to the left or
right, and you'd be back there dying with the rest."

3

Jigonsaseh slung her bow and turned to Deru where he stood beside her on the catwalk, batting out the sparks that alighted on his hair and shoulders. The sweat had mixed with ash and filled in the hollow of his crushed cheek, and it created a black oval that extended across his squashed nose. "War Chief? I'll return shortly. Keep a close eye out. They may return with reinforcements."

"Yes, Matron."

As she walked away, Deru began marching up and down, his red cape swinging, praising his warriors, clapping exhausted men and women on the shoulders.

The moans and cries of the wounded that had been carried to the council house drifted through the falling sparks and ash.

Jigonsaseh climbed down to the plaza where the three teams she'd organized waited for her just outside the inner gates. Her stride lengthened as she hurried toward Kittle.

"High Matron," Jigonsaseh said. "I don't like it that you are going out there. You should—"

"The scouts you dispatched will warn us if we are in grave danger. Any final instructions?" Kittle's beautiful face had a haunted expression. She used her sleeve to pound out the flickering sparks that landed on her hood. She must know, and fear, how enraged Atotarho would be when he discovered what they'd done to his army.

"Just work quickly. The enemy could be rallying to return. The mist and smoke make it impossible to know. We need to act now. Tell your party to collect as many usable arrows as you can find. Grab quivers, bows, and any other weapon you can carry."

Kittle nodded, lifted a hand, and ordered, "Open the gates. We're going out." She waved to the women in her group, gesturing for them to follow her.

Jigonsaseh shouldered through the crowd to reach Taya. Her fourteen-summers-old face had gone as pale as frost. She'd been vomiting every morning, and feeling queasy most of the day. Jigonsaseh had no doubts but that Taya carried her son's child.

"Taya, waste no time. Strip the corpses of belt pouches, packs, and water bags. If you have time, dispatch a small group with the water bags and meet Tutelo in the marsh to fill them. But hurry! Any questions?"

"No, Matron." Taya gave her a confident nod.

"Good. Be fast."

Taya called to the elders in her group, "We have to hurry! Our job is only food and water bags! Let's go." She led the elders through the gates.

Jigonsaseh turned to Tutelo, who stood ten paces away, talking with her group of fifty children. Each carried an empty pot.

"Tutelo? Are you ready to head to the marsh?"

"We are." Short black locks, irregularly layered, stuck to her cheeks.

"Go."

Tutelo and the children flooded toward the gates.

When everyone was gone, the village seemed stunningly empty. Jigonsaseh looked around. The warriors on the catwalks had their bows nocked and aimed at the billowing smoke and firelit mist. The fires in Yellowtail Village had died down somewhat, but sudden roars and hisses still erupted at odd moments, and tornados of sparks spun continually into the night sky.

Like black snow cascading from charred heavens, ash fell. It coated everything. She absently brushed at her cape. Then she marched back for the ladder, climbed up to the catwalk, and returned to her position.

Outside, villagers worked in grisly silence, jerking quivers and packs from shoulders, racing across the meadow collecting arrows, rolling corpses over to find belt pouches and water bags. Tutelo's children in the marsh had already started streaming back through the gates with filled water jars. They lined them up neatly along the walls of the Deer Clan longhouse.

As Jigonsaseh unslung her bow and nocked an arrow, her gaze drifted out across the marsh to the hills in the distance where enemy campfires sparkled. They'd still be picking up the pieces, caring for their wounded and assessing what went wrong. But tomorrow morning...

"Matron?"

Sindak trotted down the catwalk. He carried his bow nocked. "We must talk."

"I want to know everything."

"First, did Papon and Wampa make it back?"

"Yes, unharmed."

He heaved a sigh of relief. "Next, Gonda is wounded. He—"

"Badly?"

"The small bone in his lower leg is broken."

She gripped his arm. "So he can't walk. Did he make it back?"

Sindak gave her a wry smile that barely cut the sadness in his eyes. "He's in the council house. It—it's a long story. When the shooting stopped, two of my warriors carried him there."

She loosened her grip and let her hand drop. Relief flooded her veins. "Then Bahna, our Healer, is already caring for him. I'll check on him later."

"We need to speak, Jigonsaseh. What is your plan for dawn?" His soaked cape conformed to his muscular shoulders.

Jigonsaseh surveyed the people flooding back through the gates with armloads of arrows, packs and belt pouches. Tutelo was also herding her flock of children with the last water pots toward the gates. Soon, everyone would be back inside, and she could at least get a deep breath into her lungs.

"You think he'll hit us just after dawn?" she asked, fixing him with tired eyes.

Sindak used his wet sleeve to wipe soot from his nose. "I think we'll be lucky to make it to dawn."

She leaned back against the palisade. Warriors lined the catwalks, talking, ruffling ash from their hair. Bone-weary, there would be little rest tonight. She had to think despite that. "How will he organize the attack?"

Sindak slung his bow and sank against the palisade beside her. "Right now, news is passing around every campfire. Rage and indignation are building...as well as fear. Few of Atotarho's warriors will be able to sleep, and they're already exhausted. Even more than we are."

"More than we are? How can you say—"

"Please let me finish. Negano is definitely War Chief. Gonda and I heard his warriors talking about him." He took a deep breath. "Even though we struck him hard tonight, Negano knows he still greatly outnumbers us. But he'll be cautious tomorrow. He won't commit all of his warriors to the assault on the palisades."

"Five hundred shooting at us will keep us plenty busy."

"My guess is he'll commit one thousand, Matron. With our losses today, he'll be wagering that the terror alone will be enough to shock our meager forces—"

"Yes, and we will have our hands full dragging the dead and wounded off the catwalks." A familiar sinking sensation invaded her belly.

Sindak leaned closer to her. Softly, for her ears alone, he said, "That means Negano will be leaving two or three hundred in camp, as reserves. If he's smart, they'll all be grouped together, but if he's not..."

She fixed him with intense eyes. For a while, she didn't say anything. "Do you think Negano knows which Hills warriors switched sides?"

"No. Many fled the battle. He knows that most

probably went home. But I suspect Negano hopes a few just ran away briefly and plan to return."

She massaged her forehead as she forced her exhausted brain to think.

Sindak said, "It's a suicide mission. I don't know how many we can kill, but getting away again—"

"I don't want you to kill anyone." She lowered her hand and considered him. "You've enough on your souls, old friend. We need another way. A smarter way. I want you to help me make them sick to death of Atotarho."

Sindak's bushy brows pulled together over his hooked nose. She could see him sorting through the possibilities of what else she might want him to do. "Are you thinking of kidnapping the old man, poisoning cook pots? Whatever it is, if we're going to do it, we have to hurry. My warriors need to get out of this village and into the forest before—"

"I agree. But I have another idea. Meet me under the porch of the Bear Clan longhouse. I'll be right there."

"I'll get them organized as quickly as I can." He spun around and jogged down the catwalk, tapping his warriors on the shoulders, speaking with them briefly, moving on.

Down in the plaza, Kittle's arms moved, pointing to people, assigning them duties. Already, women searched the belt pouches and packs they'd looted from the battlefield, separating out anything edible. Elders stacked arrows and quivers along the palisade walls. Tutelo had groups of children carrying water jars, making sure they were equally distributed to each longhouse and the council house.

Jigonsaseh turned and walked down to where Deru stood speaking with Wampa. The woman warrior shivered in her wet dress.

"War Chief Wampa, you did excellent work tonight. Now, I want you to return to your chamber. Warm up, eat, get some sleep. Deru will wake you in a few hands of time. Until this is over, I want one of you on the catwalks at all times. Switch off sleeping when you can."

"Understood," Deru said.

"Yes, Matron." Wampa nodded respectfully and wearily walked toward the ladders.

Deru gave Jigonsaseh a quizzical look. "What about you? Are you planning on sleeping any time soon?"

They'd been friends for twenty summers. He knew how she thought. "We've seen some terrible battles together, haven't we?"

"Don't try to distract me. You have to sleep."

"I will. I give you my oath. There's just...much to be done. What kind of shifts are you planning for your warriors?"

Deru used his bow to scratch his chin. "I'll have

blankets brought up to them. They can sleep on the catwalks. But I was thinking I'd keep one hundred on duty at all times."

"Good." She clapped him on the shoulder. "You were brilliant tonight, War Chief. The way you targeted the piles of debris in the plaza, then when Negano's forces arrived and you hit them squarely the instant they rounded the palisade wall..." A proud smile twisted her lips. "No one could have done it better."

He nodded briefly. He'd always been uncomfortable with praise. "Every warrior, even the children, performed exceptionally. They know the survival of our nation is at stake."

Deru seemed to be considering his next words. Finally, he said, "I was just wondering what you plan to do about Sindak?" He gazed at her through slitted eyes, as though he expected to be reprimanded for asking.

"What do you mean?"

"He disobeyed your direct orders. You told Sindak and the others to leave the wounded behind and get back to the gates as soon as they could. Even though everything worked out, it sets a bad example."

"Worried that other warriors may now think they can disobey me, too?"

"Our warriors, no." He shook his head. "But his?"

If Sindak was close at hand, she'd no doubt they'd obey him, not her. But what if Sindak wasn't at hand?

"You're right, Deru. I'll speak with Sindak about it."

"Thank you, Matron."

As she walked away, heading for the Bear Clan longhouse, she pulled CorpseEye from her belt.

4

Seething, Atotarho gripped his walking stick, longing to use it as a club. He glared at Negano and Nesi as they strode toward his camp on the hilltop. Both men kept coughing, their lungs struggling to get rid of the thick, acrid smoke they'd inhaled at Yellowtail Village. The gaudy glare cast by the fires illuminated their tall, muscular bodies. Gray ash coated their shoulders and hair, and filled the lines in their faces, making both appear to be much older men.

Atotarho's jaw hurt from clenching his teeth. War Chief Negano hadn't looked at him yet. The man had seen thirty-two summers pass—many as the head of Atotarho's personal guards. He had little actual battlefield experience. Elevating him to his current position had, perhaps, been a grave error.

When the two men arrived at his fire, Nesi dipped his head respectfully to Atotarho, and split off from Negano, leaving the war chief to face Atotarho alone.

Negano stiffened his spine and braced his feet. "My Chief, I—"

"How did it happen?" Atotarho asked in a chilling voice.

"No one knows yet. Tomorrow, we will question the survivors. All I can say is that Joondoh must have missed something."

Atotarho repositioned his walking stick and gripped the antler head with both hands. His knees and hips throbbed in agony. "Is he dead?"

"I haven't seen him, so I assume he is."

"Well, then, he's lucky, isn't he?"

Negano's eyes tightened. He did not look away, which demonstrated true bravery...or perhaps foolishness. He coughed again, then choked out the words, "Joondoh was a loud-mouthed fool. I should never have placed him in charge of the Yellowtail defense."

"It's a little late to realize that."

"Yes, my Chief." Negano sounded truly apologetic, almost obsequious.

"How many did we lose?"

Negano started to answer, but bent forward suddenly, hacking and wheezing for several moments before he gained control again. A shiver ran through him.

"Forgive me." He straightened to his full height, but his expression was that of a man fighting a sudden and consuming nausea. "The fires were so intense and the smoke so thick we couldn't count tonight. However, maybe around six hundred fifty. Perhaps a few more."

"Six hundred...!" Atotarho's veins seemed to be on fire. "*You* killed one-third of our forces?"

"My Chief, I hope you will take into account that I was not personally in charge of the Yellowtail defense. If I had been—"

"Do you think it makes me feel better that more than six hundred warriors would be alive if you'd had the good judgment to lead the defense yourself?"

Negano swallowed hard but said nothing. Was he searching for a response?

"*Answer me!*"

Negano spread his arms in a gesture of helplessness. "In the future, I will not trust such situations to anyone else. I will assume the duty myself."

Atotarho gritted his teeth and looked out over the camp. No one slept. Every warrior who could stand was on his feet talking. The drone of their voices had a low, angry timbre. Their discontent had been growing. Every day, his warriors seemed a little more surly and rebellious. As the scent of their friends' and relatives' rotting bodies strengthened, more and more people clamored to go home. Their truculence would be worse after tonight. Much worse.

Atotarho's eyes slid back to Negano. "I saw the hunting parties return today. How much food did they shoot?"

"Not much, my Chief. Bur Oak Village has been here a long time. All of the nearby game was hunted out long ago. Tomorrow, I'll dispatch more hunting parties to go further afield, hoping—"

"How much food did today's party shoot?" he repeated with lethal exactness.

Negano clenched his fists at his sides. "Enough to feed our army for two days."

Atotarho's grip tightened on his walking stick, as though strangling the life from it. "And what do you think High Matron Kittle is doing right now?"

He appeared mystified by the shift in subjects. "I—I can't say."

"Well, I can. She's a leader. She's out stripping the bodies of our dead for food and weapons. She's refilling every empty pot and bag with water." His voice went hoarse with restrained emotion. "Now she has another three or four days that she did not have this morning. The spirits of her villagers are running high. My hopes of starving her out in less than one-quarter moon are gone." He extended a finger that resembled a knobby twig and stabbed it at Negano's chest. "Because of you."

In an unnaturally high voice, Negano said, "Chief, as I said, I know I am at fault. If possible, I would like to discuss our attack plan for tomorrow. We need to take our revenge quickly. To hearten our warriors. If we do not, I fear—"

"Tell me your plan." Atotarho lowered his hand to grip his walking stick again. "It had better be good, War Chief."

5

As the garish halo of firelight swelled over Bur Oak Village, the longhouses turned burnt orange and seemed to slip in and out of existence, light then dark, as though tugged at by the winds of nothingness.

In the shifting smoke, Jigonsaseh found Sindak standing to the left of the Bear Clan longhouse porch, speaking with his warriors. He'd lost four in the battle, and another five had been wounded. Thirty-one crowded around him, their expressions somber. Distinctive clan symbols decorated their painted capes. She could make out the wings of the Hawk Clan, bear claws for the Bear Clan, and interlocking green and blue rectangles for the Snipe Clan. All had mourning hair. Sindak had not yet changed out of the clothes he'd worn in the marsh. His black shirt clung wetly to his body and wet clothing made a warrior's movements awkward, sluggish.

Jigonsaseh walked up behind him, gripped CorpseEye, and in one powerful swing, struck Sindak in the back of the knees. He landed with a grunt that knocked the breath out of him. She didn't give him time to respond, but leaped on top of him, straddling him, with CorpseEye jammed down across his throat.

Shocked cries of outrage erupted from his men. Several jerked stilettos and clubs from their belts.

Sindak's eyes widened when he looked up at her, then widened even more at something over her shoulder. He choked out, "No! Lower your weapons!"

She allowed Sindak to push the club away from his throat enough that he could speak, and he casually asked, "Have I done something to offend you, Matron?"

"I gave you a direct order that anyone who fell behind was to be left behind. No trying to rescue friends. I told you I didn't need dead heroes, I needed living fighters. Yet you went back for Gonda."

"I apologize. It was arrogant of me, not to mention dangerous and stupid. In this village, you give the orders."

She paused with her eyes narrowed. "You practiced that, didn't you?"

"Well, I knew I was going to have to use it at some point."

Jigonsaseh climbed off him and rose. Sindak's warriors' expressions were a combination of indignation, disbelief, and killing rage. She watched them from the corner of her eye. In a voice filled with deepest respect, the kind of respect she reserved only for her own war chiefs, she said, "Sindak, you are one of the finest warriors I've ever known, but if you ever disobey my orders again, it will be the last time." She tied CorpseEye to her belt, and extended a hand to him.

Sindak grabbed it and let her pull him to his feet. As he dusted away the old leaves and twigs that stuck to the wet leather, he said, "You're faster than I remember."

"A fact you'd be wise to ponder."

He rubbed his aching throat and turned to his men. "Never disobey one of Matron Jigonsaseh's orders, or she will—without a shred of shame—publicly humiliate you before your friends."

Several of his men broke out in laughter, shook their heads, and slipped their war clubs and stilettos back into their belts.

Sindak gave her a sly look from the corner of his eye. Both of them smiled faintly, remembering times past when they'd had similar discussions. Men expelled breaths. Expressions relaxed.

Sindak spread his feet and turned back to face

his warriors. "As I was saying before the arrival of the only war chief that I respect more than myself" —more laughter—"Negano doesn't know which of our warriors pledged allegiance to our true high matron, Zateri. He doesn't know who has given up and gone home, or who has fled into the forest to fill his belly before he returns to duty. If we can get into position tonight, we can use that against him."

"Sindak," Saponi said abruptly. Burly, with a pockmarked face and a nose like a flattened beetle, he looked uneasily at the other warriors. He was Snipe Clan. Interlocking green and blue rectangles ran across the middle of his cape. He had a rocks-rubbing-together voice. "You can't go into that war camp. Negano may not know the identities of the men who joined you, but he does know for certain that you betrayed Atotarho. Every man saw you switch sides at the end of the battle and side with High Matron Zateri."

"That's right Saponi. I'll remain in the forest, coordinating—"

"Respectfully, War Chief, you shouldn't go at all."

Whispers passed between his warriors.

Sindak's expression tightened. "Why do you say that?"

When Saponi propped his hands on his hips in defiance, it caused his cape to flare and sway. He appeared hesitant to speak.

Jigonsaseh filled the uncomfortable silence. "I agree with Saponi. I know you wish to lead your warriors, Sindak, but it's too risky."

"Too risky?" he objected. "You don't mind having me crawl around the base of Yellowtail Village while hundreds of Atotarho's warriors are staring over the edge of the palisade at me, but you—"

"War Chief?" Saponi softly said. "May I speak with you alone?"

Sindak nodded, and the two men walked a short distance away. Sindak let Saponi talk while he listened for twenty heartbeats. Jigonsaseh caught the phrases "death would be devastating," and "dishearten our men."

Jigonsaseh strained to hear more. Saponi was right: Sindak was the one thing that held his men together. They fought for him—not for her, not for the alliance.

When Saponi stopped, Sindak's mouth tightened into a line, and he grudgingly nodded. Loud enough for everyone to hear, he said, "I don't like it, but I yield to your judgment."

He started to walk back, but Saponi gripped his shoulder. "Now that we've settled that, I wish to volunteer for the duty. Allow me to lead our warriors. I'll make certain the task is accomplished."

Their gazes held. "I know you will."

As they walked back, Saponi added, "Once you tell us what the task is, of course."

Sindak stopped at Jigonsaseh's side. When he shoved wet hair behind his ear, a black smear striped his cheek. Ash falling from the night sky blended with mist so that where it alighted on skin and clothing, it ran like watery charcoal paint.

"Matron Jigonsaseh," Sindak said, "tell us your goal tomorrow, and we will figure out how to accomplish it."

She scanned the faces of his warriors, meeting each man's gaze. From their expressions they undoubtedly thought she considered them as more expendable than Standing Stone warriors.

"First, let me make a few things clear. We're fighting for more than the survival of the Standing Stone People, or the Hills People. We're struggling for something greater. Sky Messenger's vision of a Peace Alliance. We're fighting for a better future for our families."

Saponi spread his hands. "Matron, don't worry. We'll attack with all of our hearts."

She gave him a smile filled with appreciation. "Saponi, you are a brave man. But I don't want you to attack anyone unless you're forced to defend yourselves. If everything goes well, no one—on either side—will die in this raid. If it goes wrong? Well, make your own decisions. Pretend you are Atotarho's loyal warriors, blend in with his army or head home and find your families. Do whatever is necessary to stay alive. Does everyone understand?"

Heads nodded, but warriors shared uncertain glances with one another.

Saponi looked confused. "What kind of a raid is this?"

"As soon as we're finished here, I will order every pack in the village emptied and delivered to you. All I expect you to do is find a way to fill them."

Saponi's brows drew together. The warriors looked around at each other.

Sindak laughed suddenly, and a slow, admiring smile came to his lips. "Blessed Spirits, if you're thinking what I think you're thinking, the effect will be utterly demoralizing. I can't believe I didn't think of it myself."

6

Gonda lay on the third row of benches in the council house, surrounded by around fifty men and women wounded far worse than he, many dying. Most of the victims were children and elders, not trained warriors. Their moans and tears tore his heart.

He squinted up at the ceiling poles and gritted his teeth, trying not to yell as the Healer, Old Bahna, set and splinted his broken leg with oak staves.

"The bone is aligned, so now I'm going to tighten the cords to secure the staves," Bahna warned.

"I'm ready. I think."

Bahna had survived fifty-three summers. His deeply furrowed face cradled kind eyes. Gray hair draped like spiderwebs over his ears. He'd been working all night, Healing, and his brown cape bore the evidence of his efforts. Blood and gut juices spattered the buckskin. It had probably absorbed a river of tears as well.

Gonda concentrated on the roof poles. Like spokes, they radiated outward from the smoke hole. Coal-black soot coated them. The mist outside must be thickening. He could see it glistening through the smoke hole, reflecting the fires outside.

Bahna grunted as he jerked the five cords tight, and Gonda gasped, "Blessed Ancestors!"

"All right, Gonda." Bahna placed a hand upon his forearm. "That's the best I can do for now. I want you to remain here for at least one hand of time, so I may see how you're doing, then you may return to the Hawk Clan longhouse. Tomorrow, I will send poultices to your wife, Pawen. Ask her to place them on either side of the arrow wound. And be glad," he added pointedly, "that you were not shot with one of the feces-coated arrows, as so many others were. We found many such arrows lying in the plaza, arrows that missed their marks."

Gonda propped himself up on his elbows, grimacing as pain shot through him. The five cords around the oak staves had been woven together, creating a kind of net. His left leg was one gigantic aching throb. A minor concern compared to the wounds of everyone else.

"I can leave now, Bahna. I'm all right."

"No," Bahna said firmly. "Your leg is going to swell. I need to check on you later to loosen the cords, if necessary. If Evil Spirits slip into the arrow wound and fester it, I'll be forced to cut off your leg to kill them. You don't want that, do you?"

Gonda scowled at him. "I'll stay. But only for one hand of time."

Bahna nodded and moved on to the next victim, a little boy of perhaps ten summers. He'd taken an arrow through the head. Gonda did not understand why he was still breathing—but he'd seen similar enigmas on the battlefield, things he'd rather not remember.

Firelight streamed around the entry curtain, and Gonda turned to see Jigonsaseh enter the council house. She stood for a few moments, allowing her eyes to adjust. Still slender and muscular, her beautiful face had just begun to crease—lines around her full lips, crow's feet at the corners of her eyes. She spotted him as he sat up and walked forward.

As it had for many summers, the sight of her was like the feel of a war club in his hands; it eased his fears. He could not count the number of times she had saved his life—and he hers. If truth be told, there was no one he trusted more.

Jigonsaseh's cape, covered with wet ash, moved pendulously as she came to a stop at his side, looking down at him with concerned eyes.

"Sindak told me you'd been wounded."

Gonda braced his hands on the bench to look up at her. "I swear he's the worst warrior I know. I ordered him to leave me in the marsh. Instead, he dragged me home. The fool could have been killed in the process, and we need him more than we need me. He's a powerful symbol of our alliance with Zateri's—"

"Yes. Yes. I've already attended to Sindak's errors in judgment." Jigonsaseh sat beside him. "Someday, I hope to tell him how much I appreciate his gross disobedience. Assuming any of us live that long. How's your leg?"

Gonda stared down at it. "Bahna ordered me to stay here for one hand of time, or I'd already have hobbled back to the Hawk Clan longhouse. Tell me how the battle went. How many did we kill?"

Jigonsaseh's gaze scanned the other benches, taking time to examine and identify faces, before she lowered her eyes and expelled a disheartened breath. "Hard to say. My guess is over six hundred."

A potent blend of relief and triumph surged through him. "Blessed Spirits, that's more than I'd hoped for."

She whispered, for his ears alone, "Yes, but it means they've no choice now but to hit us hard tomorrow. It's a matter of honor."

He jerked a nod. "Very true, but we'll be ready

for them. Has Sindak lined out what he thinks may happen tomorrow?"

"He says Atotarho will throw one thousand warriors at us. At dawn, or just before."

Gonda squeezed his eyes closed for a few heartbeats, absorbing the news. The sobs that filled the council house seemed louder. Before he opened his eyes again, he said, "We have to get as many of these people back on their feet as we can. We're going to need every one of them on the catwalks with a bow."

"I'll speak with Bahna. Now, I should get back to..."

When she started to rise, he gripped her hand. "I have to tell you about the Flint massacre."

"What massacre?" She eased back down to the bench. "Which village?"

Gonda kept his voice low. "Not a village. As I was moving around the palisade wall, setting fires, I overheard two warriors talking. Apparently, Atotarho's warriors ambushed a Flint war party and killed four hundred warriors."

Her face slackened, and her gaze darted over the council house while she thought about it. "Cord's war party?"

"Probably."

Jigonsaseh bowed her head and massaged her brow. "Blessed gods, they left here with around five hundred warriors, if Atotarho killed four hundred..."

Gonda gave her a few moments.

When she lifted her head, he said, "The survivors should be getting back to Flint country tomorrow. After they've told their story, the Flint Ruling Council will act."

"Yes, but what action will it take?"

"How many warriors do you suppose they have left?"

She waved a palm through the air. "If I know their chief"—Gonda winced when she did not say Cord's name as it meant she thought he was dead—"he talked the matrons into leaving a significant number at home to guard their three villages. I don't know...I suspect they have perhaps one thousand five hundred warriors remaining in the nation. Five hundred guarding each village. A pittance, compared to Atotarho's forces."

"Yes, even if they know we're in trouble, they will not wish to risk any of their remaining forces to help us."

Her lips tightened into a white bloodless line. "No."

They both exhaled at the same time, and their breaths frosted in the cold, firelit air. When she looked back at him, it was as though the summers had rolled back and he was still her deputy war chief. She depended upon him to give her good advice, advice that would save lives.

Gonda squeezed her hand and released it. "Tomorrow morning, we must get every person on the catwalks that we can. Even the members of the Ruling Council must take up bows."

Her head moved in a barely visible nod, but her eyes were focused elsewhere. He knew from long experience that her thoughts had turned to strategy and tactics, already envisioning what her enemy might do at dawn, and planning how to counter it. She had an unnatural ability to place her souls inside her enemy's body and see through his eyes.

He softly interrupted her thoughts, "Sky Messenger should have reached the villages of the People of the Landing yesterday or today."

"Only if he's been able to run the whole way. We can't count on that. We don't know how many war parties or other obstacles he might have faced. And even if he did, even if they joined the alliance, our son has no idea we're in a fight for our lives. There's no help coming, Gonda. Get used to it."

Gonda's head waffled in uncertainty. "Don't underestimate the Traders who've passed by here and seen what's happening. I suspect the news of our struggle is racing down the trails like wildfire. If we can just hold out—"

"We have to destroy our enemies by ourselves, Gonda."

Her beautiful, exhausted face had set into determined lines. He nodded. "You're right. What do you need me to do?"

She glanced at his splinted leg. "When you are able—"

"I'll be able tomorrow. I may have to get around on a crutch, but at dawn, I'll be right there on the catwalk beside you."

7

Opalescent gray light fell through the dark trees, weaving a gigantic spider's web of shadows across their camp on the densely forested hillside.

Baji sunk her water bag through the hole in the icy pond, filling it while she watched Gitchi. He lapped water from the other side of the pool, but his yellow eyes clung to the lone wolf out in the trees. The pack had moved on a little while ago, pouring in a silvery flood down the hillside and across the valley. From far away, their faint, sharp yelps rose as they trotted up the trail that crested the tree-covered hill to the west. This wolf had remained behind. He stood motionless, as if carved of starlight. Long and lean, he seemed strangely curious about Gitchi. As well, he kept casting odd glances at Baji, tilting his head, as though not certain what she was.

Baji lifted her dripping bag from the hole, pulled the laces tight, and tied it to her belt. Then she lowered Dekanawida's water bag to fill it. He still slept, rolled in their blankets five paces away, unaware that she and Gitchi had started the day without him. She'd been standing guard most of the night, adding branches to the fire to keep him warm. One hand of time ago, she'd started breakfast. The tripod with the suspended cook pot hung at the edge of the fire. Flames licked gently at the soot-coated bottom, keeping it at a slow boil. The mixture of *tic'ne*—powdered red corn—along with beechnuts, dried raspberries, and leftover chunks of last night's muskrat would make a hearty breakfast.

She pulled Dekanawida's filled water bag from the hole and snugged the laces. She would keep it on her weapons' belt until he rose. As she tied it beside her bag, the row of stilettos and knives rattled. It didn't seem to disturb the lone wolf. He kept his shining eyes on Gitchi.

Baji adjusted the bow and quiver slung over her left shoulder. Her headache was gone, and she felt so much better, she wondered if this sensation was akin to being Requickened in a strong, healthy body after a long illness. The shapes of the waking forest appeared clearer and crisper. The Faces of the Forest might have carefully chosen the background shade to highlight the massive chestnut trunks and dark branches that laced over her head.

Gitchi finished drinking and turned to face the wolf. The stranger took a step forward, stopping with one paw lifted while he scented the air. Gitchi curled his lip in a snarl, just a warning, and his big paws crackled in the ice that skimmed the low spots. Every fallen leaf and twig sparkled with a white coating of ice.

The lone wolf whined softly, then backed away, yielding the dominance contest to Gitchi.

It occurred to Baji that it might be a female, perhaps out examining the packs for a future mate.

When she whined again, Gitchi must have tired of her advances, for the hair on his neck and shoulders stood straight up, and he sprang forward with a ferocious growl, chasing the wolf out into the trees and down the hill. Branches cracked in their flight. Baji saw the wolves, stretched out full, shooting between the smoke-colored trunks like pewter lances.

Her gaze returned to the forest shadows, searching for odd shapes, textures, and the slightest movement. Trees rocked in the breeze. Occasionally, an old leaf detached from a branch and fluttered through the air. The pungency of frozen bark wafted around her.

A short time later, Gitchi trotted back with his

head held high and dropped to his haunches beside her.

Baji stroked his soft back. "You protected the camp, Gitchi. Thank you."

He licked her face.

Above them, the shimmering Road of Light that the Standing Stone People called the Path of Souls had begun to fade. As night edged toward day, its cold crystal brilliance paled to a faint white swath, dotted here and there by the largest campfires of the dead.

She whispered, "What do you think the Road is like, Gitchi? Is it winter there? Or summer? From the number of campfires, it looks crowded. I'm not sure I'd like that. You wouldn't either, would you?" She scratched his neck, and he half-closed his eyes in enjoyment. "Your ancestors are wilderness people, too. On cold nights, they point their noses at Grandmother Moon and howl long and hard, complaining about the frozen forests and the dark, but you and I know they wouldn't trade it for anything."

Gitchi looked up, following her gaze, and seemed to be contemplating her soft words as he surveyed the sky, perhaps remembering litter mates and friends who had turned to dust long ago. A pained wistfulness filled his yellow eyes.

"Don't worry, old friend, you'll see them again. You'll romp with them in fields of wildflowers and be able to run for days without your paws hurting at all."

Baji reached down and gently petted his sore legs and feet.

Gitchi wagged his tail, and she slipped her arms around him and hugged him, resting her throat across his thickly furred neck. He vented a deep sigh and leaned into her embrace. They sat like that, loving each other, until Dekanawida's soft voice called, "When we get home, I'm going to paint that image on a rawhide shield."

At the sound of his voice, Gitchi slid from Baji's arms and trotted to where his best friend lay, propped on one elbow in the warm folds of blankets. Dekanawida scratched Gitchi's ears. "I saw you chase away the invader wolf. Well done, Gitchi."

Baji swore that Gitchi's yellow eyes gleamed brighter when he gazed at Dekanawida. Their love for each other was palpable. She could feel it warming the cold morning air—or perhaps it was just in her heart.

Dekanawida rose, straightened his cape, and knotted his belt around his waist. It disturbed her to see his belt strung with Power pouches instead of weapons. He adjusted the four different-colored pouches to their proper position, then spent a moment petting the red pouch that dangled like a cocoon on the far right. He touched the red one often, and she always wondered why? What did it contain? He knelt to roll up their blankets.

She just watched him. The familiarity of his movements eased the peculiar loneliness that tormented her. Sometimes, when he was out of her sight, even for a few instants, panic set in, as though she'd suddenly found herself abandoned, left alone in an alien forest utterly empty of other human beings. The experience bore a striking similarity to sitting in a death vigil, which she'd done many times on the war trail. As a person watched his friend's eyelids flutter, and listened to lungs rattle, friendship seemed to momentarily strengthen... then thin like the last beautiful note of a flute, dying into silence so complete its loss stunned the soul. She wondered if all loneliness was a death vigil.

"Breakfast smells wonderful," Dekanawida said as he tied the blankets to the top of his pack.

She stood. "You need to eat well this morning. By afternoon, we'll reach Shookas Village, and then your troubles really begin."

"I'm ready. I've been thinking a lot about the things we discussed."

"You are ready. I'm sure of it."

Baji untied his water bag from her belt, and walked forward with it dangling from her fingers. Dekanawida rose, said, "Thank you for filling it," and tied it to his belt.

They stood side-by-side in companionable silence, listening to the crackle and snap of the fire and the rustle of wind through the winter trees. Deep in the forest, deer hooves rattled on stone.

Baji's gaze drifted over the predawn mosaic. Black pools of shadow dappled the grayness, but quaking aspens glowed in the dark tangle of tree trunks, their ivory bark shining. Her ears tracked the sounds, the low *shish* of windblown dead ferns, branches sawing, mice feet whispering beneath the piles of old autumn leaves. Nothing unusual.

She leaned over to view the contents of the bubbling cook pot. The dried raspberries had combined with the red corn to turn the mush a deep purple color. "It will be ready soon."

"I love the fragrance of raspberries on a winter morning."

She smiled at him. "I know you do."

He put his arm around her shoulders, holding her close. "How's your headache today?"

"Gone, for the moment. Once we start running the trail, we'll see how long that lasts."

"Is the swelling down?"

"Yes. Some."

He removed his arm and slipped his hands beneath her long hair to gently probe her head wound. His expression tensed.

"What's wrong?"

"It's better, but before we leave camp this

morning, I want to wash it thoroughly again. You're sure you are feeling better?"

"I am. Truly."

He gave her a suspicious look, as though he sensed there was something she wasn't telling him. "I want the truth."

She sighed. "Nothing's wrong. Actually, I feel very good. I'm just afraid you might assume that means I'm about to fly away."

"Any numbness or odd pains in your body?"

"For the sake of the Spirits, I'd tell you if there were!"

"All right." He put his arm around her again and hugged her close. "It's just that I know you. If your leg had just been amputated, you'd tell me you felt fine."

What she didn't want to tell him was that something had happened to her last night. That's why she'd risen. Her senses had become remarkably intense. Even in deep sleep, the faintest sound had disturbed her, and she'd known instantly whether it announced danger or calm. When she'd opened her eyes, the forest had appeared translucent, shining as though every shred of bark and blade of grass were sculpted from quartz crystals. And the night scents! They'd struck her like blows. She didn't understand it, but she'd had the feeling that ancient instincts, long buried, had begun to stretch and move, awakening. She knew, *knew*, that somewhere inside her, her soul trotted through a primeval forest, running down food as her distant ancestors had done, hunting with fang and claw, rather than bow and knife, and it left her feeling more alive than she'd ever thought possible.

Dekanawida's stomach squealed, and she smiled. "It sounds like you're ready for purple corn-meal mush."

"Obviously."

Baji bent and retrieved their cups and spoons from where she'd stowed them beside the hearth-stones. As she spooned their cups full, raspberry-scented steam encircled her face. Never before had the fragrance of raspberries been so overpowering. She might have been wandering through an endless field of ripe berries.

When she rose and handed him a cup with a spoon sticking in it, she asked, "I wonder where Hiyawento and Zateri are today? I'm worried about them. Do you think they've reached the safety of Canassatego Village yet?"

"I hope so. They should be close."

"Gods, I pray their villages made it to Canassatego unharmed and all is well."

"As I do." He picked up his wooden spoon. After he'd tasted the mush, he smiled. "This is delicious. That was a fat muskrat we snared last night. The flavor of his meat goes well with the raspberries."

"I gave Gitchi one of the muskrat legs. I doubt he tasted it at all. He wolfed it down in four bites."

When he heard his name, Gitchi ambled over to sit on his haunches beside Dekanawida, looking up with soulful eyes, probably hoping for another leg.

As Dekanawida ate, his short black hair fell around his face, framing his slender nose and brown eyes. "Speaking of Hiyawento, I've been thinking about Shagoniyoh coming to you on the trail."

A thread of unease went through her. "What about it?"

She ate the rich cornmeal mush, and tried not to look at him. Her fear of discovery had not ebbed, but only increased as the days passed.

"Did Hiyawento ever tell you about Shagoniyoh coming to him?"

She lowered her spoon to her bowl where it clacked against the wood. Surprised, she said, "No. When did this happen?"

"Twelve summers ago. Soon after we all escaped from Bog Willow Village. At the time, you and I would have either been on the trail with Mother and Father, tracking the old woman, or maybe canoeing the river. I'm not sure about the timing."

A swallow went down his throat, as though

memories filled the space behind his eyes, and they hurt.

"What happened?"

He tilted his head and frowned. "He said he was lying in the old woman's canoe. He was very sick. You recall how badly they'd beaten him after he killed the warrior and made sure we got away."

"Yes." Love for Wrass filled her.

Dekanawida rubbed his eyes. "He thought he was dreaming when the man waded through the water to get to him. The man wore a black cape, and had a nose bent to the right. Wrass thought he might be one of the *hanehwa*."

Hanehwa were enchanted skin-beings. Witches—like the old woman—skinned their human victims alive, then cast spells upon the skins, forcing them to serve as guards. Hanehwa never slept. They warned the witch of danger by giving three shouts.

"How did he know it was Shagoniyoh and not one of the hanehwa?"

"The man spoke to him, which hanehwa never do."

"What did he say?"

Dekanawida seemed to pause to get the words right. "He said, '*We are all husks, Wrass, flayed from the soil of fire and blood. This won't be over for any of us until the Great Face shakes the World Tree. Then, when Elder Brother Sun blackens his face with the soot of the dying world, the judgment will take place.'"*

Baji frowned at Dekanawida. The Great Face was the chief of all False Faces. He guarded the sacred World Tree that stood at the center of the earth. Its flowers were made of pure light. The World Tree's branches pierced the Sky World where the Blessed Ancestors lived, and her roots twined deeply into the underworlds, planting themselves upon the back of the Great Tortoise that floated in the dark primeval ocean that spread forever around the land. Elder Brother Sun nested in the World Tree's highest branches.

"Why have you never told me this story?"

His shoulders lifted. "It's Hiyawento's story, not mine. The first time I heard it was twelve summers ago."

She studied his tormented face. "The first time? There was another?"

"Yes, just a few days ago. In Coldspring Village. I—I wanted Hiyawento to tell Taya about it."

There was a small awkward moment of silence, as though he feared she might view it as a betrayal. And perhaps it was, for he'd wanted Taya to hear the story, but he'd never felt Baji needed to hear it.

Baji playfully bumped shoulders with him. "Good. That was the right thing to do." He gave her a small apologetic smile, and she said, "The images are different, though. From your Dream, I mean. In your Dream, Elder Brother Sun turns his back on the dying world and flies away into a dark hole in the sky. In Hiyawento's, Elder Brother Sun covers his face with the soot of the dying world. Are they the same event, or different?"

He took a bite of mush and chewed it. "I've wondered that same thing for many summers."

"Any conclusions?" She spooned mush into her mouth and ate it while she waited for him to answer. The sweet flavor of the red corn penetrated through the tang of the raspberries.

"A few. Despite the differences, there are also striking similarities. Elder Brother Sun vanishes into darkness. The flowers of the World Tree are shaken loose. The actions of humans are judged and condemned."

"What do you think it means?"

He frowned. "I'm not sure, but have you ever noticed that people on the same path see it a little differently? Some focus on the tracks in the trail. Others see only the campfires of the dead visible through the trees over their heads. Others ignore the sky and ground completely and notice the birds and deer."

"So, you're saying it's possible they are the same event, just seen through different eyes?"

"Maybe." He shrugged.

Gitchi stood up and stretched. He was a beautiful old wolf. The white hair that had grown around his eyes gave him character, like the wrinkles of a wise old face.

Baji ate a few more bites of mush, then scooped the last chunks of muskrat out onto the frozen ground for Gitchi. He gulped them while he wagged his tail.

As Baji started to straighten up, sharp, birdlike chirping echoed nearby. Her head jerked around in time to see a flying squirrel leap from the tallest branches of a chestnut tree. Its enormous eyes shone. Using the fold of skin between its wrists and ankles to slow its descent, it glided down to land on the trunk of a maple, then quickly scampered up it and disappeared.

Baji set her bowl on the ground, quietly pulled her bow from her shoulder, and nocked an arrow. When she lifted her nose to scent the wind, the pungency of fear sweat wafted to her.

Dekanawida set his bowl down beside hers and tried to follow her gaze out into the trees. He whispered, "Did you see something?"

"There's someone out there. Let's move out of the firelight."

Dekanawida glanced down at Gitchi happily licking their bowls clean. "Gitchi doesn't seem to smell anything."

"Trust me."

She led the way around the pond to stand half-hidden behind a sycamore trunk as wide as three men standing shoulder-to-shoulder. Dekanawida took a position just behind her, peering over the top of her head.

The noise of Gitchi licking bowls suddenly stopped.

Baji glanced back at the wolf. He stood absolutely still, his tail straight out behind him, his muzzle pointed at something in the aspen grove on the other side of the pond.

8

SKY MESSENGER

My heartbeat quickens as I follow Baji's gaze to a dense grove of aspens that shine faintly white in the dark forest weave. Gitchi growls, barely audible.

Baji hisses, "Keep Gitchi here until I've circled around behind the fool. Once my arrow is in flight, we'll both rush him."

"I don't see anything. Where is he?"

She half draws back her bow. "Standing right there in the aspens."

With the silence of Eagle hunting Rabbit, Baji eases into the trees and vanishes amid the warp and weft of branches and trunks. Her steps are completely silent.

I slide around the massive sycamore to get a different view of the forest, and softly call, "Gitchi, lie down. Don't move."

The wolf flattens out behind the hearthstones with his ears laid back. His yellow eyes dance with reflected firelight, still focused unblinking on the aspens.

I don't understand why Gitchi and Baji see the intruder, and I do not. I cast a quick glance to my right at the thin, spiral-twisted pines where Baji disappeared. The morning air smells of hickory smoke and raspberries, almost obscuring the tangy forest fragrances.

I search for recognizable threats—human shapes like rounded heads, extended hands and legs amid the saplings. Often, strands of hair fluttering in the breeze or the swaying of a cape gives an opponent away. This murderer must be especially skilled, for I see absolutely nothing.

Then, far to the right of the aspens, a glint flashes and vanishes. It flashes again, moving through a thicket of chokecherries.

Jewelry? Cape decorations? Maybe a white arrow point being aimed at Baji or me?

I keep my gaze on the location, and slowly work my way through the frosty ferns that cover the forest floor. Each movement of my feet stirs a faint *shish*. Slipping from tree trunk to tree trunk, my gaze scans for movement. Where is Baji? She should be somewhere in the maples to my right. Can she see the light? Gitchi lies in the same place, at least partially sheltered behind the largest hearthstones. As the morning sky begins to shade deep purple, angled layers of snow-sheathed limestone appear and glisten amid the patchwork of shadows. Grass stems cluster at their bases. In the trees, fluffed out for warmth, birds hunch on the branches like small circular boles.

The light winks again and vanishes, heading into a grove of birch saplings. I glance back at Gitchi. He hasn't moved. His coat shimmers in the newborn light as though strewn with crushed amethyst. From this position, I can't see where his eyes focus. He seems to still be looking at the aspens, some fifteen paces ahead of me and to my left. If so, he's not looking at the flashes, but at something else.

Maybe there are two men out there.

I squint at the dense stand of birch saplings that create a slatted white wall, interrupted here and there by black streaks of forest background. The only motion now is a tremble of old leaves clinging to branch tips. The flashes are gone. Which may mean the man has stopped moving because he's sighted his prey. *Me.*

Wind Woman's breath carries the rich mineral scent of the forest floor at dawn, which tastes like iron on my tongue.

If I continue on this path, the space between my hiding place and the next tree trunk is three paces. Without knowing where my opponent stands, that is a killing space. By the time I reach the next maple, I will have been in the clear for three heartbeats. He can easily aim and let fly.

I'd be smiling right now if I were him. I'd inhale through my nostrils, and hold my breath, anticipating the moment my enemy tried to step to the next tree. Brush thrashes, followed by a hoarse, surprised cry, then a man shouts, "Stay *back!*"

He lunges from the aspens, releases two quick arrows at something behind him, then whirls and flees through the maples with his buckskin cape flying. He keeps glancing over his shoulder in terror. When he charges into the open, he sees me, gives me a wild look, and shouts, *"For the sake of the gods, don't you see it? What is it?"*

The faint whisper of an arrow lances the dawn, followed by a meaty splat.

The man grunts and careens forward, tumbling face-first to the ground, rolling several times before he can stop himself. The arrow has punched its way through his cape just above his heart. His voice turns into a high-pitched, breathless wail. *"It—it's coming! Help me!"*

Sobbing, he manages to shove up on his hands and knees and struggles to crawl away.

I shout, "Gitchi!" and burst from cover, pounding for the man as I search the forest for whatever has so terrified him. There must be another warrior out there, or perhaps a bear, or one of the flying heads—fearsome Spirit creatures with long trailing hair and great paws like a bear's.

Gitchi leaps up and streaks out ahead of me, his lean, muscled body cutting a deadly swath through the pale lavender light. At the very edge of my vision, I catch sight of Baji leaping deadfall as she dashes for our enemy. Gleaming waist-length hair bounces across her back as she runs.

"Gitchi, don't kill him!" I shout. "Just guard!"

Gitchi leaps around the man in a snarling, bristling blur. If the warrior even tries to grab for a weapon, Gitchi will tear his throat out.

I reach the man before Baji does. Hills People markings cover his cape. He lies on his back, his panicked eyes wide and unblinking. Blood already bubbles at his lips, rising from his wounded lung. He has a severe triangular face with a nose so thin the bones appear to have been removed. When Baji arrives holding her bow nocked and aimed down at his head, the man lets out a shrill cry and tries in vain to slide away from her.

I kneel beside him. "Who sent you? Chief Atotarho?"

Only his eyes move, sliding to me in dazed confusion. He chokes out the words, *"What…is…it?"*

Thinking that he means he didn't hear me, I repeat, "Did Chief Atotarho send you to murder me?"

His gaze returns to Baji and his eyes go so wide they resemble those of the flying squirrel, too huge for his face, bulging slightly from their sockets. He tries to speak again, but falls into a coughing fit that spatters gouts of blood across his chest and face. As the life drains from his eyes, a red pool spreads around him, looking faintly blue in the murky gleam.

Baji slowly releases the tension on her bowstring and her aim moves aside. "He was less than one heartbeat from killing you," she says, "when he suddenly went crazy and started shrieking. What do you make of that?"

I rise to my feet and frown down at him. "I think his soul was loose, Baji. That explains the strange light I saw."

"You saw a light?"

"Yes, winking in the trees. When a person's after-life soul is loose, it tries to stay as close to the body as it can, hoping to be allowed back inside. The flashes must have been his soul chasing after him."

Gitchi growls and edges forward to sniff the man's eyes. Bits of wind-blown forest duff stick to the wide orbs. After Gitchi has convinced himself that the enemy is dead, he backs away and drops to his haunches, patiently awaiting whatever comes next.

Baji and I stare at each other. The white knife scar that cuts across her pointed chin has picked up the bluish tint of the coming dawn. Black wavy hair frames her beautiful oval face and flutters over her buckskin cape. Her knee-high black leggings are speckled with old pine needles, collected in her mad dash through the forest. Seeing her standing there over the body of the man who was about to kill me is ethereal. Her hair blows softly in the breeze, feathering over her shoulders.

"You are so beautiful."

She tilts her head reprovingly, and her mouth quirks. "We were talking about insanity and murder."

"Well, I'm past that now. I'd rather talk about you, about how you look in the blue morning light, your long legs spread and your bow half-drawn. The image is heartrending."

She tucks her arrow back in her quiver, slings her bow over her left shoulder, and walks around the dead man to step into my arms. As she embraces me, a warm sensation tingles through my muscles. I rest my chin against her temple, and drown for a time in the silken texture of her hair. The glossy strands smell of campfires and leather, things that comfort me.

"I'm glad you're here with me," I whisper. "Being with you is all I've ever wanted."

She hugs me harder, her strong muscular arms like granite bands, but says, "I think you want peace more than me."

The soft words remind me of my duty to our Peoples. I heave a sigh. "I take it that you do not wish to stay here in my embrace any longer than necessary."

She laughs and looks up at me with shining eyes.

"If I could wish for anything, that would be it. But we do not have the luxury of wishing, Dekanawida.

We still have to pack up our camp. As it is, we won't make it to Shookas Village until late afternoon. And I have the feeling, somewhere deep inside me, that we *need* to get there. I don't know why, but I want to hurry."

She pushes away from me and clasps my hand. We walk back toward our fire with Gitchi at our heels.

As the day brightens, the scent of pine suffuses the cold air.

Out of curiosity, I ask, "Baji, where were you when the man burst from his hiding place in the aspens?"

Black waves dance around her face as she looks up and gives me a hesitant smile. "In the birch grove, why?"

"No reason. I just didn't see you out there. I…"

She smiles again and looks away. She's avoiding my eyes. Why?

My heart starts to pound harder as a strange, weightless sensation comes over me. The light. *No, no, it's not possible, but…*Images cascade. *Baji appearing on a trail I didn't even know I would take… running all the way to find me with a head wound that would have killed most men. No…I—I would know.*

I look down at her, my gaze searching for some sign…

As though my unspoken words are bludgeoning

her, she stops and a shiver goes through her. "What's wrong?"

"Nothing, I...I was just wondering..."

She looks up and the lines around her eyes tighten as though she senses my thoughts. Her gaze shifts, scanning the forest as she sighs, "Dekanawida, before we leave, there's something I need to tell you." She clutches my hand tighter.

"About what?"

Her black eyes glisten like jewels. "About what Shagoniyoh said to me on the trail."

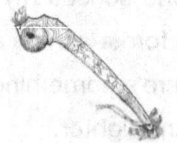

9

A short while later, Baji crouched across the ashes of the campfire, staring at Dekanawida in the resplendent predawn glow. Gitchi lay between them, his gray muzzle propped on his forepaws, watching in utter silence. Occasionally, when their voices grew strained, his tail lightly tapped the ground, trying to ease the tension by showing them he loved them.

Baji pulled a branch from the woodpile and toyed with it to keep her hands busy. Dekanawida's handsome face showed barely endurable pain. She could feel every shifting thought that moved behind his eyes. Like obsidian-sharp lances, they stabbed and jerked, cutting and carving her souls. Is this what strong emotions felt like in the afterworld? Is that why the Land of the Dead was beautiful and peaceful, and people only made war for sport? They couldn't bear anything else?

She gripped the branch harder. Generations of civilization, of corn and squash, had fallen away from her, leaving the sublime purity of the wild behind—and like an ancient wolf, she could smell the storm coming. The air tasted of snow and cold sweat. If it had been nightfall, she'd be digging her den in a snowbank, on the leeward side, where later she would be sheltered from the freezing darkness that engulfed the world outside.

"Baji, listen to me," Dekanawida insisted. "It means nothing. I tell you, it doesn't. Shago-niyoh frequently asks cryptic questions. He does it to teach—"

"I know. You've told me. But this is different. You and I both know it. I don't think he was trying to be cryptic. I think he came to help me find my way."

Dekanawida clamped his jaw to keep it still, and gazed at her like a man who refused to believe in the Faces of the Forest, though he saw one hovering right before his eyes. He balled his fists. Stubborn, he enunciated, "I—would—know."

She smiled. All the love in her heart must have shone on her face, for his tight jaw hardened. "All right. I just needed to tell you. I was tired of carrying the weight of it by myself."

She rose to her feet and adjusted her bow and

quiver where they draped her left shoulder. Her weapons belt clacked. "I'm ready to go if you are."

He drew a shallow breath and stood up. Short black hair blew over his face, and jet strands glued themselves to his high cheekbones. She hadn't realized he'd been crying.

Baji walked around the fire and embraced him hard enough to drive the air from his lungs. "Promise me that if you're wrong, you'll always take the time to stop and speak gently to old trees."

He crushed her against him. In her ear, he hoarsely whispered, "I'm not wrong."

10

As Sonon watched them trot away, moving up the snowy trail that led to Shookas Village, he placed a hand on the ancient oak beneath which he stood and caressed the cold bark. It had a rough, ridged texture. He could feel the brave soul of the warrior who slept inside, breathing deeply. All around him, massive sycamores and giant chestnuts dotted the forest, each filled with an old, old warrior. They towered above the rest of the canopy, their winter twigs like dark, trembling fingers grasping for wisps of drifting Cloud People.

Though Baji and Sky Messenger had vanished into the indigo shadows, the faint drumlike rhythm of their moccasins carried.

He closed his eyes to listen.

It was, perhaps, a strange truth that for most of their journey, human beings lived as impostors, wearing fear masks to ward off true intimacy. When their disguises at last failed, and they became truly present with one another, everything sensed it. Animals and trees turned to look. Great Grandmother Earth heaved a sigh. The universe itself tilted, balancing on each precious moment.

He didn't wish to disturb it. Better than most, he knew that great beauty and tears were inseparable, bound together in a crystalline shimmer of longing that tore the heart. Even at the end, love was the only thing that turned suffering into a beauty too great to be borne. Perhaps especially at the end.

A low bark split the morning.

Sonon opened his eyes to see Gitchi loping back down the trail. The old wolf stopped and cocked his head at Sonon, waiting, as though to say, *"What's taking you so long?"*

As Sonon lifted his hand to the wolf, signaling that he was coming, his black hood waffled around his face. Gitchi's bushy tail wagged, then he turned and trotted back the way he'd come, returning to Sky Messenger's side.

Sonon expelled a deep breath and stepped onto the trail.

Carefully, so as not to smudge them, he placed

his sandals in the tracks they'd left in the snow, hoping to touch their luminous paths, knowing that the dying world lay just ahead.

11

A totarho stood before his campfire, gripping the head of his walking stick with crooked aching fingers. The icy morning air had turned pink with the coming dawn. The heads of war clubs and arrow points glimmered as his warriors marched up the rise in the distance, weaving drunkenly across the old battlefield, avoiding the frozen corpses that covered the ground.

A smile turned his lips. Right now, High Matron Kittle must be shuddering, her knees quaking at the sight of over one thousand warriors surrounding Bur Oak Village. If he...

"My Chief?"

He turned to see Qonde and two wounded warriors climbing the slope to reach his camp. Atotarho had sent Nesi off to fight, which left

Qonde in charge of his personal guards for the day. A short, stocky man, Qonde's hawkish face bore streaks of soot. The tall man behind Qonde had his left arm in a sling, and the other man wore a bloody head bandage. Several other wounded warriors stood waiting thirty hands away. From the looks of them, they'd probably been injured in last night's fiery debacle at Yellowtail Village. As Qonde got closer, Atotarho called, "What is it?"

Qonde spoke to the men and came forward alone. "Forgive me, my Chief. War Chief Negano ordered the wounded to rest today, but these men would like to be of some use."

"So put them to use."

Qonde spread his arms. "I realize this is an intrusion, my Chief." He respectfully bowed again. "But I cannot countermand Negano's orders without your approval."

Annoyed, Atotarho waved the tall, wounded warrior forward. "What is your name, warrior?"

"Saponi, my Chief." The man bowed.

"Tell me what you wish to do? The battle is about to begin. I have more important duties than assigning menial tasks."

Saponi shifted his slung arm as though it hurt, and his narrowed gaze went over the camps. His face was so blackened with ash and soot that the whites of his eyes seemed to glow. Only about two hundred warriors remained scattered around dozens of fires. Most were wounded, useless. Several slept, curled as close to the fires as they could safely get. Somewhere, he heard corn popping.

Saponi said, "My Chief, it's hard staying out of the battle. There are many small duties we could accomplish to stay busy, carrying water, gathering branches for firewood, organizing the food stores."

Saponi gestured, and Atotarho's gaze slid to the stockpiled food guarded by two exhausted warriors who appeared to be asleep on their feet. Haunches of venison lay on the ground before them as though dropped by men too tired to stack them. All around, pots of nuts and seeds canted at angles, about to topple over if someone didn't right them. The baskets of high cranberries that had been collected yesterday had been left uncovered. In the night, raccoons and other animals had strewn many across through the frosty grass. *Negano is so incompetent!*

A shout went up. Atotarho turned.

Shrill calls carried across the hills as the first wave of his army began to move, at a slow march, closing in around Bur Oak Village. Far off, in the trees to the east and south, he saw the second and third waves slithering like long serpents, silently walking forward, their nocked arrows gleaming, readying themselves to lay siege. Clan flags of many colors hung slack in the morning stillness as men marched into position. Atotarho's blood began to surge in his ears.

"My Chief?" Saponi said softly.

Atotarho flicked a hand. "Yes, I place you in charge of such things. Now go away and let me concentrate."

"Yes, my Chief. Thank you." Saponi bowed deeply, then nodded gratefully to Qonde for allowing him to approach Atotarho.

Qonde sighed and went back to his position with Atotarho's other guards. He could hear them joking, but couldn't make out the words. Nervous laughter erupted.

Saponi rejoined the group of wounded warriors, where he seemed to be assigning duties. Heads nodded, and warriors plodded off to obey whatever orders he'd given.

As Elder Brother Sun lifted from the World Tree, his shining face crested the eastern horizon and sunlight swathed the tallest branches with gold. Moments later, his light flooded across the valley, sparkling through the frost, turning it the palest of yellows.

Negano's voice rang out, giving the call to advance. Atotarho searched for his War Chief, but saw only his warriors charging forward. Atotarho had ordered Negano to hit hard immediately, hoping it would shock the enemy into submission. As the first line, men carrying ladders, raced to the exterior palisade, and attempted to climb up and over into the village, the second line, all archers, let fly. Up and down the Bur Oak catwalks enemy warriors fell, but it didn't stop the Standing Stone warriors. They concentrated their fire upon his warriors, scaling the ladders, cleanly picking them off, leaving them lying in bristly heaps at the base of the palisade. From every direction, cries wavered in a singsong of agony. The Bur Oak defenders shoved away the ladders. Where they fell upon the frosty ground, they resembled crisscrossing sticks. The second line moved up and a third line of archers took its place, preparing to let fly. The fourth line, still in the trees, appeared to have frozen solid. They resembled human-shaped ice sculptures, white and still, watching.

"F-forgive me, my Chief," Qonde said from behind Atotarho.

He swung around in rage. *"What?"*

Qonde's shoulders hunched defensively. He extended a hand to point at a white-haired man with a battered face, scarred around the mouth like an old fighter. He wore a grim expression.

"Who is that?"

"Chief Wenisa of the Mountain People sent him to speak with you."

"Tell him to come forward. Quickly."

Qonde waved and the man came forward in a half-crouch, as though he couldn't straighten up.

"What is your name?"

The old man bowed. "I am Wasa, Beaver Clan of the People of the Mountain, and messenger for the great Chief Wenisa."

"Yes, what is it?"

The square-headed elder took a breath, as though about to deliver a lengthy message. "Our Ruling Council wishes you to know that it received your message asking if we wished to participate in the final destruction of the Standing Stone nation—"

"Is it sending forces?"

"Yes. They should arrive in two days, if the weather—"

"How many?"

The elder shifted, as though not accustomed to being interrupted. "Two thousand will be at your disposal, providing we can come to an agreement. Our Ruling Council assigned me to negotiate with you."

"Negotiate?" Atortarho glared. "I offered to split Standing Stone territory equally between our peoples. There's nothing else to negotiate. Either your Ruling Council wishes to accept, or it doesn't." But a vague unease went through Atotarho. If two thousand Mountain warriors were on their way here, the situation could rapidly deteriorate. After today's battle, he estimated that he would have perhaps nine hundred warriors left. If

Wenisa wanted, when he arrived, he could turn his forces on Atotarho's.

"With respect, Chief," Wasa said. "Your offer of half the territory was enough to get us to send warriors, but not enough to guarantee our full support."

From the corner of his vision, Atotarho saw his warriors launch a shimmering wave of arrows into the morning sunlight. He gritted his teeth, longing to watch, but kept his attention on the messenger.

"I see. What would be enough?"

Wasa took a moment to watch the volley strike Bur Oak Village. Screams, shouts, and cheers rose.

"Should we decide to give you our full support, the Mountain People's Ruling Council will wish to have your full support in return."

"My full support to do what?" Atotarho gripped his walking stick, ready to strike the old hunchback if he didn't get to the point.

Wasa straightened slightly, as though sensing Atotarho's patience was at an end. "Just as you wish to completely destroy the Standing Stone nation, we wish to obliterate the Landing People. After we're finished helping you here, we ask that you lead your army back to the Landing villages and help us wipe them from the face of Great Grandmother Earth. In exchange, we will give you half of their territory."

He needed time to consider the ramifications of

such an arrangement. "When do you require an answer to this request? My Ruling Council—"

"Perhaps we are mistaken." Wasa tilted his head as though he knew he was being toyed with. "We have heard you have supreme control of the Hills nation. The Ruling Council merely advises you. Is that wrong?"

Atotarho's livid expression must have worried the elder, for the old man's eyes narrowed to slits. With deadly softness, he said, "I have control."

"Then, since you do not have to send a message to your Ruling Council seeking permission for this agreement, we require an answer immediately."

Atotarho took a new grip on the head of his walking stick. The impudence was stunning! Not only that, it would outrage the Ruling Council if the Hills army destroyed the Standing Stone nation today, and no longer needed the Mountain People's help. Chief Wenisa would arrive expecting to be awarded half the Standing Stone territory for coming as he'd asked, and Atotarho would be forced to give it to him, lest Wenisa turn his army on Atotarho's decimated forces.

Which the greedy fool might do anyway once he sees that his forces greatly outnumber mine.

Cheers echoed from across the valley, high-pitched, pounding the air. Atotarho kept his gaze on Wasa's.

"Tell your Ruling Council its offer is acceptable."

Wasa bowed deeply and smiled. "Then our army will be at your disposal."

Wasa backed away and hobbled toward four men Atotarho had not seen before. They stood just on the other side of his personal guards, carrying the litter that must have borne Wasa here.

Atotarho watched the old man climb onto the litter, then his bearers carried the old man off toward the trail to the west.

He turned back to the battle. The Bur Oak palisade was on fire in several places. Warriors scurried along the catwalks, dumping water onto the flames. Every drop brought them closer to destruction.

A low laugh shook Atotarho.

No matter how many warriors he lost today, with the two thousand that he'd instructed Kelek to send back to him, and the two thousand Mountain warriors already on their way...the Standing Stone nation would soon be nothing but a despicable memory.

12

Clusters of black willows and yellow birches whiskered the slope in front of Hiyawento and Towa, running like a rumpled blanket down to Shookas Village. In the late afternoon light, the windblown branches created a vista of constant movement where shadows leaped and danced across the hills. Fortunately, the forest fire had not reached here. This was the first time since dawn that Hiyawento had been able to get a breath of fresh air into his ash-choked lungs.

Hiyawento gripped his war club and studied the hastily constructed camps that completely encircled the village palisades. Most were composed of scavenged branches that had been tied together at the tops and covered with hides, and they resembled small rounded huts. From this perspective, he couldn't see inside Shookas Village, but warriors crowded the catwalks of the double palisade. He tried to estimate their numbers. Maybe eight hundred on the walls?

They're expecting an attack.

To the west of Shookas Village, Sapling River cut an arc that paralleled the curve of the oval palisades. The dark green water glinted with sunlight as it wound its way across the countryside.

"Blessed Ancestors," Towa said in a dire voice. "The entire nation must have fled to Shookas Village."

"My guess is that there are two or three thousand people outside the walls, living in the huts. How many usually live inside?"

Towa shrugged and his long black braid, which hung like a frizzy rope over his left shoulder, bobbed up and down. "After the fever that devastated them last moon? Maybe two thousand. There are six longhouses, each is six hundred to seven hundred hands long. Before the fever around three thousand people occupied the village. If there are three thousand outside, plus two thousand living here, and even more refugees from other villages in the plaza...there are probably another three or four thousand people inside the walls."

"Then six or seven thousand people total? Of

those, around two thousand are trained warriors. What do you think is going on?"

Towa shook his head. "I don't know. Perhaps, like our own faction of the Hills nation, they've abandoned all their other villages and joined forces to protect each other."

"Or every other Landing village has been destroyed, like Agweron Village."

"Yes, that's possible." Towa's brown eyes narrowed as he surveyed the thousands of people roaming between the huts. Children darted around, playing games, as though nothing was wrong. Occasionally dogs barked. "Where are we supposed to meet Sky Messenger?"

"About where we're standing, on the eastern trail into Shookas Village."

Towa rubbed his jaw with his sleeve. "I don't like the looks of this. There are too many warriors on the catwalks. I think they're expecting a raid."

"I agree. Which means they're going to be especially vigilant. Are you sure you can get us through that crowd and into the village to see High Matron Weyra?"

"Well"—Towa gestured uncertainly—"no one has ever tried to stop me before."

"No, but have you ever entered their village with a Hills War Chief at your side?"

"I'm still alive, aren't I? Of course not. And I

won't today, either. As of this instant you are not a war chief. You're my new assistant, a young Trader from the Standing Stone People on his first visit to the Landing villages."

Hiyawento shifted uncomfortably. "Why the Standing Stone nation, and not—"

"Because they hate the Hills People almost as much as they hate the Mountain People, though not quite. They're attacked far more frequently by Mountain raiders. And your Standing Stone accent may help us. Matron Jigonsaseh and Matron Kittle routinely feed Landing war parties as they pass through Standing Stone country. As a result, a small amount of goodwill exists between the Landing and Standing Stone nations."

Hiyawento thought about that. Not so long ago High Matron Kittle had made a point of telling him that he had no name among their people. He was Outcast. Forgotten. When he'd allowed himself to be adopted into the Hills nation so that he could marry Zateri, he'd committed treason. It had been a moment of generosity on Kittle's part that she had not carried out his death sentence on the spot. Of course, that was before he'd switched sides and fought shoulder-to-shoulder with Sky Messenger against Atotarho. But he still felt uncomfortable about pretending to be a Standing Stone Trader. However, if such a deception would help Sky

Messenger? Well, his feelings were of no consequence. "Very well. What's my name?"

Towa gazed at him thoughtfully. "I'd go by my boyhood name: Wrass. It's easier to remember. You're Bear Clan of Yellowtail Village, just as you were before you wed Zateri. And when Sky Messenger arrives, he will be Odion."

"What if someone recognizes us? Most war chiefs know each other."

"True, but many of their war chiefs died when the fever swept their villages. Still, I think we should paint our faces before we approach the camps."

Towa shrugged out of his Trader's pack and knelt on the trail before it. As he pulled out his paints box, Hiyawento glimpsed the black pointed shapes of buffalo horn sheaths. Since they were worth a fortune, Hiyawento was surprised that Towa hadn't hidden them somewhere, waiting for a more opportune time to Trade them.

"Are you hoping to Trade here?"

"Absolutely. That's why we're here. And you'd better remember it." As he opened his paints box, the cold leather hinges squealed. "As we Trade, we will talk about the great miracle that occurred during the Bur Oak battle, but we'll just be gossiping, passing along the news of other nations, as Traders do."

"What about Sky Messenger's vision? Shouldn't we—"

"Really, Hiyawento." Towa looked up and his mouth quirked. "How poor a Trader do you think I am? Since I first heard of his vision, I've been carrying the story everywhere I go. The last time I was here, the Ruling Council called in every storyteller. They asked me to retell the story over and over, to make sure they had the details right, so they could go home and repeat it."

"Do they believe his vision?"

Towa rose with his paints box in hand, studied Hiyawento's eagle-like face and dipped a fingertip into the white paint. A mixture of clay, crushed shell, and bear fat, it had a pleasing sparkle. As he began painting Hiyawento's face, he answered, "I happen to be a very good storyteller. When I was finished with the fifth telling, no one with a soul could have doubted its truth. Every jaw in the council house hung slack with awe. Even the children had hushed and stared at me with huge eyes."

Hiyawento smiled. "Sky Messenger will appreciate that, old friend."

"He'd better. Retelling the story forced me to remain in the midst of the sickness far longer than I'd intended. I had to stay away from Riverbank Village for another five days to make sure I hadn't been infested with the Evil Spirits. The last thing I wished to do was carry them home to Riverbank

Village." In a sad voice he added, "Though when I arrived I discovered sickness had already entered the village, carried in the bodies of Flint captives taken during the latest raid on Monster Rock Village."

Concerned, Hiyawento asked, "How are your wife and son?"

"Both were sickened, but got well. I was fortunate. Many others perished."

The expressions on Towa's handsome face shifted as he scrutinized his painting, then decided to add black circles around Hiyawento's eyes and mouth. "There, not even Sky Messenger would recognize you."

While Towa painted his own face, red on top and gray on the bottom, Hiyawento's gaze returned to the village. As Elder Brother Sun descended in the west, the colors of the late afternoon began to shade toward dusk. The yellow sunlight that had illuminated hundreds of huts only moments ago had turned deep amber, and the lengthening forest shadows pointed eastward like black lightning bolts zigzagging across the hills.

When the breeze shifted, the scent of hundreds of campfires blew around him.

Towa tucked his paints box back into his pack, tugged the laces tight and slipped it over his shoulders again. As he rose, he exhaled the words, "I think we should get a little closer. Their scouts will already have spotted us. If we just keep standing here they will become suspicious that we are Mountain People spies. Are you ready?"

"Yes."

"Then let's go, Wrass."

Towa led the way down the hill at a slow trot.

13

Matron Jigonsaseh stopped long enough to tuck grimy black hair behind her ears. As the hush of evening settled over Bur Oak Village, small fires continued to burn, mostly in the longhouse roofs, sending ash floating across the plaza in waves. The cool air was pungent with the odor of charred slippery elm bark, and redolent with the cries of the wounded and grieving. Their losses had been devastating. When they were attacked again, *not if,* they'd be overrun. She suspected it would take Negano less than four hands of time to completely destroy the last survivors of the Standing Stone nation.

She propped a hand on CorpseEye where he rested in her belt, and continued toward the wounded where they were laid out in rows. The few remaining pots of water had been stashed close to them. From this point on, only the wounded that were certain to live would receive water. Her long-empty stomach—empty of both food and water, for she would not eat or drink if her warriors couldn't—had been playing tricks on her souls. Sometimes the screams and sobs seemed far away and tiny, like the incoherent dreams born of a fever. Later, they bombarded her like huge fists, beating her heart to dust. She was tired, so tired, but she could not lie down until this was finished.

A curious numbness had begun to filter through her body at noon, and totally possessed her by sundown, killing her emotions. She should feel glad that they had survived another day, but the only thought that came to her was that she had to figure out a way to make it just one more. *One more day, my ancestors, just let me fight for one more day.*

The only good news was that the major fires had been doused...but it had required almost all of their precious water to keep the village from becoming one gigantic fireball.

"Matron?" a wounded warrior called from where he lay on the ground. "Matron, a moment?"

Jigonsaseh knelt at his side. She'd seen Bahna working on his wound earlier. He was one of Sindak's men. Barely seventeen summers old, with long filthy hair draped around his narrow face in stringy locks, the youth had kind brown eyes. She suspected he had a family back home in Atotarho village. He must be worried about them. "What is it, warrior?"

"I know we have...very little water, but...one sip?" He tipped his head to the pot that rested just out of his reach with a cup over the top, and gazed up at her with a pained expression.

She reached for the pot, poured a small amount into the cup and gently lifted his head to tip the cup to his lips. He drank the three swallows greedily, then sighed, "Thank you, Matron."

She gently eased his head back to the blanket and reached to return the cup to its place over the water pot.

"Matron?" the warrior asked in an exhausted voice. "I can't feel my legs. Tell me why?"

She did not hesitate. "The arrow struck close to your lower spine." His face visibly paled, and she added, "It didn't sever your spine. Our Healers say you will heal and walk again, perhaps in one moon. Be grateful. You will live to see your family again. Many others lying in the plaza will not."

His gaze scanned the bodies, arranged in rows, and lingered for a long time on the wounded children and elders who'd stood on the palisade firing their bows until the very last. "I appreciate hearing the truth, Matron."

She gave him a confident nod. "You fought bravely today. Your service to the alliance will never—"

"Will there be an alliance after tomorrow, Matron? Or will it die with us?"

Jigonsaseh stared into his eyes. Given the severity of his wound, it surprised her that he realized the truth of their situation. She reached down to take his hand in a powerful grip. "No one will forget what we did here today, warrior. What *you* did here. Our sacrifices will be the glue that will bind the alliance and keep it together for generations."

He smiled at the absolute certainty in her deep voice. "Thank you, Matron." When he released her hand, he sank into his blankets to close his eyes as though he couldn't stay awake for another instant.

Jigonsaseh rose to her feet. The warriors on the catwalks had begun to walk around briskly as their voices rose in pitch. To the east, she saw High Matron Kittle standing between Sindak and Gonda. Gonda leaned heavily on his crutch, trying to relieve the pain in his splinted leg, but he was pointing at something.

She put her head down, and marched to the closest ladder to climb up to the catwalk. As she made her way toward them, warriors buzzed with excited conversation. Out across the old battlefield hundreds of campfire had glimmered to life. Negano was taking no chances. He'd moved his entire army into a ring around Bur Oak Village, bottling them up tight, making certain no one could reach the marsh again. Just out of bowshot, hundreds of Hills warriors paraded around, some shouting. Others waved their arms furiously.

As she walked up, Gonda turned. His round face had a pain-stricken expression. He maneuvered his crutch so he could hobble around to face her. "Something's going on out there."

She squinted out across the battlefield. The commotion was spreading through the ranks, men and women stalking around like stiff-legged dogs while they cursed.

Kittle said, "What do you think is happening? It looks like a riot."

A grim smile turned Sindak's lips. He laughed softly and looked at Jigonsaseh. Ash coated his lean face. "Saponi did it." Pride filled his voice. "He did it."

"What do you mean all the food is gone! Our warriors are starving!" War Chief Negano shook both fists in the face of the warrior hunching before him. Qonde's hawkish face had a tortured expression, as though he expected Negano to strike him. "What happened to it? When I left before dawn, we had plenty—"

"Negano, it's not my fault!" Short and stocky, Qonde bravely straightened to his full height and clenched his fists at his sides. Sweat matted his black hair to his cheeks. "After you left, a group of wounded warriors came to me asking to speak with the chief! They said they wished to be useful, and Atotarho told them to reorganize the food stores. They said they were hauling the deer haunches into the forest shadows to keep them cold. It made sense, and the battle had just started, I was watching—"

"When did you discover all the food was gone?"

"Not until late afternoon! I sent warriors to search the ground, even the tree branches, thinking they might have—"

"Dear gods." Negano rubbed a hand over his stunned face.

His warriors had fought hard all day long. Exhausted and with empty bellies, most had just miserably walked away when the news had come. But around two hundred had encircled Negano. Shouting curses, they shook war clubs and fists in the air, ready to kill whoever was responsible for denying them a well-deserved supper.

Fear twisted deep in Negano's belly. "Where is the chief?"

Qonde's shoulders hunched again. He swung around to point to the northern end of the camp. "I warn you. He's not happy, Negano."

Negano squeezed his eyes closed and massaged

his forehead. "It's too late to send out hunting parties, which means there will be no food for breakfast tomorrow, either. Tell the chief that I expect many warriors will desert tonight, and more will vanish tomorrow. Even if we—"

"You want *me* to tell him? I'm not War Chief, you are! You tell him!"

His nerves humming, Negano grabbed Qonde by the front of his cape, shook him violently, and shouted in his face, "Do it! *I gave you an order!*

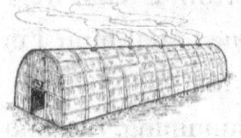

14

Baji and Dekanawida had avoided the main trail that led to Shookas Village, choosing instead a narrow trail that wound through the eastern hills. The acrid scent of forest fires clung in the air.

She felt a new stirring in the land. Oddly, the knowledge came to her not by sight and sound, but something deeper. As though she could extend her soul beyond her body and out into the forest, every part of her, muscle and sinew, felt the land awakening. The animals felt it, too. Bounding deer chirped the news, squirrels leaping between branches chittered about it, Great Grandmother Earth tried to beat the awareness into Baji each time her moccasins struck the ground.

When she broke into a run, passing

Dekanawida on a downward slope, he gave her a curious glance and pounded after her.

He must sense it, too. We are almost there. The last meadow in the belly of the clouds awaits us.

As they careened down the slope and headed up the next rise, Shookas Village appeared. Dekanawida let out a low confused sound and staggered to a stop, staring at the fire-devastated landscape. His round face streamed sweat. Breathing hard, Baji halted beside him to assess what they saw. Hundreds of camps dotted the flats around the village, and thousands of people milled around them.

"Why are so many people here?" he asked.

"It looks like the end of the world to me. And I feel it, don't you?"

Sky Messenger sucked in a breath and exhaled the words, "All I feel is scared, Baji."

Gitchi growled as he paced back and forth in front of them with his neck fur bristling and rippling. The old wolf had lived a long, strong life, filled with battle, and bitter cold, and hunger that stalked the souls. He knew without being told that war was in the air he breathed.

"I fear," Baji said, "that they are preparing a giant war party." Her gaze scanned the crowded palisades and lightly skimmed across the hide huts. "Weapons are everywhere."

Dekanawida said, "I don't see Hiyawento."

The dread in his voice made her smile. She reached out and clasped his hand. "Has he ever let any of us down? No. Not even when we were children. He's here. I'm looking forward to seeing—"

"Baji, I want you to stay here," he said suddenly. He turned to stare down at her, and his cape flapped around his tall body, whipping into snapping folds when the wind gusted just right. His broad chest expanded and shrank with his panting lungs.

Calmly, she asked, "Why?"

"When this is over, if I survive, I'll meet you on this very spot."

She tilted her head. "Why do you want me to stay behind?"

"Because"—he reached out to still the long black hair that blew around her face—"if things go wrong in there, I'll be so worried about you that I will forget everything else I must do."

"Is that it, really?" she asked mildly. "Or are you afraid that no one else will be able to see—"

"That's not it. I swear it." He shook his head as though denying something he knew in his heart. "Please do this? Just stay here and wait for me."

She searched his taut expression. "I'll do whatever you need me to. You know that."

He heaved a relieved breath, as if she'd removed a great weight from his shoulders and bent down to kiss her. His lips were warm and soft, caressing. When he drew back, he said, "I'll return as soon as I can. No matter what happens, never forget how much I love you."

Baji smiled and gestured to the trail. "Stop stalling. I'll be waiting right over there in the trees, watching for you."

Dekanawida backed away and his eyes narrowed. "Gitchi, stay. Guard Baji."

The wolf trotted over to Baji's side and stood looking up at her. She scratched his head.

As Dekanawida trotted away, Gitchi's big front paws nervously kneaded the ground, as though eager to run after his best friend.

Baji looked down at him. As he leaned against her leg, she said, "He's afraid to lose you, too, you know?"

Gitchi's ears pricked, listening attentively. She petted the wolf's neck for a long time, letting his soft warmth seep into her, before she walked off the trail through the frozen brown leaves to stand beneath the arching branches of a beech tree.

She braced her shoulder against the smooth gray bark and gazed upward at the crows sailing through the sky with their ebony wings flashing in the sunlight. Gitchi stood beside her, his nose up, sniffing for danger.

Baji tingled. She didn't understand it, but every time she got off the trail and stole cat-footed into the forest shadows, a supernatural vitality filled her. Life seemed to rear up and charge through her veins with such exquisite freedom she felt she would burst with the sheer ecstasy of it.

I feel so alive.

Her entire life, in one form or another, she had existed in perpetual fear of things seen or unseen. Now all that was gone. Like white water rushing away down a river, it had receded into the far country.

Gitchi whimpered.

She lowered her fingers to absently stroke his head. As though the wolf understood more than she did, he whimpered again.

Baji looked down. His yellow eyes had a tight look, as though he sensed her leaving him, and didn't want her to go.

"I'm still here, fool," she teased.

Gitchi gently licked her hand.

15

When they reached the eastern-most periphery of the camps, Towa slowed to a walk and lifted his hand to every person he saw. Almost everyone recognized him and smiled in return. Hiyawento carefully examined them. These people's capes hung about them in shreds, and their moccasins and leggings were a patchwork of sewn-up holes. No jewelry clicked or glinted.

Towa whispered, "Let's just walk along the edge of the camps. That will look perfectly normal to the warriors on the palisades."

"I understand."

As they passed each fire, Hiyawento tried to identify the thin soups that filled the supper pots: dried milkweed and ferns were the main ingredients, but occasionally he caught sight of mushrooms or chunks of desiccated grasshoppers.

Hiyawento said, "They have no meat? No corn, beans, or squash? No sunflowers?"

Towa shook his head as he weaved between two huts. Four women sat outside, talking, using bone awls threaded with cordage to sew up the holes in badly worn hides—hides anyone else would have thrown away.

"A pleasant afternoon to you," Towa said warmly.

One of the women lifted a hand, and they fell back into their conversation, barely glancing up at Towa and Hiyawento as they casually walked by.

"A little rude," Hiyawento murmured.

"Don't blame them. They have nothing to Trade. My presence just reminds them of how poor they are."

The remnants of last autumn's cornfields stood along the riverbank. The stalks—hacked off at the ground—had barely grown to the size of Hiyawento's little finger. They'd obviously gotten no corn from these fields. They'd cut the stalks to weave into mats, baskets, dolls, ropes, or sandals, maybe even boiled them to extract what little nutrients they contained, but they hadn't fed many people, if any.

A group of five boys walked by, and Hiyawento stared at their bulging eyes. Their heads appeared huge, wobbling on bony necks. When Towa noticed Hiyawento's undue attention, he whispered, "Take a good look. The next time you think your people are hungry, remember these children."

Hiyawento swallowed hard. "No wonder the Mountain People have been hitting them so hard."

Every nation was struggling to survive, so they viewed the troubles of others as opportunities. Any village that was sick or starving became a target. Their neighbors waited until they were too weak to fight back, then they attacked, ransacked the food stores, and killed their enemies.

A memory slipped from the locked door where Hiyawento kept it buried...*last spring...boiling maple sap with my three daughters...pouring the syrup into wooden molds...waiting until it hardened and turned to sugar...sweet treats and laughter...so much love in their eyes...*

His steps faltered as he forced their smiling faces away. Jimer and Catta had been so beautiful.

"Are you all right?" Towa asked. He gazed at Hiyawento in concern. "You just made an agonized sound."

"Sorry. I..." He took a breath and held it for a few heartbeats. "I was thinking about last spring. We made maple sugar candy in Coldspring Village."

"Yes, we did in Riverbank Village, as well. I know for a fact that the Landing People didn't have a chance to. Mountain raiders tapped all their trees long before they could get to them."

To Hiyawento's right, he glimpsed a tall man striding between huts, heading straight for them, his short black hair flapping over his high cheekbones.

As he trotted up, Sky Messenger said, "I almost didn't recognize you." He embraced Hiyawento and for the first time in days, Hiyawento smiled in true happiness.

He pounded his friend's back. "It's good to see you. I've been worried. We've spent half our time dodging war parties."

"Me, too."

When they separated, Hiyawento said, "We should probably paint your face before we try to—"

"No, not me." Sky Messenger turned abruptly to embrace Towa. "Gods, it's good to see you."

"And you, my friend."

Then Sky Messenger looked from Towa to Hiyawento, and his smile faded. "Tell me everyone made it safely to Canassatego Village."

"Yes," Hiyawento answered, "though Canassatego was attacked shortly after they arrived. But that's a long story for another time. It will be dark soon."

Sky Messenger's eyes shifted to the village gates. "We have more important duties."

Towa sternly said, "All right, listen to me, both

of you. Let me do the talking. Sky Messenger, until you reveal yourself, I will introduce you as my new assistant, Odion. Do you understand?"

"Perfectly." He nodded.

"All right. Follow me and act obsequious, like you worship me."

Towa walked up to the gates and cupped a hand to his mouth. "Towa, the greatest Trader in the land, requests entry to Shookas Village!"

Laughter ran down the catwalks, and a man with a shaved scalp leaned over to look down at them. Tattoos covered his face, including a spiral on the tip of his long nose. "Towa! You're back sooner than we thought. Who are these men with you?"

"My new assistants, Wrass and Odion, both are from the Standing Stone nation. I am training them in the great and noble art of Trading."

"And what worthless trinkets have you brought this time?"

"Many worthless trinkets, Nokweh! You will be amazed and delighted by the price I ask, I assure you!"

"Oh, yes," the man said doubtfully. "I'm sure I will." He signaled to someone Hiyawento couldn't see, and said, "The gates will be open shortly."

Towa grinned up. "I'm glad to see you alive, Deputy War Chief. I feared you'd fallen to the—"

"I'm War Chief now, Towa. Our former War

Chief is traveling the Path of Souls." Grief twisted the man's bony face.

"Ah," Towa said sadly. "I will miss him. Did the fever take him?"

"No. The Mountain People have been ravaging our country, killing anyone they can. Our women and children are afraid to go out to fill pots at the river for fear that they'll be ambushed by the vile beasts. Our former War Chief fought to his last breath to protect his people; he fell to one of their arrows."

Towa glanced back at the huts that extended for as far as they could see. "Is that why so many people are camped around Shookas? Are these all refugees from destroyed villages?"

"A few survivors ran here from Agweron Village. The others are not refugees. Three days ago our scouts reported a huge Mountain army on the move. We assumed they would be coming here to finish us for good. Decanasora Village and Elehana Village chose to abandon their homes and move here to consolidate our forces. It makes strategy easier."

"Strategy?"

"Yes, my friend. Haven't you heard? It's the news of the camps. We are organizing the largest army in the history of our People. Apparently the Mountain army was not on its way here, but headed elsewhere. That means their villages are

poorly defended. We are going to attack and annihilate every Mountain village in the land."

Towa gave Nokweh a pained nod. "I'm sure
you will, too. Landing warriors are the best in the
world."

Nokweh glanced to his left and said, "Get
ready. The guards are opening the gates."

"We thank you!" Towa lifted a hand again.

The gates swung open and Towa, Hiyawento,
and Sky Messenger passed by the guards with
respectful nods, and walked out into the crowded
plaza.

Sky Messenger softly said, "If they destroy the
Mountain villages, it will provoke a war of annihi-
lation. You know that, don't you?"

"Yes, of course," Towa whispered. "But look
around you. No parent can peer into the eyes of a
starving child without picking up weapons and
doing whatever is necessary to keep that child
alive."

"Attacking the Mountain villages will not
accomplish that. They are as bad off, or worse,
than—"

"I know that, Sky Messenger. I've been
there."

Five longhouses encircled the broad plaza,
each stretching six or seven hundred hands long,
and forty wide. Chunks of the elm bark walls had
been ripped out, while others were charred. Fire-

light gleamed through the holes like the campfires of the dead.

Forty paces ahead of them, in the middle of the plaza, people packed shoulder-to-shoulder around a large bonfire, apparently listening to an ugly little man. The fellow shouted from where he stood on a massive hickory stump overlooking the assembly. He wore his hair in a traditional Flint roach, shaved on the sides with a black bristly strip in the middle. Few teeth remained in his mouth and they were yellowed and half-rotted. To the speaker's left, the Ruling Council of the Landing People, composed of twelve elders, sat on log benches, listening. They each wore a white cape, decorated with the symbols of their clans.

"Who's the orator?" Sky Messenger asked softly. "I can't tell from here."

"That's Tagohsah," Towa said. "I wonder what he's doing here? His rounds usually bring him to Shookas Village in the middle of the moon. I try to arrive several days before just to avoid him."

Hiyawento whispered, "Let's move closer so we can hear what he's saying."

The crowd's attention, riveted on Tagohsah, didn't shift as Hiyawento, Sky Messenger, and Towa weaved through the tightly packed bodies, stepping into any gap that opened. Tagohsah must have begun talking only a short while ago, because fragments of the story had just begun filtering back through the listeners, relayed in awed whispers.

A young woman in front of Hiyawento said, "Atotarho attacked Bur Oak and Yellowtail villages with eight thousand warriors..." Then she turned back to hear the next few words being repeated, and said, "The Standing Stone army was cut down like blades of dry grass..." She turned to listen again.

Sky Messenger and Hiyawento exchanged a look, and slipped closer, shouldering between two men. Towa followed along behind them.

A toothless old man whispered, "Atotarho's forces killed over two thousand five hundred Standing Stone warriors...that's when the Hills nation crumbled to dust...Coldspring Village, along with Riverbank and Canassatego villages, turned against Atotarho and fought on the side of the Standing Stone nation."

Hiyawento murmured, "They're talking about the battle five days ago."

"Yes," Towa replied, and stepped into a slim space that allowed him to move two steps closer.

Hiyawento and Sky Messenger followed. A young warrior carrying a war club propped on his shoulder said, "Then a Flint war party appeared, lined out on the hills to the east...the Flint warriors, too, fought on the side of the Standing Stone nation...the battle was so great and terrible it shook the ground...just when it looked like the Standing Stone alliance was about to be overrun, killed to the last person...the Prophet stepped out..."

Sky Messenger's expression changed, as though the sense of wonder in the youth's voice had made his heart thunder.

Hiyawento clung to his friend's side, his hands invisible beneath his long cape, holding tight to his belted war club. A low hum of awed voices spread across the plaza, coming in waves, each portion of the tale repeated from one person to the next, but there was always someone who didn't believe. Someone who longed to earn a reputation by killing legends. Well, he'd have to kill Hiyawento first.

The youth swung around again, his starved face alight. "The Prophet, the human False Face known to the Standing Stone nation as Sky Messenger, lifted his hands, ordering the armies to stop fighting...Elder Brother Sun saw him...he sent a great monstrous storm crashing down upon the battlefield, scattering Atotarho's army like old leaves in a hurricane! Atotarho's forces ran. *They ran!*"

Hiyawento slid into a new gap in the milling crowd and managed to get four steps closer. Sky Messenger and Towa were right behind him.

"Blessed gods!" a woman half-shouted, "the Prophet alone remained to face the storm! Just before the spinning darkness swallowed him, his cape transformed into billows of white clouds, and he rode the winds of destruction like one of the Cloud People. When the storm had passed over the battlefield, the Prophet appeared again, hovering over the battlefield like one of the Sky People. Not a single hair upon his head had been disturbed!"

Towa leaned sideways to murmur to Sky Messenger, "I heard it a bit differently."

A tight smile tensed Sky Messenger's face. "Someone should tell them the truth."

Towa shook his head. "Bad idea. Look at them."

Reverence lined every face and filled every voice.

Hiyawento looked around, trying to hear words through the general noise of thousands of voices.

"...the human False Face has come...he is among us right now...the Faces of the Forest walk with him..."

There was a momentary hush, then an old man with a deeply wrinkled face turned and repeated, "Atotarho attacked them again...just a few days ago. He's there now trying to starve the last survivors to death!"

Towa jerked around to look at Hiyawento and Sky Messenger. "Dear gods. Did you know this?"

"No." Sky Messenger's voice had gone deep with shock.

Hiyawento clutched his war club tighter. He had to get word to Zateri. She'd probably already sent back as many warriors as she could afford, as she'd promised Kittle she would, but—

"I wish to speak." High Matron Weyra stood and lifted a hand to the crowd. Thin white hair fluttered around her wrinkled face. She'd seen perhaps fifty-five summers, and had a fleshy nose that rippled when she scratched it. After the voices died down, she called, "It seems the Hills People have the same designs on Standing Stone territory as the Mountain People do on ours, and neither nation will stop at anything to achieve its goals. We must—"

Sky Messenger shouted, *"That's because we have an amnesia of the heart. We've forgotten that we were once one People!"*

Towa hissed, "It's unhealthy to interrupt the most powerful woman in the nation."

Sky Messenger boldly shouldered through the crowd. As he passed, eyes went wide, men and women shuffled backward, and a stunned chorus began to whisper across the plaza, *"It's him... Blessed Gods, it's the Prophet...it's Sky Messenger!... No, it's not, you fool...I tell you, it is! Look how tall he is. He fits the descriptions..."*

"Let him through!" High Matron Weyra called. "Who are you?"

Sky Messenger stopped long enough to meet

and hold her gaze. His brown eyes blazed so brilliantly that people gaped at him, their faces immobile, as though afraid to move in his presence.

In a strong, powerful voice, he said, "I am Sky Messenger, called Dekanawida by the Flint People. I've come to offer you something better than battle, better than death! Reason and righteousness must prevail, elders, or none of us will survive the coming darkness!"

As he strode forward, the crowd fell back before him, shoving one another to get out of his way, and opening a narrow pathway that led straight to the Ruling Council.

Hiyawento and Towa had to hurry to stay close.

"It's him! I fought against him once...look at the cut of his cape...definitely Standing Stone..."

Hiyawento clutched his war club as he scanned every face they passed, noting those who scowled and sneered, paying special attention to hands that rested upon belted weapons.

Sky Messenger bowed deeply before the elders. In a deep, respectful voice, he said, "Council Members, I ask your forgiveness for disturbing this meeting."

Most of the elders stared at him slack-jawed, almost certain they sat in the presence of a living legend, but not quite. One or two gave Sky Messenger wary looks.

High Matron Weyra said, "You really are Sky Messenger, the son of Matron Jigonsaseh and Speaker Gonda?"

"Yes, High Matron. I am Bear Clan, from Yellowtail Village. If you will allow it, I would request an audience with your Ruling Council."

Ghostly silence possessed the inside of the council house. The warm air was still. Only the firelight wavered as elders' hands clenched, or feet shuffled.

Hiyawento and Towa stood to the left and right of Sky Messenger, ready for anything, their gazes scanning the small gathering. High Matron Weyra had wisely limited the audience to just the Ruling Council, but thumps sounded around the walls outside as people shifted, pressing close, ears to the walls in an attempt to hear anything. Sky Messenger had just finished relating his Dream, and a low-awed drone penetrated the elm bark walls.

Where he sat on the log bench on the opposite side of the fire, Sky Messenger leaned forward. He propped his elbows on his knees and laced his fingers before him. As he gazed across the flames at the twelve most influential people in the Landing nation, worry cut lines across his forehead and around his wide mouth. He appeared much older than his twenty-three summers. A stranger entering the house just now, seeing him for the first time, would guess Sky Messenger's age at perhaps forty summers. Each layer of Sky Messenger's hair caught the glow and created short, jagged lines around his head. His long black cape had fallen into folds on the floor.

"There is one point I do not understand," High Matron Weyra said. Her white hair, thinning on top, hung limp over her ears, but it was her wrinkled face that held a man's attention. Shadows darkened the cavernous hollows of her cheeks, and filled in her skeletal eye sockets. Wiry gray eyebrows created bushy tufts above her kind, thoughtful eyes.

"You said that just before Elder Brother Sun turns his back on the world, there will be gray shades drifting through the air around you, their voices hushed like those of lost souls. But are they lost souls? Do you know?"

"I was wondering the same thing," an old man said with a tottering nod. "It sounds to me as though all lost souls will be found. That they are the last congregation."

Sky Messenger's eyes tightened. "The shades are the dead who still walk and breathe, elders. More than that, I don't know."

The old man said, "But the dead do not walk and breathe, Prophet. They are dead."

Sky Messenger bowed his head to stare briefly at the flames dancing around the logs in the fire hearth. A thick bed of red coals glowed around the edges. "Are they? I'm not sure, elder. I can't explain these things."

When Sky Messenger paused, the council members, six men and six women, shifted silently, waiting for him to continue.

"But I know that the darkness will swallow Great Grandmother Earth." Sky Messenger looked up to meet their gazes. "I can't stop it without your help, elders."

More shifting as soft voices discussed what they'd heard.

"How may we help?" Weyra asked softly.

Sky Messenger seemed to be listening to the voices outside, perhaps to the barking dogs. "I have come to believe that compassion is the highest form of politics, elders. Many of you are much older and wiser than I am. I'm sure you've known this truth since long before I was born, but it is new to me. As many of you have heard, I spent most of my life as a warrior. Killing my enemies was the only form of politics I knew. Elders, we must replace blood revenge as a means of justice. It has to end."

"Replace it with what?" the old man snapped, as though appalled by the notion. His lips puckered over toothless gums. Bear claws decorated the throat of his cape. *Bear Clan*. "The Law of Retribution gives us the right to—"

"Yes, it does." Sky Messenger respectfully dipped his head, silently apologizing for interrupting. He hesitated as though preparing himself, then in a deep resonant voice, he said, "When I look across this fire, I see that there have been deaths in many of your families. I grieve with you, elders. If I could, I would wipe away your falling tears and take the sorrow from your hearts, so that you might open your minds and look around peacefully, without hatred. I know this is not an easy thing. The spirits of our bereaved nations are tired. We all starve. We all lash out in fear. There *is* a better way. A peace alliance between all of our peoples."

One of the younger elders, a very thin man with black-streaked gray hair and close-set eyes, laughed. "And how many nations have you convinced to join this alliance?" Wolf tracks scattered his white cape. *Wolf Clan*.

"The alliance is currently composed of the Standing Stone nation, the Flint nation, and three villages of the Hills nation."

"The same three villages that broke away from Atotarho to fight on your side in the recent battle?" Weyra asked.

Sky Messenger nodded. "Yes, High Matron. Coldspring Village, Riverbank and Canassatego Village have joined us."

"I suppose at some point you plan to tell us the benefits of this alliance?" the Wolf Clan elder pressed. "Why don't you get to it? If Tagohsah can be believed, your own people are under attack, and likely to be destroyed in the next few days. Which means the Standing Stone nation will be of no use to us in our current situation."

Sky Messenger unlaced his fingers and opened his hands to them. "I'm not sure I believe his words, but even if my People are not under attack right now, they will be soon. Just as yours will. It is inevitable. This winter is going to be desperate for every nation. If we don't join forces to help each other survive, I fear that by springtime we will all be dead."

Hiyawento watched the expressions. Two elders clearly opposed the alliance. From their cape decorations, Heron Clan and Beaver Clan. Their eyes had turned dark and brooding, and they sat rigid on the benches. The other ten council members, however, watched Sky Messenger with such hope in their eyes, it hurt to look at. They wanted peace more than anything on earth.

"Will you ask the filthy Mountain People to join the alliance?" the frail old woman from the Beaver Clan demanded to know.

"I will."

"Well, I do not wish to be part of any alliance that allows the Mountain People to live," she said.

"They *must* be destroyed! My clan will accept nothing less."

Sky Messenger spread his arms in a quieting gesture. "Let me explain the alliance. First, each nation that joins must pledge to give its life, and the lives of its people, for every other member. Second, any alliance member that violates this oath will be punished by the combined might of the alliance. If the Landing People join, the alliance will help to protect your borders. We will also send more Traders to you, so that you may exchange the magnificent bowls you make for our corn, or our blankets. When necessary, the members of the alliance will pool a portion of their harvests and redistribute the food to needy villages, no matter their nation. We—"

"How quickly could you send food?" Weyra asked almost breathlessly.

Ravenous looks entered the eyes of every council member.

"Once you join us, we will begin pooling what little we have so that we may take care of hungry villages like yours. I won't lie to you. No one has much this winter. But we will do the best we can."

Weyra blinked around the house, as though judging the mood of the other council members. "I have doubts about the alliance's ability to keep its promises. Does anyone else?"

Nods went round.

Sky Messenger said, "Please explain these doubts."

Weyra looked back at him. "Prophet, we are far away from the countries of the current alliance members. What if the Mountain People refuse to join you? They are our closest neighbors, and they wish to destroy us. How will the alliance get here in time if we ask for help to defend ourselves?"

Sky Messenger sat back and squared his broad shoulders. "Details will have to be worked out, of course, but I think the wisest course may be to have each nation assign warriors to your borders to block raids into Landing country."

Elders whispered behind their hands.

The Beaver Clan elder said, "And how will you feed such huge numbers of warriors? You don't expect us to provide for them, do you?"

"No, that would be too great a burden. I think each nation should be required to contribute equal amounts of food to sustain the army."

Council members cast glances at one another, unwilling to openly state their opinions at this time.

Sky Messenger lifted his hands. "Allow me to say one final thing, and then I will go and leave you to your deliberations. Elders, I truly believe that no nation can create an empire by conquering its enemies. Empires arise when enemies forget their own interests and become of one mind, one heart, and one body."

The Bear Clan elder sneered. "And how can such a thing be accomplished? We have too many different clans—"

"We must remember the truth of our origins. We are all relatives. Clans of alliance members shall recognize each other as such. Every member of the Bear Clan, no matter his or her nation, will be my relative, and I will treat him as such. Wolf Clan will be Wolf Clan. Turtle Clan will be Turtle Clan. We will return to the ways of our Blessed Ancestors." He laced his fingers and squeezed them together in one hard fist. "One mind, one heart, one body. We will become one *Haudenosaunee,* one People of the Longhouse."

High Matron Weyra's elderly face slackened, as though she was beginning to understand the kind of alliance he proposed. "So, the clans will be the binding that holds the alliance together?"

"As they are in individual nations, clan mothers will be the heart of all decisions. In my vision, I see clan mothers from every nation sitting around the same fire, guiding the course of the alliance, assisted by a Ruling Council of chiefs."

The elders began a spirited discussion.

Sky Messenger rose to his feet and slowly took the time to meet each gaze. "I must return to my home. I am needed there. If you wish to join us, please send word to me as soon as possible, and I will begin organizing the alliance to help you. Or better yet, send emissaries from your Ruling Council to Bur Oak Village so that you can meet with alliance representatives personally. We hope to welcome you soon."

He bowed deeply and walked around the fire. Hiyawento and Towa followed him down the central aisle, through the leather door hanging, and stepped outside into the crowd. Six guards, including War Chief Nokweh, stood just outside the council house door with worried expressions on their young faces.

Hiyawento swore another thousand people had squeezed into the plaza. He stepped in front of Sky Messenger, shielding his friend with his body. "Stay close behind me," Hiyawento ordered.

"Blessed Spirits, I can't believe—"

"You'd better start believing, my friend. As things become more desperate, this is going to get much worse. The only thing they have is hope."

Towa called, "Hiyawento! I'll cover Sky Messenger's back. Go!"

They started walking through a writhing sea of reaching hands.

"*Stop! Let me touch him. I must touch him!*"

"*Move! Please, I have to get close...*"

"*I just need to speak with the human False Face for a moment...get out of my way!*"

"*Let me through! I must tell him something. He must hear this! Stop pushing me!*"

"Gods!" Hiyawento shoved a man away. The panicked insanity of the crowd would smother them if they didn't get out of the village.

Towa yelled, "Hiyawento! Use your war club if you have to!"

He pulled his club from beneath his belt and waved it over his head. "Move, or I'll start crushing skulls! The Prophet must leave!"

"No, don't take him...belongs to all of us, doesn't he...let him go! He's tired, he needs to stay here for the...we'll kill you if you try to take him!"

People, many of them weeping, stumbled over each other trying to move as Hiyawento bulled through the mass of humanity, clearing a path to the gates. When he neared the plaza bonfire and saw Tagohsah still standing there, Hiyawento shouted, "Tagohsah! Meet us outside!"

"Why? What do you want?" The man's voice was shrill, frightened. He kept looking around at the eddying crowd as though he knew he'd be crushed long before he made it to the gates.

"If you're not out there in one-quarter hand of time, I'm coming back in to find you!" Hiyawento glared at the ugly little Flint Trader, then turned back to forcing his way through the grasping sea of hands.

16

"Gitchi?" Baji whispered and cocked her ear to the forest. "What's that sound? Do you hear it?"

The wolf, who lay curled in the grass at her side, blinked up at her, as though he sensed nothing wrong, or perhaps he didn't hear the strange wistful cry that had begun to seep across the land the instant Elder Brother Sun passed below the horizon. Riding the wind like a falcon, it rose and fell, sometimes seeming very close, other times vastly far away.

The cold quiet forest stood perfectly still. She listened. A fox over the next ridge? No, she didn't think so. Tremulous, descending in pitch like an eerie wail of longing, it seemed not to be of this earth.

Baji hesitated, listening for a time longer,

then she tiptoed into the forest. Nightfall had drained the colors from the land, leaving it slate gray. Downy woodpeckers peeked at her from holes in the trees, their feathers fluffed out for warmth.

She stopped. The woods had gone peaceful. A screech owl sailed through the trees barely six hands over her head, so silent it might have been a shadow rather than a living creature hunting the pine-scented evening.

Baji watched it alight in a red pine twenty paces away. Small, no longer than her hand, he lacked the usual rusty ear tufts. Probably a young owl. When he turned to study her, his eyes glowed with a silvered brilliance.

The call came again, stronger, trying to pull her deeper into the growing darkness.

Baji placed her hand on her belted war club and took another step. The arrows in her quiver uttered a faint rattle, like a rattlesnake's warning.

Gitchi's paws crunched behind her. He whimpered, urging her to go back to the trail, to return to a place where Dekanawida could find her, but the call was too powerful. It continued to pull her into the falling darkness where towering trees turned black, and frost grew like quartz crystals on rocks and deadfall. The astonishing fragrance of wet bark melted into her body. Her nostrils quivered. Just the movement of breath in her lungs filled her with such gladness she might have become one of the sailing Cloud People.

"Wolves?" she whispered. "Maybe that cry is a pack of wolves in the distance?"

The cry turned into long drawn-out wailing. The chorus seemed to resonate in Baji's chest, wild and free, and she strained so hard to hear it that her throat ached. As though untold generations of ancestors Sang to her of a primeval time before fire and roof, of a time before Elder Brother Sun existed, her souls thrilled to the melody. In her heart, she was running with them, hunting the cold and dark in the frost dance of constant winter.

Barely audible, she murmured, "I don't think it's wolves, Gitchi."

He nosed her hand.

"Don't worry," she said softly. "I'm fine. Everything is fine."

But it wasn't, and she knew it. Something was happening to her.

As evening blanketed the forest, dove-colored and iridescent, patches of snow became radiant, turning the air liquid and faintly blue, and shivering light upon the delicate ferns that hid between the rocks. The ache in her heart had become too much to bear.

Baji had to squeeze her eyes closed against it. *What is that unearthly crying?*

Against her leg, Gitchi's tail wagged.

She opened her eyes. In the small clearing surrounded by fire cherries and pawpaws, she caught movement. She kept her eyes on it. When she could make out darkness rippling around a black cape, she quickly called, "I don't need you! Leave."

No sound. No response.

The quiet of evening seemed to intensify. The call faded, leaving behind a huge maw of silence.

As he started to turn, to leave, she swallowed hard. "No, wait. Just tell me one thing."

He turned back to stare at her. Obviously trying not to frighten her, he slowly walked closer. Dark sad eyes glinted in the frame of his hood. He stopped three paces away, folded his arms beneath his cape, and gently asked, "What do you need to know?"

"Tell me why I feel so alive?"

He blinked, and his gaze shifted. He seemed to be staring over her shoulder, seeing something far away. "It's part of preparing."

"Preparing?"

He nodded. "Yes. You're at a place where every step you take is illuminated by the Road of Light." He glanced up at the twilight sky where the brightest campfires of the dead had just begun to shine. The contours of the Road were dimly visible. "It wakes a person up, and that's necessary, because to live your dying fully you must wake up."

To live my dying fully...

She braced her feet. "So I'm dying?"

A faint smile turned his lips. "That's all any of us ever do, Baji. When the deer come for you, if you let them, you will understand that the Road is all there is. We set foot upon it long before we're born."

Gitchi slid around her leg and went to stand in front of Shagoniyoh, looking up with loving eyes. When Shagoniyoh smiled down at him, the wolf stretched and wagged his tail again.

"All right," Baji said as though dismissing a war council. "You can go now."

He hesitated. "Don't you want to ask me about the strange many-voiced cry?"

Her heart stuttered. She took a quick step toward him, breathlessly asking, "What is it? Do you hear it? Is it human?"

He cocked his head in a curious birdlike manner, examining her with only one shining eye. "They stand at the foot of the bridge. They start calling very early, when we are children. Their Song changes over the summers, as more and more come and lie down, to wait. They're trying to guide you to them so you won't get lost on the way. If you find them, they will protect you as you cross to the other side."

The animals who wait at the bridge that spans the dark abyss...

Her eyes burned. She wiped them on her sleeve. "So, I'm still alive?"

He stood for a long time, gazing up at the evening sky. Wind waffled his black hood around his face and sent icy fingers probing beneath her cape. When she shivered, he looked back at her.

Baji said, "I'm not sure anymore. I was when I started, but...I'm not sure now. Tell me."

Shagoniyoh waited for a time, staring at her with kind eyes, then he turned and walked away into the deepening shadows with his cape swaying about his long legs.

She watched until he disappeared. "He knows, Gitchi. Why won't he tell me? I'd still be doing exactly what I am. It wouldn't change a thing."

The wolf stayed very close to her side as they walked through the old leaves, listening to the wavering moans and sobs that seemed to flutter in the air around them. The cry grew fainter with each step, until it thinned to nothingness across the distances, and the forest felt suddenly hollow beyond words.

17
SKY MESSENGER

As twilight settles over the forest, I hike up the
steep trail behind Hiyawento, heading
toward the crest of the hill where I know
Baji and Gitchi wait. My friend's broad back sways
with his long stride. He has his war club clenched in
his fist. Each time he glances over his shoulder at the
rumbling crowd that trails behind us like a great thun-
derstorm, worry and near-panic fill his face. We move
rapidly, trying to lose them. The camps surrounding
Shookas Village emptied out as we wound our way
between the fires, coalescing into a ragged horde of
six or seven hundred people. They follow like walking
skeletons. Enormous sunken eyes ringed with black
circles peer at me from inside ragged hoods.

Hiyawento's nerves are fraying. He keeps looking
back, his jaw grinding. His beaked nose glistens with
sweat. He doesn't like this any more than I do.

Crowds are unpredictable, and none of us is certain why they follow us.

Towa calls, "Hiyawento, let's stop. It's getting dark. We need to speak with Tagohsah."

"All right, but let's get the information we need quickly, so we can move on. It's impossible to know how many people in that crowd wish to kill Sky Messenger."

Dusk has coaxed the fragrances of night from the trees and earth and set them loose on the breeze.

Towa's gaze fixes on the ugly little Flint Trader. He waits until Hiyawento strides back to tower over Tagohsah like an avenging Earth Spirit, then the three of us close ranks around him, pinning Tagohsah inside our small circle.

Tagohsah hunches like a trapped packrat pushed into a corner by predators. His roached black hair has picked up a coating of dust that gives it a gray tint. The red porcupine quill chevrons across the front of his cape flash with his uneasy fidgeting.

Tagohsah blurts, "What do you want? If you don't hurry we'll all be trampled to death!" He runs a pink tongue over his rotted teeth and stares in horror at the crowd moving up the slope.

Hiyawento's voice is iron: "You told the Landing People that Bur Oak Village was being attacked. How do you know that? Did you hear it from another Trader? Is the story running the trails?"

"I saw it with my own eyes," Tagohsah insists.

"Towa, you know my rounds take me to Bur Oak and Yellowtail villages around the first of the moon. As I came down the hill, heading toward the valley, two of Atotarho's warriors stepped out and blocked the trail. They told me to go home, that there was nothing left of the Standing Stone nation."

Towa grimaces. "Then you saw nothing except two warriors."

"Don't be ridiculous! Do you think I actually turned around and left? I'm a Trader. I need good stories. I sneaked through the trees until 1 could see down into the valley." He shakes his head grimly. "Your People are in trouble, Prophet."

"Describe what you saw," Hiyawento orders.

Fear has begun to beat a stark refrain inside me. Since I first heard Tagohsah speaking, my souls have been conjuring images too terrible to believe. *Bur Oak Village burned, littered with dead bodies, all my family, my friends...*

"I saw around two thousand Hills warriors surrounding the last smoldering villages of the Standing Stone nation."

Towa glances back at the crowd. The leading edge has arrived and begun forming up into a murmuring multitude, crowding closer and closer. "How do you know they were Atotarho's warriors?"

"I saw the evil chief himself! He stood like a hunchback, wearing the black cape covered with circlets cut from human skulls. It was him. I'm sure of it."

I'm breathing hard when I turn to meet Hiyawento's tight eyes. "After the battle, he must have split his forces, sending some warriors to punish the rogue Hills villages, while the rest of his army circled back to finish the job at Bur Oak."

Hiyawento nods, and glances uneasily at the crowd pushing in around us, listening to our every word. Wide eyes stare up at me, as though I'm no longer human, but some strange otherworld phantom. Their hushed voices tremble with awe and fear.

Hiyawento pulls his war club up and menacingly props it on his shoulder for all to see. "If he returned the day after we left, the villages have been under siege for five days. Do you think they could have held out so long?"

Fire seems to rush in my veins, burning a path through my body. "I don't know." *But I don't think so.*

Towa hisses, "Don't forget that Matron Jigonsaseh is there. Sindak, too. He knows how Atotarho's army thinks."

"If they've made it this long, they need help badly," Hiyawento replies. "Their water and food must be gone."

I say, "Do you think Zateri sent the warriors that High Matron Kittle requested?"

"Even if she did, there's no way to know how many she could spare. But it won't be enough to make a real difference. Not if what Tagohsah says is true." He glowered at the ugly Trader.

"It is! I swear it."

Towa turns to me. "What of the Flint nation?"

"1 doubt they even know the Standing Stone nation is in trouble. Chief Cord's army was attacked by Atotarho right outside—"

"What?" Towa and Hiyawento shout at once.

They crowd closer to me and Hiyawento says, "When? How do you know that?"

"Baji escaped the massacre. She came after me."

"She's here? With you?" Hope strains Hiyawento's voice as his eyes scan the trail and the trees. "Where is she?"

I gesture vaguely over my shoulder and am surprised when the entire crowd goes still and turns to look up the hill. "Hiding in the trees up there. She has no idea if any other survivor of the massacre made it home to the Flint nation."

"Massacre?" Towa's eyes went hard. "How many were killed?"

As the crowd pushes closer, hemming us in, I whisper, "Hundreds."

"Dear gods." Hiyawento rubs his forehead. "Then Cord may be unable to—"

"If he lived," I say. "Baji says he was badly wounded."

Tagohsah's gaze darts over the hungry faces surrounding us. "Whether he's alive or dead won't matter. The Mountain People will reach Bur Oak Village long before Chief Cord could pull together a war party and get there to help them."

We all turn to stare at him.

"What are you talking about?"

He gestures to the east. "On my way here, I passed a huge Mountain army. They said they were on their way to join Atotarho's forces. They told me they were going to annihilate the Standing Stone nation and split up the country between them."

Rage fires my veins. "How many warriors did you see?"

"They were scattered through the trees, I don't know. Thousands."

Towa and Hiyawento whisper to each other. My gaze shifts to the tree line, searching for Baji and Gitchi. Where are they? My eyes are trained to identify Gitchi's coat even in a tight weave of grass. I don't see him.

Hands touch the back of my cape, subtle, almost not there. Then people grow more bold, pushing one another to get closer to me. Whispers pass from mouth to mouth: "...*the Mountain People have joined Atotarho...great darkness is almost upon us...Elder Brother Sun is ready to turn his back...that's where they were headed...Hills People going to destroy the Prophet's nation...we should help...starving...not enough warriors to...*"

I ignore the grasping hands, reach out, twine my

fingers in Tagohsah's cape, and drag him close. When our faces are less than one hand's breadth apart, I hiss, "I want you to deliver a message for me."

"What message?"

In a voice loud enough for everyone around me to hear, I call, "Run to every village in the land. Tell them I have foreseen the destruction of Chief Atotarho. Tell them it happens just outside Bur Oak Village!"

I shove him away, and the crowd rumbles, a mixture of gasps and voices relaying the message through the ranks.

Tagohsah stumbles and looks at me with half-panicked eyes. "Is it true? Have you?"

I straighten and let my eyes roam the masses. Hundreds of gazes are riveted to my face, as though waiting for me to continue.

I lift my hands, and shout, "*I have foreseen the destruction of the evil Atotarho, the man who murdered so many of your loved ones, and it happens right outside Bur Oak Village! Landing warriors are there standing shoulder-to-shoulder with the rest of the alliance! I have seen it! We stand as One. Together, we will do this!*"

An awed hush falls, then several people shove through the crowd and run back to Shookas Village, carrying my words, hopefully, to the Ruling Council.

"Sky Messenger," Towa says as he steps around behind me and begins shoving people back, "we have to get out of here. Now."

"Wait." Hiyawento steps in front of me, and shouts, "I need thirty of the greatest warriors of the Landing People to serve as personal guards for the Prophet! Come forward! Who will help me protect him from his enemies?"

Men and women murmur and blink. Feet shuffle, creating an ominous rumble. There seems to be a discussion going on, people talking between themselves about what they should do. I see several heads shake violently and men and women back away.

"He is the greatest Dreamer our Peoples have ever known! Help him!" Hiyawento lifts his war club and waves it over his head so people can see him. *"I need thirty warriors!"*

Hiyawento has placed them in a difficult position. In essence, he has asked them to swear loyalty to me without the approval of their Ruling Council. It could be construed as treason. Not only that, each knows that Shookas Village needs every warrior in the nation now. The Landing People are more vulnerable than they have ever been, and despite what Tagohsah says, no one can be sure that the huge Mountain army won't return here to destroy Shookas Village.

"Hiyawento, you know they can't—"

"These people chose to follow you up the hill without the approval of their elders," he answers. "I have to know now how much faith lives in their hearts. Enough to willingly follow you all the way back to Bur Oak Village? Let them make the decision, my friend."

Towa's back presses against mine, and I wonder if he's been crowded against me, or just chosen to stand so close. When he stumbles, shoving me into Hiyawento, I know the answer. The crowd is growing too brave.

Hiyawento cups a hand to his mouth. "I'm only asking for thirty warriors. Just thirty! The rest of you must return home to help protect your nation."

Slowly, as though accepting their fate, a handful of warriors come forward. Then more. One by one, they shoulder to the front of the crowd, circling me. Most are big burly men with quivers and bows slung over their shoulders. A few are strong women with hard eyes. I count only sixteen, but their eyes glow when they look at me.

Hiyawento studies them, deciding their worthiness. He pounds fists into arm muscles judging strength, scrutinizes bows and arrows to see how well they've been cared for, and looks into each person's eyes assessing something far more subtle, character. He is a renowned War Chief, greatly feared by the Landing People. These warriors clearly respect him, but several glare into his eyes. Have they fought against him? Will they obey him when the time comes?

A tidal wave of questions rolls through the crowd. People shift, arms extend to point.

I turn.

At the top of the hill, Baji stands with her long hair

blowing around her broad shoulders in the soft winds of evening. She has her bow nocked and aimed at the ground, but her chin is held high as she scans the crowd. Gitchi lopes nervous circles around her, hair bristling, guarding her. I know without a doubt that he will fight to protect her until he cannot fight any longer. The sight of them standing together is like a Spirit plant rushing in my veins.

Everyone sees her! Look at them. They're all looking at her. She's here...Blessed Spirits...she's here.

Hiyawento lifts a hand to Baji, and she lifts a hand back and gives him a firm nod.

Hiyawento yells, "Guards, we have to move up the trail to that hilltop in the distance where we can protect the Prophet. Do whatever you have to to keep the crowd back as we walk!"

18

As High Matron Kelek made her way across the dark plaza of Atotarho Village with her guard, her old heart thumped. She felt weary beyond exhaustion. White hair hung about her wrinkled face like a cloud of spiderwebs. The meeting with the village councils from Turtle-back and Hilltop had not gone well. All day long Atotarho Village had been in an uproar. Accusations had flown about like diving falcons. No one had been left unscathed, especially Kelek. She felt as though she'd been pecked to pieces by a flock of rabid turkeys.

The sight of the Bear Clan longhouse made her utter a deep sigh. She longed to sleep. As she parted the entry curtain, she shivered in the sudden warmth, and headed toward her chamber at the far end of the house. Her guard dutifully stuck close behind her, his war club in hand.

At just past midnight, the six-hundred-hand-long house appeared still and quiet. Less than a dozen people sat around the thirty fires that sparkled down the center aisle. A few of the curtains had been drawn closed across chambers, but most remained opened to the warmth from the hearths. People slept beneath piles of hides with dogs curled up beside them.

When she reached her chamber near the south entry, Kelek turned to her guard. Thirty summers old, with short black hair, he wore a greasy cape streaked with soot. He'd just returned from the Standing Stone battle, like so many other warriors, and looked as though he hadn't even changed clothes. It was disgraceful.

"Be vigilant, Hakowane."

"I will, High Matron."

His voice was utterly devoid of emotion, which she found peculiar after the day's emotional turmoil.

Kelek scrutinized him. He was slender now, but as a child, he'd been known as a glutton. He'd seemed to spend every waking moment shoving food into his mouth, which is why she'd never really liked him. Not only that, he had a pointed face that resembled a long-tailed weasel's, the eyes dark and beady, the nose pink, and ears too big for his small head. When he smiled, his pointed teeth resembled fangs.

"You're from the Eti'gowane's lineage, aren't you?"

"Yes, Matron."

"*High* Matron," she corrected.

"Forgive me, High Matron." He bowed in apology.

"The Eti'gowane has been a good Matron of the Cornfields."

"It's kind of you to say so, High Matron."

The man seemed distracted, his eyes shifting around as though he expected monsters to emerge from the night shadows. She reached over to unhook her curtain from its peg. As it fell closed across her chamber, he vanished, but as the curtain swung, she glimpsed him slip his war club into his belt and draw a chert knife. An odd choice. Any warrior worth his reputation would have stood guard with his war club. It was more threatening.

At this moment, however, she didn't have the strength to care.

Kelek walked over and sank down on the deer-hide-covered bench that lined the rear wall. Her chamber was large, four paces long by three wide. Pots and baskets nestled on the floor beneath the bench, and sacred masks hung upon the divider walls.

As she tiredly leaned her head back, a soft groan escaped her lips. The Wolf and Snipe clans had been especially vindictive today, going so far as to threaten to Outcast the entire Bear Clan, but she'd paid them little attention. It was the Bear Clan elders who had stunned her. For the first time in her life, her relatives had accused her of shaming them. It had been a difficult fight, almost unbearable.

"The old fools have no vision. If they'd leave me alone, I would make our clan legendary!"

She blinked up at the dried plants that hung from the roof poles. The cornhusks had been peeled back from the ears and braided together into long ropes, allowing the kernels to dry faster. Each time someone walked by outside, his or her shadow danced over the corn braids, sunflower heads, and bean vines. Occasionally she heard soft voices, people briefly speaking with Hakowane.

Cold and desperate for sleep, Kelek didn't bother to undress. She stretched out on her sleeping bench and pulled the hides up over her cape.

Some time later—she couldn't say how long— Kelek was jerked from deep sleep by what sounded like someone entering her chamber. Her eyelids felt like granite weights as she fought to open them. The fires must have burned down to ashes. The only light in the longhouse came from the campfires of the dead. Streaming down through the smoke holes, their gleam coated Kelek's chamber like a faint wash of gray paint.

She blinked at the dimness, saw nothing, and closed her eyes again. The door curtain had probably just been carelessly brushed by Hakowane.

She was almost back to sleep when she heard someone breathing close by. Barely audible, the rhythmic puffs fluttered her hair across her cheeks. Like slow poison, terror crept through her veins. Her eyes jerked open.

Less than two hands away, wide feral eyes blinked down at her. She tried to scream, but a heavy hand clamped over her nose and mouth.

He whispered in her ear, "I have been instructed to tell you that I am not Wolf Clan. I am Bear Clan, sent by our clan elders."

He struck like lightning, the sharp knife slicing her throat in one clean stroke. When he removed his hand from her mouth, she tried to scream, but her lungs didn't seem to have air. For twenty heartbeats she flailed on her bench, while warm blood spurted over her shoulders and chest.

Her murderer stood by watching, apparently ordered to remain until it was over.

Anger filtered through her panic. *The Bear Clan bargained with the Wolf Clan. To prevent a war of retribution, they must have offered to eliminate the problem themselves...*

As her vision started to go gray and sparkling, her muscles relaxed and her body went featherlight, floating.

She faintly heard her door curtain whisper when her murderer left.

19

The Path of Souls glittered brilliantly across the dark night sky, sparkled through the forest, and reflected from the branches with a liquid-silver intensity. Voices and laughter rose from around the hundreds of campfires that scattered the valley below. The air felt warmer tonight, cold, but not bone-cold, which probably meant they had a few warm days coming. Winter solstice was still about two moons away. If they were lucky, they'd have more than a handful of unseasonably pleasant days before winter's frigid presence arrived in earnest.

Saponi lay on his belly in a dogwood thicket, staring down at Bur Oak Village. The palisades had been devastated. Glowing orange gaps flared as the breeze shifted. A short distance away, Yellowtail Village stood like a black burned-out husk.

"Gods, the battle was terrible. I really felt for them today." Disu, who lay stretched out beside him, shook his head. "I wonder how many they lost?"

Saponi didn't answer for a time. "More than Matron Jigonsaseh could afford to lose."

"That's for certain. If she lost only one-third of her trained warriors, that means she has less than two hundred left."

"Two hundred against perhaps one thousand Hills warriors...and there are another two thousand Mountain warriors on the way."

When they'd heard the story racing through Atotarho's camp, it had stunned them. Mountain warriors joining forces with their old enemy, the Hills People? One moon ago, no one would have believed it possible. Not just because they'd spent half of last summer killing each other, but the Mountain People were in a bad way. The plague had hit them hardest of all. Many Traders had carried the tale far and wide. The Mountain People had been so sick, they hadn't even been able to harvest their crops. Their corn had moldered in the fields, and their sunflowers had been plucked clean by birds and squirrels. Any other crops that had survived had been taken in raids by their neighbors.

"I hate to say it, Saponi, but it's hard to imagine

how the Standing Stone nation can survive another assault."

Saponi turned to look at his old friend. Disu had seen twenty-four summers. A thin, lanky man, he stood two heads taller than Saponi, but what Saponi lost in height, he made up for in muscles. His burly shoulders spread twice as wide as Disu's.

This was the first either of them had spoken since they'd made it to the southern hilltop at midnight, less than a hand of time ago. The future was just too terrible to think about.

"I believe in Sky Messenger's Dream, old friend," Saponi said with a sudden fervency. "I *believe* he can stop this war. Whether he can do it before his own people are gone...I do not know. Perhaps the destruction of his nation is what triggers the unfolding of his Dream. If it is, he'll pay a terrible price."

Disu hesitated. His hood, which lay upon his back, waffled in the wind, creating a soft thumping sound. "We're never going to make it back into Bur Oak Village with this food. You know that, don't you?"

He squinted at the campfires. "I know."

War Chief Negano had apparently decided to take no chances. He'd lost many warriors today. Though Saponi couldn't guess how many, at least two hundred bodies were visible in the flickering firelight. That meant many more lay freezing in the darkness beyond. Rather than moving his forces back to their camps across the valley, Negano must have known that he had to keep the noose tight, or Matron Jigonsaseh would manage to restock the village with food and water. The noose was tight indeed. Camped approximately one hundred paces from the walls, Negano's warriors completely encircled the village and the marsh. No one could get in or out.

Saponi shifted to brace himself on one elbow so he could look back over his shoulder at the twenty-eight warriors gathered in the shadows.

Sixty packs of food made a dark hump behind them, piled in a small clearing surrounded by leaf-less maples. Soft voices eddied, his men talking over supper, finally able to eat after a long day of tireless effort. They couldn't build a fire, but they'd filled their fire pots with coals before they'd left Atotarho's camp. The scent of roasting crickets, being tossed with hot coals, wafted on the cold breeze. That had been the real find today. Ten pots of crickets! Negano must have had warriors out in the forest kicking over every pile of leaves to find them. When parched in ceramic bowls, the crickets had a crunchy exterior and creamy interior that tasted just like crab legs. His mouth watered. They were all starving. They'd spent most of the day hauling food into the forest, supposedly to transfer it to shadowed area beneath the trees where it would stay frozen. Instead, they'd filled as many packs as they could carry back, two each, and buried the rest beneath piles of leaves and branches: bags of nuts and acorns, venison haunches, and rabbits that had yet to be skinned.

Their mission today had been a great success. He hadn't lost a single warrior, nor had they been forced to kill any of their relatives in Atotarho's camp.

Disu propped his cheek on a fist, and stared at Saponi with tight eyes. "From what I could see today, they poured a lot of water on the palisade."

He left the question of *how much* to Saponi's reckoning. The glowing holes in the exterior palisade of Bur Oak Village stood as a mute testament; they'd probably been forced to use every drop they had to quench the flames. "Yes, and since we can't get back with our packs, they have very little food left, too."

As Wind Woman's daughter Gaha softly moved around the village, fanning the smoldering logs, reddish light wavered over the bodies piled against the base of the palisade. Including the dead from the battle six days ago—corpses they hadn't had time to bury—there had to be six or seven hundred bodies total. Even from his position on the hilltop, he could see the contorted arms and legs, bent-back heads, and gaping mouths. White teeth glistened. Over the next few days, as the temperature warmed up, the stench of rotting corpses would become unbearable.

If they have a few days, which I doubt.

Disu said, "How many do you think deserted tonight?"

"I counted a group of around one hundred trotting away up the trail before it got too dark to see. More probably left under the cover of night."

"I was surprised that Negano didn't try to stop them."

"He didn't want to split his army in half. People would have been forced to take sides. If he'd tried to stop them, another two or three hundred warriors would have sided with them and left, too."

"You're probably right. I always liked Negano. To tell you the truth, I feel sorry for him."

Saponi toyed with the grass beneath his fingers, absently stroking it while he thought. "Don't feel too sorry. His army still outnumbers the Standing Stone nation by at least three to one, and he has reinforcements coming."

Disu heaved a taut breath and sat up. "Well, there's nothing more we can do about it tonight. Let's go grab a bowl of roasted crickets before they're gone."

20

SKY MESSENGER

I n the middle of the night, Gitchi growls softly, and I hear Hiyawento call, "Sky Messenger?"

I roll over and sleepily blink up at the three people standing over me. Hiyawento, Baji, and an unknown Landing warrior, a tall square-jawed man wearing a ragged buckskin cape, stare down at me. Hiyawento has his jaw clenched.

I sit up in my blankets and rub my eyes with the back of my hand. Gitchi lays on the foot of the blanket, his yellow eyes fixed on the Landing warrior. While he knows and trusts Hiyawento and Baji, this man poses a threat, and he knows it. "What's wrong? Where's Towa?"

Hiyawento squats beside me and props his war club across his knees. Exhaustion lines his tight eyes. "He's in charge of the guards tonight."

Below Hiyawento, I see men and women standing

in a ring around the small hilltop with war clubs clutched in their hands. Their attention is focused on the people bedded down on the slopes below. It's dark. No campfires glow. Snores and coughs ride the wind that sweeps up the hillside.

Hiyawento extends a hand to the Landing warrior. "This is Deputy War Chief Tiyosh, formerly of Agweron Village." The man bows respectfully. I nod back. "We've been talking. We think you and Baji need to get away from here as soon as possible. If you run most of the night, you should be far ahead of the crowd by morning."

Baji kneels beside Hiyawento and gives me one of those distinctive, *don't argue* looks. Wind flutters long hair around her beautiful stern face. "Tiyosh says most of the people who followed you when you left Shookas Village are desperate. Their villages were just destroyed. They're sure the Mountain People are coming to kill them. You are their only hope."

Desperation can drive even the best of people to madness. "I understand, but how do you propose that we get out of here? We're surrounded."

"Yes, Prophet," Tiyosh says with soft reverence, "but most people are asleep. You and I are about the same height. I think if you exchange capes with me, and keep your hood pulled up to shield your face, you and War Chief Baji may be able to make it out without being recognized."

My limbs feel like dead weights as I throw back

my blankets and rise to my feet. Hiyawento and Baji stand up and move to either side of me, protecting me. I hate being treated like a fragile pot...but I know they're right. 1 saw the glazed, almost stunned, looks in my followers' eyes, and felt them shoving each other just to get close enough to touch my clothing. I pull my cape over my head and hand it to Hiyawento to hold, while Tiyosh removes his own cape and gives it to me. As I slip it on, I ask, "How long will Tiyosh be forced to feign being me? I'm not comfortable with this. I'm putting him in danger."

Hiyawento looks at Tiyosh, who shrugs. "Before dawn, we will hit the trail and run hard. The new guards will keep Tiyosh surrounded so that no one can get a good look at him. Hopefully we will lose most of the crowd on the way."

"Before we do this, I want you to consider what the crowd will do when they discover Tiyosh is not me. They will feel betrayed."

Hiyawento's mouth curves into a half-smile, a determined expression I know well. He will do whatever it takes to keep me safe. He always has. "I have considered it. As has Tiyosh. All of your new guards discussed the matter thoroughly. We will tell them something. Now, you and Baji need to go. By the time you reach Bur Oak Village, we should be no more than a few hands of time behind you. I'll send a messenger ahead to tell you when we'll arrive."

"How will I know the message is from you, and not someone claiming to—"

"I'll send you this." Hiyawento's hand slowly drops to his shell-bead belt and he caresses it, his fingers slowly moving over the small human figures that decorate the front near the ties. Deep purple, they have childlike shapes. "I'll send my belt with the messenger so you know he speaks the truth."

Gitchi rises and stretches, preparing his aching joints for the run ahead.

His yellow eyes and thick fur glow silver in the light cast by the campfires of the dead.

Through a heavy sigh, I say, "All right. I'll be expecting the Truth Belt. We'll see you there day after tomorrow."

Hiyawento's head dips in a firm nod. "Yes, you will."

As he hands my cape to Tiyosh, the man's expression slackens. He puts it on and smoothes it down as though it is a sacrament, a rare ritual object with a soul of its own that must be handled with great care.

Baji flips up her hood and gestures for me to do the same. I hesitantly comply. All of this...this ruse... makes me feel dishonest, as though I'm pretending to be something I am not.

Baji grabs Hiyawento in a bear hug, and says, "I'll take care of him."

Hiyawento hugs her back. "I know you will. I'll see you soon."

Baji scratches Gitchi's ears and gestures to the winding deer trail that leads down the steepest side of the hill, where only a few people are camped because of the slope. "Gitchi, you go first. I'll guard his back."

Gitchi looks at her with adoring eyes, then trots out into the starlight.

21

Two hands of time before dawn, Baji lay snuggled beneath the blankets with Dekanawida's muscular arms around her. His soft breathing warmed her ear. They'd run until they'd started stumbling. As soon as they'd made camp at the base of a gray rock wall and crawled between the blankets, he'd fallen into a dead sleep.

Baji, on the other hand, had been staring out at the glistening forest, listening. The intoxicating far-off cry lilted through the darkness. It was especially powerful tonight, calling to her like a lover's summons, begging her to come. It had grown constant, echoing across the distances, sometimes barely audible, other times so loud it rang inside her as though the callers had their muzzles pressed to her ears.

At such times, Gitchi's gaze never left her.

The wolf lay close beside Baji, watching her as the campfires of the dead wheeled through the sky high above them. His yellow eyes were alert, attentive to the slightest change in her expression, looking up into her face with keen unfathomable interest. He seemed to be concentrating on her breathing, as though he greatly feared it might cease. Even when she tried to sleep, the strength of the old wolf's gaze woke her. Each time she blinked and yawned, his tail wagged, and his whole heart shone in his eyes.

Trying not to wake Sky Messenger, she eased her arm from beneath the blanket to scratch Gitchi's chest, and he sighed in that way that only a contented dog can. As she petted him, images fleeted across her souls. He'd been so small and scared when they'd found him tied up in that bag on the shore of the river outside of Bog Willow Village. She remembered it as though it had happened moments ago.

She, Odion, and Tutelo had heard Gitchi crying, and had followed the sound down to the riverbank. The shore had been strewn with refuse. Victorious warriors with packs of new plunder had cast their shabby old belongings on the ground just before they'd shoved off in their canoes. Threadbare packs and capes, blankets with too many stitched holes, and hide bags filled with who-knows-what, had littered the shore.

As they'd walked, a soft muffled "woof" erupted.

A short distance ahead, a sack wriggled. They'd all charged up the bank and encircled it. At the time, she'd seen twelve summers, Odion eleven, and Tutelo eight summers.

"Hurry, open it and let him out," Tutelo had urged. "There's no telling how long he's been in there. He may be dying of thirst."

Odion had hesitated, taking a few moments to gently pet the warm body inside. Barks had erupted as the sack had flopped around like a big dying fish.

Baji had taken Tutelo's hand, preparing to drag her away if the puppy emerged in a flying snarling bundle of fur.

As soon as Odion loosened the laces, a soft gray nose poked up through the opening. The little wolf had wriggled the top half of his lean body out onto Odion's lap and looked around with bright yellow eyes. He'd seen perhaps four or five moons.

"I'll bet the puppy was supposed to be dinner." Tutelo had said as she'd edged forward to pet the puppy's silken back. "He's the color of a ghost. Maybe his name was Ghost."

"Or *oki*," Baji had suggested.

Odion and Tutelo had turned to stare at her.

Oki were Spirits that inhabited powerful beings, including the seven Thunderers, rivers, certain rocks, valiant warriors, even lunatics. Oki could bring either good luck or bad. People who possessed supernatural powers—shamans, witches—were believed to have a companion spirit, an oki, whose power they could call upon to help them.

"He definitely has some special power," Odion had said, "or we'd never have found him. He called us to him. Oki sounds like a good name."

Tutelo had shaken her head vehemently. "I don't like that. What if somebody thinks he's an evil spirit? If somebody's having a bad day, that name could cost him his life."

"Well...then think of something else," Odion had said.

Baji smiled at the memories.

Gitchi.

Yes, Gitchi. Baji had named him those many summers ago. *Gitchi Manitou* were words she'd heard from a Trader who'd come from north of Skanodario Lake. She had no idea what it meant, but she'd always liked it.

She lowered her hand to stroke his sore foreleg and Gitchi licked her fingers with his eyes half-closed in gratitude.

Gitchi had grown up on the war trail, and his white face testified that he was far older than the number of breaths he had drawn, or the long winter nights he'd slept curled beside Dekanawida. When Baji looked at him an old, old soul looked back, one that had witnessed far too much, and loved too deeply to ever be quite ordinary again.

Odion had been right. Gitchi did have a special power. She thought that maybe her souls, and his, were intertwined. Baji had been born Wolf Clan. Though Cord had adopted her into the Turtle Clan when she'd seen twelve summers, some part of her still heard the wolf songs that seeped up from the primeval darkness between her souls. Often, she wondered if Gitchi could hear them, too. It was a strange thing. There had been many nights last summer when she'd been lying in Dekanawida's arms, blinking dreamily into Gitchi's eyes, and she swore they had both drifted out of this world to somewhere beyond. Perhaps they'd sat together beside one of the campfires of the dead? She knew only that he was there with her, standing guard, keeping her safe. They'd scented the wind together, shared blankets, and listened to that far-off cry that Baji swore was the same cry she heard tonight. His devotion, in this life and the life beyond, was both wonderful and wrenching.

Last summer, she'd seen the effects firsthand when two Flint warriors, Ogwed and Yondwi, had gotten into a fight on the war trail. Baji had been a deputy war chief. She'd stepped between them to shove them apart and started shouting at them to stop. Gitchi, as usual, was curled up on the ground at Dekanawida's feet ten paces away, but he'd been watching. Ignoring Baji, Ogwed had swung a fist into his opponent's temple, and Yondwi responded by grabbing Baji's shoulders and hurling her aside like a cornhusk doll so he could get to Ogwed. She'd hit the ground so hard it had knocked the wind from her lungs.

The other warriors standing around watching the fight heard neither snarl nor growl, but a sound that more closely resembled a soul-chilling bellow, and they'd seen Gitchi's gray body streak across the ten paces and become airborne, launched straight at Yondwi. Yondwi had been in the process of drawing back his arm to throw another punch, when Gitchi slammed into the chest, toppled him backward to the ground, and grabbed him by the throat. Yondwi lived only because Dekanawida had shouted, *"Gitchi, no!"*

While friends rushed to Yondwi's side to examine his bleeding neck, Gitchi had run circles around them, his fangs slathering foam, snarling ferociously. Every hair on his body had stood straight up. The threat had been clear: *Don't you ever touch Baji again.*

The story had traveled through every camp, up and down the war trails even into enemy villages where Gitchi's name was whispered in the same breath as *Oki* and *Witch Dog*. Gitchi had become legend. No man or woman dared lay a hand on Baji if Gitchi was in sight.

"Maybe I should have named you Oki after all," she murmured to him.

Gitchi wagged his tail and propped his muzzle on her blanket so that his black nose almost touched Baji's. For a long time, they breathed each other's souls. In his yellow eyes she saw stars reflecting, one in particular, bright and faintly reddish.

When the mournful many-voiced cry blared again, Gitchi pricked his ears to listen, but his gaze remained fixed upon her. She felt strangely certain that he was convinced she could not possibly leave him as long as he could see her with his own eyes.

Baji gently slid forward to hug him. His thick fur smelled of old leaves and campfires. "You're a good friend," she whispered.

Gitchi licked her shoulder and vented a deep sigh.

In a sleepy voice, Dekanawida whispered, "Are you awake?"

"Yes, but you should sleep."

As she lay down again, he shifted to cup his body against her, bringing his knees up behind hers, and encircling her with his muscular arms.

"Why are you awake?" he murmured. "What are you thinking about?"

Baji's gaze drifted upward to the Road of Light

glittering across the belly of Brother Sky. "I was looking at the fork in the trail."

Confused, he said, "Hmm?"

"The fork in what your people call the Path of Souls, and mine call the Road of Light."

He nuzzled his chin against her long hair. "What about it?"

"Do you believe there's a bridge at the fork? A bridge where all the animals you've ever known wait for you? The animals who loved you protect you and help you across, while the animals you've hurt chase you, trying to force you to fall off the bridge in the eternal darkness below."

She felt him smile. "I believe."

Baji's gaze returned to Gitchi. He was still staring at her with that worried expression, something akin to grief, in his yellow eyes. She reached out to stroke the white hair beside his left eye.

"Do you think the animals call to you?"

Dekanawida's arms tightened around her. "You mean just before you die?"

"Or after."

Where his wrist rested just below her heart, she felt his pulse speed up, thumping against her ribs. After ten heartbeats, he firmly said, "First, I've never heard any of our storytellers say that. Second, everyone saw you today. *Everyone.* Third, why did you ask? Do you hear something?"

Baji grasped his arm and pulled it more tightly

around her. "No, but a holy man told me that once. I was just wondering if you'd ever heard of such a thing?"

"No, and I really wish you'd stop thinking about death."

"Me?" she said in a teasing voice. "You're the one who keeps Dreaming the end of the world. How can you expect me to think of anything else?"

Offhandedly, he replied, "Well, there is that," and tenderly kissed her hair. Then his lips moved down to her throat, warm and inviting.

Baji rolled to her back to look up into his eyes and found so much love shining in those brown depths that her heart ached. She smoothed her fingers down his side and slipped them beneath his cape and shirt to touch his bare skin. "My head is much better, you know."

He reached around to feel her head wound, frowned a moment, then said, "Yes. It is."

They laughed together.

As Grandmother Moon rose above the dark hills, the ghostly pewter landscape took on an opalescent sheen that painted every swell and hollow with an edge of silver fire.

Baji looked up into his face, haloed by short black hair, and her gaze slipped across his slender nose and blunt chin, coming to rest at the lines that cut deeply around his eyes. He had seen only twenty-three summers, but so many had been difficult. Her hand lifted to massage his left shoulder, broken by a war club when he'd seen eleven summers. It still hurt him on cold winter nights.

He whispered, "Baji, don't think about those days," and rolled over to kiss her.

As his lips grew more passionate, she yielded completely to him, letting herself drown in the tingling warmth of his hands gliding over her breasts, trailing down her waist to her thighs, lifting her war shirt and whispering like ermine fur across her bare skin. *One moment of perfect happiness...*

As if a fever had been lifted from her, she wept.

His whisper sounded loud in the buried stillness of the moonlit night. "Are you all right?"

"Happy." She wrapped her arms around his back and pulled him hard against her, holding him desperately. "I want this to last forever."

He kissed her and said against her lips, "I'll do my best."

Their touching drifted with the silence of river mist into love. As Grandmother Moon rose higher in the sky, her light brightened and streamed through the forest. Baji never closed her eyes. She watched his leisurely movements repeat in vast amorphous shadows on the rock wall to her right. Gitchi kept wagging his bushy tail, and Baji kept smiling at him. All the way to the enchanted lavender dawn, she ached with joy.

22

Kwahseti stood beside Gwinodje on the catwalk of Canassatego Village, overlooking the main trail below. Six hundred men and women with bows aimed, manned the catwalk around them. Another four hundred lined the trail that led to the village, standing in neat rows. Their nocked bows glimmered in the newborn sunlight that filtered across the valley. In the distance, two clan matrons, one from the Wolf Clan and one from the Bear Clan, walked at the head of a procession of approximately two hundred warriors—enough to protect the matrons, but not enough to threaten Canassatego Village. *No show of force. Interesting.*

A messenger had arrived late last night informing them that the Hills nation would be sending a delegation to negotiate with the New Hills nation. They'd spent most of the night discussing what they would say. Gwinodje wore a plain doeskin cape with no decorations, as did Kwahseti. If they were forced to become a separate nation, they would immediately change their cape designs, and wanted to foster no wrong ideas about their loyalty in the minds of the delegation from Atotarho Village.

Gwinodje gripped the palisade. "Is that Yi? Her white cape has red paw prints."

Short gray hair blew around Kwahseti's eyes when she turned to look at Gwinodje. Her friend's heart-shaped face had flushed with excitement. "Yes, that's Yi."

Leafless maples and a few towering chestnuts swayed along the path, casting windblown shadows over the delegation's distinctive capes.

Kwahseti scrutinized the face she saw in the white hood. Yi had seen forty-eight summers. Silver strands glittered in her short black hair. She walked with her back straight, her bearing stately, demanding respect. Deep wrinkles cut around her mouth and across her forehead. Yi had her gaze focused on the catwalk where Kwahseti and Gwinodje stood, already taking command. In clan meetings, Yi traditionally said little, but each careful word had a knifelike quality, cutting to the heart of the matter.

Kwahseti was of Yi's lineage, but she lifted her chin and stared back at the leader of her ohwachira with defiance. Kwahseti had been instructed by the Ruling Council of the New People of the Hills to give no ground until she knew where the Old Hills nation stood on two issues: the position of the High Matron, and the Peace Alliance.

Kwahseti leaned over the palisade and called, "War Chief Thona, allow only the matrons inside the gates. Their warriors remain outside. No exceptions."

He craned his neck to look up at her. The web of scars on his face had a white sheen. "But what if they wish to have guards, Matron?"

"As a sign of good faith, we agreed to speak with them, but we owe them nothing. No guards, Thona."

Thona bowed obediently. "Yes, Matron."

As Yi approached, her eyes narrowed, and fixed upon Kwahseti. Kwahseti did not bow in respect, as was customary. She kept her back stiff and straight. A slight smile touched Yi's lips.

Yi called, "Matron Kwahseti, we wish you a pleasant morning." She extended a hand to the Bear Clan matron standing beside her. "This is Little Matron Adusha."

Without further delay, Kwahseti said, "A pleasant morning to both of you. Order your warriors to lay down their weapons."

Yi stared at her with her mouth open. When she finally found her voice, she cried, "That is an *outrageous* demand. Surely you don't expect us to leave our war party completely vulnerable?"

"We do, Matron Yi. Your forces attacked us only a few days ago." Kwahseti's hand swept across the vista. "As you can see from our charred palisade and the freshly dug graves to the east of the village, you killed many of our people."

Yi's mouth pressed into a hard white line. Indignant, Yi's face turned ugly. She looked like she might turn around and leave. But after five heartbeats, she called, "War Chief, order your warriors to lay down their weapons."

A commotion rose across the field, disgruntled warriors crying out in opposition...but they did it. Clattering sounded as bows, quivers, war clubs, and other weapons were all placed on the ground.

Kwahseti said, "War Chief Thona, allow the matrons inside our gates, but only the matrons."

"*What?*" Yi cried. "I will not enter this village without guards!"

"You will, Yi, if you wish to address the Ruling Council of the New People of the Hills. Our wounds are still bleeding. We will allow no enemy warriors inside these gates."

After a staring match where Yi's eyes blazed like freshly flaked mahogany chert, she said, "Very well. Open the gates."

Kwahseti nodded to Thona who pulled the gates open just wide enough for them to enter one at a time. After Yi and Adusha slid through, he closed them tight, and the warriors dropped the locking plank into place with a loud thump.

Gwinodje started to hurry down to meet them, but Kwahseti subtly gripped her arm to stop her. "Make them wait for us. They are not our leaders. We are not part of their nation."

Gwinodje wet her lips nervously. "You're right."

Kwahseti and Gwinodje continued to stand on the catwalk, watching as their four hundred warriors completely encircled Yi's two-hundred-strong escort. As expected the Old Hills warriors called and glared threateningly. The New Hills warriors had been ordered to say nothing to their enemies. They stood in perfect silence with arrows nocked and ready to be loosed at their enemies' hearts. It was a magnificent sight.

"All right, Gwinodje. You lead the way to the council house—slowly. We are in no hurry. They requested this meeting, we agreed with reluctance. I'll walk at Yi's side. Since she has always been the leader of my ohwachira, I owe her that much."

"I understand."

They climbed down the ladder to the plaza and walked shoulder-to-shoulder toward the two enemy matrons. Yi, her eyes half-slitted, watched Kwahseti's every move. Little Matron Adusha had a thin face and sharply pointed nose. Her expression was subdued, even apologetic. Kwahseti didn't know her well, but she'd always liked her.

When Kwahseti and Gwinodje stopped before them, Adusha bowed and remained down for a long time before she straightened to face them. In a soft voice, she said, "I offer my deepest condolence for your recent losses, matrons. Let me tell you that the Bear Clan requested this meeting. We beg that you hear what we have to say."

"We will hear you, Adusha. Please follow Matron Gwinodje to the council house." She extended a hand toward the round log structure squatting to the left of the plaza along the eastern wall.

Adusha looked at the hundreds of people crowding the plaza, and swallowed hard at the hatred that contorted her relatives' faces. Canassatego Village had just finished burying its dead. Their hearts were raw. They had no love for these women who, as members of the Ruling Council of the Old People of the Hills, had undoubtedly given the orders for the attack that killed their loved ones.

Kwahseti walked to Yi's side and gestured for her to follow Adusha and Gwinodje. Yi complied.

As they walked, Yi spoke in a quiet voice, for Kwahseti's ears alone, "Where is Matron Zateri?"

"*High* Matron Zateri is not available today."

Yi gave her a look that would have frozen lava. "Are you telling me that she refuses to meet with us? That is unaccept—"

"You have no rights here, Yi. None at all. If our High Matron deems it unnecessary to—"

"The former Bear Clan High Matron is dead."

Kwahseti stopped dead in her tracks to stare wide-eyed at Yi. *"Dead?"*

Yi glanced around, studying the inquisitive faces of the people crowding in around them. "Let's keep walking. There may be Bear Clan members standing close. They need to hear this from their own clan. I just wanted you to know that I, too, keep my promises. I gave you my oath that I would do what I could to help you."

Kwahseti stared dumbly at Yi, not certain what to say. *Kelek is dead?* She felt herself deflating like a water bag being emptied.

In a friendly gesture, Yi slipped her arm through Kwahseti's, and they continued toward the council house as though close companions of many trials—which they had been until recently.

Blood pounded in Kwahseti's ears. "How did it happen?"

Yi murmured, "The Bear Clan has honor. We brought forward the witnesses. When they grasped the problem, they took care of it."

"Because they wished to avoid a blood feud with the Wolf Clan?"

Kwahseti stood one head taller than Yi. When Yi tilted her head to look up at Kwahseti, the bruised crescents beneath her dark eyes shown purple. She'd endured many sleepless nights of late. "No one wanted it to come to that, least of all our clan."

As they rounded the curve of the council house and the leather door curtain came into view, Kwahseti asked, "So, she's dead. What now?"

Yi's head waffled. "That remains to be seen. Are you of my lineage, or have you founded your own lineage, as well as your own nation?"

Kwahseti's chest moved with a low disbelieving laugh. She walked ahead, leaving Yi to catch up with her. Four guards stood outside the entry, including War Chief Waswanosh. She dipped her head to him, drew the entry curtain aside, and held it back while Yi entered the council house. Yi exchanged a potent glance with her before she stepped inside.

Kwahseti turned to Waswanosh. "For the moment, this is a closed council meeting. Let no one enter without permission from a member of the Ruling Council."

"Of course, Matron."

Kwahseti let the curtain fall closed behind her.

As it swayed, dawn light flashed through the council house, illuminating the three circles of benches around the central fire, and the fifty council members seated upon them. Yi had not waited for her. She'd resolutely marched down the central aisle alone and gone to stand beside Gwinodje and Adusha in the orange gleam of the flames. They made an interesting trio. Gwinodje's slender frame looked childlike standing stiffly between the two taller women. Gwinodje and Adusha both had coal-black hair that almost disappeared in the darkness, while the silver threads in Yi's hair glittered like sunlit webs.

Kwahseti silently walked forward to take her place on the first ring of benches with the other elders from Riverbank Village. Chief Riverbank sat to her right. He had seen fifty-four summers. Wispy white hair clung to his freckled scalp. He was a large man, larger than life, black-eyed, ominous, and slow-talking, he'd lost his entire family in last moon's plague, then he'd been forced to abandon his village, leaving it to be burned to the ground. Yet he looked at her with clear calm eyes, ready for anything. Over the past five summers, since Kwahseti had become the Village Matron, she had come to appreciate him greatly. He would speak his heart. Always his heart. He engaged in neither guile nor fits of temper.

Riverbank gave her a questioning look, as though he sensed she had news.

Kwahseti beckoned him to lean down, and whispered in his ear, *"The Bear Clan High Matron is dead at the hands of her own clan."*

Riverbank drew back suddenly. He gazed at her as if for confirmation. Kwahseti nodded, and he squeezed his eyes closed and bowed his head. She couldn't tell if it was in mourning or overwhelming relief.

Kwahseti had both galloping through her veins, so perhaps he did, as well.

Gwinodje raised her hands to the assembly, and called, "We come together at the request of the Bear Clan of the Old People of the Hills. Matron Yi from Atotarho Village and Little Matron Adusha of Turtleback Village have been empowered to speak on behalf of the old Ruling Council."

Every time Gwinodje had used the word "old," Yi had flinched. She squared her shoulders and stared boldly out at the congregation of elders seated on the benches around her.

Gwinodje turned to Yi. "Matron Yi? As the eldest great-grandmother here, would you address this council first?"

Yi extended a hand to Adusha. "I yield the privilege to Little Matron Adusha of the Bear Clan."

Gwinodje nodded for Adusha to proceed.

Adusha wet her lips and stepped forward. As she clasped her hands before her, she called out, "I believe, regardless of the terrible injustices that have been committed by a handful of traitors, that this is one nation, and I will address you, with all the love in my heart, as my relatives."

Whispers passed around the benches. Many heads shook violently. A general din of competing voices arose.

Gwinodje lifted her hands again. "Please, Little Matron Adusha entered our village unarmed and without guards. She deserves our utmost courtesy. I ask that you listen carefully to her words before you make any judgments."

The assembly reluctantly hushed, anxiously awaiting the next volley from the other side.

Adusha seemed to have prepared herself for the hostility. She mildly looked around, meeting and holding gazes as she scanned the fifty people seated upon the benches around the fire. In a deeply apologetic voice, she continued, "You were betrayed. We know that now."

Another flurry of voices rose and dwindled.

Adusha continued, "I am not your enemy. I give you my oath. I was one of the witnesses who testified on *your* behalf before our Ruling Council. You see, I was there in the Wolf Longhouse when Matron Zateri's grandmother was murdered." She patiently waited until the voices died down.

"Though I didn't know who he was at the time, I saw the terrible witch, Ohsinoh, enter her chamber. He left very quickly, and when we went to check on the High Matron we found her dead."

The council house hummed with conversation. Rumors that High Matron Tila had been murdered had been flying about like summer bats, but no one in the New Hills nation knew their truth until this moment. Kwahseti was as stunned as everyone else.

Adusha called, "Let me tell you what conclusions our Ruling Council has come to after listening to many witnesses brought forward by the Wolf Clan elders."

Yi inhaled a deep breath and slowly let it out. Her wrinkled face had rearranged into somber lines.

"First, Atotarho's personal guards testified that they had accompanied the Chief to the Bear Clan longhouse in Atotarho Village the night before the High Matron's murder. The Chief told the Bear Clan matron that he had *a proposition* he thought she would appreciate. It seems clear that in exchange for retaining his position as chief, and being given free rein to make war on distant nations, he offered to claim that the murdered High Matron had named the Bear Clan matron as her successor." Only the crackle of the fire filled her pause. All eyes focused unblinking on Adusha. "Matron Zateri of Coldspring Village is clearly the rightful High Matron of *our* nation."

While the Ruling Council retained its dignity, the people who'd had their ears pressed to the council house walls, listening to the proceedings, burst into cheers. A riot of hoots and cries erupted, along with the sound of pounding feet, as the news swept Canassatego Village.

Kwahseti felt slightly weak in the knees. Chief Riverbank leaned to whisper to her, "I hope they know that the Bear Clan High Matron was only part of the problem."

"We will make sure they know."

Yi looked pointedly at Adusha. The Little Matron bowed deferentially and stepped back, yielding the floor to Matron Yi.

Yi walked to the edge of the benches. "The former matron of the Bear Clan, who stole the position of High Matron, is dead."

Cries of joy exploded in the plaza, while the council house was filled with gasps and murmuring.

Yi raised her voice. "There is—as you all know —another matter to be considered. Chief Atotarho. While our Ruling Council refused to send him the two thousand warriors he requested, he remains in Standing Stone country with a large war party intent upon crushing the Standing Stone People once and for all. What is your opinion of this?"

"She asks our opinion?" Riverbank noted with a frown. "As though we have already agreed to reunification and are part of her nation?"

Little Matron Tarha of the Beaver Clan rose to her feet. Hunched and gray-haired, she used her walking stick to prop up her thin body. "Before we discuss Chief Atotarho, I wish to address another matter. Riverbank Village and Coldspring are both gone, destroyed by *your warriors,* Matron Yi, and Canassatego Village barely survived. Did the Old Hills council order the destruction of our villages?"

Hateful voices rumbled around the circumference of the house.

Yi answered, "Blessed Spirits, no, Little Matron. Our council knew *nothing* of these attacks until warriors came streaming into Atotarho Village carrying their wounded. From what the warriors told us, Atotarho ordered the attacks to punish your villages for turning against him during the Bur Oak battle. It was completely Atotarho's decision."

Kwahseti thought about it for a time before she rose to her feet. "If it pleases the council, I would speak on the issue of Atotarho and his war party."

Matron Tarha sat down, and Gwinodje said, "Please do so, Matron Kwahseti."

Kwahseti didn't look at Yi. Instead, she turned around to face the other council members. "Atotarho is utterly mad. I don't know when he lost his soul, but it's been wandering aimlessly in the forest for at least thirty summers that I can recall. He must be stopped. As you all know, High Matron Zateri sent one hundred warriors back to Bur Oak Village to help protect them, as she promised she would do, but if Matron Yi is telling us the whole truth, it will not be enough to stop Atotarho from wiping the Standing Stone nation from the face of the world."

Kwahseti turned back around and stared directly at Yi. Yi's face had gone rigid. "So, we ask you, Matron Yi, will the *old* Ruling Council join the new alliance and send warriors to reinforce ours...or does it prefer to wait and see how many of its enemies Atotarho can kill?"

Yi lifted her chin and gazed down her nose at Kwahseti, but a tiny grudging smile of respect tugged at her lips. "The Ruling Council has already carefully considered this matter. We will *tentatively* agree to join the Peace Alliance, and order our forces to support yours, but only, *only*, if you agree to reunify our nation."

From the rear of the house, a flash of dawn light filled the chamber as someone entered. Kwahseti turned to see Zateri gracefully marching forward. Her long white cape gleamed in the firelight. The blue paw prints around the bottom swayed with her steps. The High Matron stopped in front of Yi with her feet spread and her fists clenched. In a powerful voice, raised for all to hear, Zateri asked, "If we agree, will the Ruling Council send word to Atotarho that his people have declared him Outcast, and he is a member of the walking dead? He must become a man with no name!"

A cacophony of shouts and supporting voices exploded inside the council house, and more outside. The entire village roared.

One of Yi's delicate black brows lifted. She gave Zateri a challenging look. In an equally strong voice, she called, "Only the full council of matrons has the right to take back his name and depose him from his position. If you rejoin the nation, and undergo the Requickening Ceremony to accept your grandmother's Spirit, I give you my oath that I will support that motion in council. But first, *High Matron*"—the assembly hissed in response to her calling Zateri the High Matron of the nation, which forced Yi to hold up a hand to get their attention—"let's make this nation whole again."

Every nerve in Kwahseti's body tingled with shock. Zateri stood like a small statue. Her cape was so still it appeared to be carved of white marble. Her face showed no give.

Gwinodje edged forward to whisper, "Blessed gods, Zateri, this is what we've been praying for."

When Yi heard Gwinodje's words, some of the fire went out of her eyes. She reached out to place a gentle hand upon Zateri's shoulder, and softly said,

"You are not my enemy. You never have been. If your people agree to reunification, we can immediately send a runner to War Chief Negano telling him to use our army to support the alliance. But it will take almost two days, running day and night, for him to get there. We must do this quickly, Zateri. Or we will be too late."

23
SKY MESSENGER

Weary. We've run almost straight through...

As the slanting rays of sundown filter through the trees, amber-tinted mist seeps up from the piles of old leaves that cover the forest floor and twines around the bases of the maples like gossamer vines. It is so quiet. Baji and I run side-by-side down the trail that leads to Bur Oak Village, listening to the sound of our moccasins striking earth. Gitchi trots behind Baji, staying right at her heels, as though he senses she's in danger. We have no idea what lurks in the forest ahead. Three more rises to go, and we will know for certain if Tagohsah told the truth and Atotarho's army surrounds Bur Oak Village. Smoke fills the air, but it is faint. It may come from the fire hearths in the longhouses, not from enemy campfires. My heart thunders in anticipation.

Sweat mats my black hair to my temples and soaks the hide of my shirt, trickling down my sides. Warmth like this two moons before winter solstice is very odd, almost supernatural. By early morning we'd removed our capes and tied them around our waists. Tiny, damp curls fringe Baji's forehead, but the rest of her long hair flies around her shoulders in sinuous, glistening locks. Her bow and quiver sway with her motions. She has tied her arrows together to keep them from rattling, and carries her war club in both hands, clutched across her chest for balance. Her candid black eyes scan the trees incessantly.

As I watch her, my heart aches. It seems impossible that we are separated by six hands distance. I feel her presence like a physical thing, a warm sea swirling around me, penetrating my body, washing against my souls in languid waves. We are both exhausted. I have no ability for long complex thoughts. The trail has turned into a series of precious moments...light dancing on the curve of her cheek... snatches of birdsong falling around us, spiraling down from the branches like wing seeds...the heart-numbing scent of her hair...my body sulking, long-ing...memories of silken textures...of skin sliding, inflaming the darkness.

The sunset-varnished air grows cool as evening comes, stroking the fevered flesh beneath my shirt. The odor of hot earth slaked with mist is strong. I breathe it in as though my lungs can't get enough and try not to let my worries overwhelm me.

Blessed gods, I love her. Since she's been at my side, I haven't had the Dream. What does that mean? Is her presence enough to stop the horror from unfolding? Or...is her presence something else?

In the hundreds of times the Dream has come to me, I have never seen her there with me at the end. The soot of the dying world does not darken her face as it does Hiyawento's. I never hear her voice or feel her touch. The possibility that she dies before the final events begin is too much to bear. It haunts me, gnawing at my vitals like a wild beast. I will do whatever I must to protect her...no matter the cost.

Nor have I seen Shagoniyoh there, or heard The Voice seeping from the air around me. Have I done something wrong? Is he gone forever?

We crest the swell in the trail and plunge down the other side into a hollow filled with oaks and dry ferns that *shish* when Caha softly breathes across the land.

Baji glances at me. I feel it like a huge hand squeezing my heart. "You have to stop worrying about me."

"How did you know I was—"

"Dekanawida, I know every expression you're capable of."

"Well, that's unnerving."

"Get used to it. Even if I die I'm going to haunt you forever."

"Promise?"

"Absolutely," she says with such dire certainty it makes me laugh.

Tension drains from my exhausted muscles, leaving me feeling slightly light-headed. The world takes on a shimmer.

"Can you feel it?" she asks.

"Yes, we're headed into it."

"What does it feel like to you?" Her head tilts in curiosity.

I think about how to describe it. The dark tingling sensation of Power swells and eddies through the trees. "It's a...fire...searing my veins. I..."

Baji suddenly cocks her head and her eyes go wide as she stares to the west with such longing that it tears my heart. It's as though she sees the Blessed Ancestors marching over the hills, coming right at us in a vast spectral army.

"What's wrong, Baji?"

Her smile is heartrending. "Nothing's wrong. I just thought I heard something."

Gitchi suddenly goes stone still in the trail, and the hair on the back of his neck rises into stiff bristles. Baji and I both stumble to a stop. His yellow eyes are focused unblinking on something...

As though they emerge from the Land of the Dead, the warriors seem to step from nothingness into this world of rich amber light. While I only see twenty or so, more move out in the trees. I hear their legs threshing ferns, coming. It sounds like thousands. These men and women have been on the trail for many hard days. Each dusty face has sleepless bloodshot eyes, and a greasy mop of mourning hair. Walking skeletons in windblown rags. Ghastly eyes that seem too huge for bony faces. As they draw back their nocked bows, emaciated muscles tremble in arms that once bulged through war shirts.

"Mountain warriors," I whisper.

Gitchi lets out a vicious growl and starts barking, preparing to defend us with his life.

Baji shouts, "Gitchi down! Stop it!"

The old wolf obeys instantly, sitting close at her side, but he can't suppress the barely audible deep-throated growls that vibrate his throat.

A big man pushes through the crowd of warriors. A dark cold man with ghastly scars, his right eye is missing, plucked out by an enemy long ago. The socket has been sewn closed and creates a shriveled pucker in his face.

"Blessed gods, that's Yenda," I murmur to Baji.

"Let's show them our empty hands."

We both slowly lift our arms.

From out of a locked chamber deep inside me, the sound of shrieks rise...*Father drags us out of our beds and orders us to run...burning longhouses... screaming people racing through the firelit darkness...*

dead bodies. Then standing in the forest, clutching my eight-summers-old sister's hand, stunned, as enemy warriors round us up and march us away...

At the command of the man who now stands before me.

Yenda, now called Chief Wenisa, led the war party that destroyed Yellowtail Village when I'd seen eleven summers. He is the reason Wrass, Tutelo, and I were captured and sold to Gannajero.

For a time, Yenda just stares at us, as though trying to confirm a suspicion.

I've fought against him many times. Bitter and angry, he is a brilliant strategist, careful to a fault, but slippery as an eel, a man who prefers to achieve his goals through torture rather than negotiation. He has no patience for words. He's built his reputation by destroying opponents.

He cocks his head in a birdlike manner, and stares at me with one blazing eye. "I know you."

More warriors emerge from the trees. It's forty to two, and increasing. Now or never...

I shout, "Baji, take Gitchi and run!" as I launch myself directly at the horde in front of me, roaring like a madman, hopefully distracting them long enough for Baji to escape.

"Shoot the dog!" a man shouts. "Quickly! It's getting away!"

Arrows hiss, loosed from too many bows to count. I don't make it ten strides before Mountain warriors fall upon me like starving panthers, dragging me to the ground. Fists knock the wind out of me. Feet slam my sides and face. I'm rolling, fighting.

Yenda calls, "Don't kill him!" and strides up to glare at me. "Yes, I know you, Deputy War Chief *Sky Messenger*."

My name flits through the war party in gasps and blurts.

Yenda lifts a hand to his warriors. "Hear me! We have just captured the infamous Standing Stone Prophet! The one known as the human False Face!"

Like a flock of frightened grouses, warriors scuttle backward to get away from me, and a cacophony of hisses and disbelieving voices erupt, filling the air.

Yenda stalks around me, smiling in diabolical glee. "You have all been afraid of this"—he thrusts a hand at me—*"this* man! Look at him. He's pathetic! He can't even defend himself."

His warriors apparently do not believe him. There is a rush of men and women retreating through the forest. Twigs and branches crack in their wakes as they flee.

Yenda roars, "You weak fools! Come back here!"

When they do not, he turns upon me like a ravening wolf. "Look at him! All of you. He has no Power. He's just a man!"

At the edge of my vision, I glimpse Yenda's war club slicing the air. He brings it down on my skull with a crack that every warrior nearby seems to feel in his teeth. Men and women flinch. Then I am hauled to my feet again, half-conscious and disoriented, still struggling. A futile bellow rises from my lungs and echoes down the trail.

With a low chilling laugh, Yenda orders, "Let's drag him to Matron Jigonsaseh. She may wish to gaze one last time upon her dying son."

24

The sound of distant voices woke Negano from a dead sleep. As he blinked up at the glittering Path of Souls, he moved his stiff limbs. His exhausted body longed to return to slumber. If he just closed his eyes, he'd be asleep again in less than five heartbeats. He felt himself sinking back and down, his muscles relaxing...

Then Chief Atotarho's voice carried: "I don't believe it! I sent two of my best warriors to kill him. Are you sure it's him? How would you..."

A man may have answered, but Negano didn't hear the response.

He exhaled tiredly and rolled to his side to look out across the dark vista where warriors slept wrapped in blankets and capes. Tree-filtered moonlight fell across their bodies in glowing streaks. When the siege had ended, his surviving warriors had fallen into their blankets like lumps of clay. Only a handful of campfires burned. The night had been so warm that fires had been allowed to die and hadn't been restoked. These were probably breakfast fires, which meant the warriors had been out hunting the darkness for owls and flying squirrels, and the mice that scampered through the piles of old leaves, anything to fill their bellies.

Thirty paces down the slope, in the very center of the camp, a ring of warriors surrounded Atotarho. He could make out Nesi, because he towered over everyone else, and Atotarho was unmistakable. The elderly Chief stood propped on his walking stick with his black cape flapping around him. The rattlesnake skins braided into his gray hair winked eerily in the moonlight.

Atotarho continued, "...and if your army arrived last night, where is it? These games are foolishness. Tell Chief Wenisa...speak with him...no more messengers."

A short, gaunt man, barely visible in the moonlight, bowed deeply and trotted away.

Negano forced himself to sit up. Gods, he longed to go back to sleep, but the mention of Wenisa's name meant the Mountain People had arrived. He didn't see them out there, but they must be close, perhaps bedded down in the valley of corpses to the west of Bur Oak Village. He shifted to look in that direction.

Two hundred paces away, down the hill, Bur Oak Village wavered in and out of sight, cloaked by the downy mist that rose from Reed Marsh and rolled across the valley bottom like moonlit clouds. The village was completely dark. Matron Jigonsaseh probably didn't want to fire-blind her warriors, just in case Negano decided to launch a night attack, or perhaps she was saving wood. Though that seemed unlikely. She must know that today would be the last day of the Standing Stone nation. Her people weren't going to need wood. By midmorning at the latest, they would be dead or slaves. It was a miracle, a testament to her skill, that they had managed to survive as long as they had. He was fairly certain he could lay the blame for the destruction of his food supplies at her feet. He shook his head as grudging respect filled him.

Nesi said, "I don't like this. Wenisa is a weasel, he can't be trust..."

Negano strained to hear more. When he couldn't, he dragged himself to his feet and straightened his cape. The unbelievable warmth of the night had made him sweat. His war shirt stuck to his chest in clammy folds. In a rumpled line on the eastern horizon, the faintest hint of blue gleamed. Soon, dawn would overwhelm the black pools of moon shadow that splotched the valley.

He reached down to pick up his weapons. While he'd slept in his weapons belt, he'd removed and placed his quiver and bow beside him, within reach. It took all of his strength to bend down, grab them, and sling them over his shoulder.

As he started down the slope for Atotarho's circle, he saw two warriors off to his right, moving through the camp, apparently kicking men and women awake. Even in the dim moonlight, he could see blankets flying when feet connected— probably warriors scrambling up and throwing off their blankets. It annoyed him. Everyone except the sentries should be allowed to sleep for as long as they could. Who had given the order to wake the army?

His gaze returned to Atotarho, and his brows drew together. Negano had lost another three- hundred-forty-two warriors yesterday. He wouldn't know for certain until dawn how many more had died from wounds during the night...but he suspected he had perhaps six hundred fighters left, and though severely damaged, the Bur Oak palisades still stood. Even with two thousand Mountain warriors as reinforcements, many more of his warriors would lose their lives today.

"War Chief?" a man called from his right.

Negano turned to see a young warrior, sixteen summers, trotting through the moonlight. The youth had a lean hungry face with shoulder-length black hair. His dark eyes looked huge. "What is it, Yekonis?"

The man slowed to a halt two paces away, as though he wanted some distance between them. "War Chief, I don't know how to tell you this. Tarha and I were walking across the camp when we noticed that many of the bundles of blankets on the ground were too small to be sleeping people. We started kicking them over." The man spread his arms in a helpless gesture. "They're gone, War Chief."

Negano tried to focus his foggy thoughts. "Who's gone?"

"The warriors. Our warriors. Sometime in the night, they formed their blankets into human-shaped bundles, probably hoping to fool us long enough that they could get far away before we discovered their ruse. They—"

Negano lurched forward to grip his shoulder hard. "How many fled?"

Yekonis nervously licked his lips. "I don't know. We've only just begun searching. We've discovered about seventy so far. I thought I should come and tell you before we continued."

Negano's fingers dug into Yekonis' shoulder. Did they have enough of an army left to defend itself? The ramifications could be deadly. "Does anyone else know about this?"

"I don't think so, but I can't be cer—"

"*Tell no one.* Do you understand? No one! When you've finished your count, report to me."

"Yes, War Chief."

Negano released him and Yekonis trotted back to join Tarha. Their faint upset voices carried through the moonlight. A short while later they returned to kicking over empty blankets.

Dear gods, I should have known. After I put down the food riot yesterday, the disgruntled warriors gathered into a knot and talked long into the night. They planned this well...

Negano lifted his eyes heavenward for several stunned moments. As the blue of dawn seeped across the sky, the campfires of the dead began to fade to soft twinkles, and the Path of Souls dimmed.

Gods, this was too terrible to think about. He felt light-headed as he turned and plodded down the hill.

Before he entered Atotarho's circle, he heard Nesi say, "Blessed Ancestors, is that the Mountain army?"

Negano swung around. As he squinted, trying to make out the movements he saw along the tree line, a premonition of calamity filled him. From three sides, Mountain warriors with nocked bows slid from the trees and slowly started forward, hemming in Atotarho's camp. The only side left open was the eastern edge of their camp, which stretched along a wavy line just out of bow range of the warriors on the Bur Oak catwalks.

Blood surged in Negano's veins as the Mountain warriors closed in. He shouted, "Rise and grab your weapons! We are surrounded! Get up! But loose no arrows!"

All across the meadow a flurry of shouts, groans, and breathless grunts erupted as men and women lunged for weapons and struggled to their feet to face the enemy. Negano repeated, "Loose no arrows! We don't know their intentions yet!"

They're supposed to be our new friends...but why would Wenisa surround us if he planned to honor our agreement?

A group of ten or so warriors detached from the line to the east and marched down the slope. Two men dragged an unconscious warrior between them. They had his arms stretched over their shoulders. His head flopped while his feet dragged behind him, generating a scraping sound.

"Negano?" Chief Atotarho called. "Join us."

Negano broke into a trot, hurrying to stand in Atotarho's circle. The mad chief glanced at him, then his gaze slid back to the man walking out front of the ten Mountain warriors. He might have been dressed in thin rags, but he wore a magnificent wolf hide headdress with the ears pricked. Negano had heard that Wenisa's long-dead evil brother, Manidos, had favored similar wear during battle. For much of Negano's childhood the two men had terrorized the world. Stories of their merciless cruelty had plagued his nightmares until he'd finally become a man and somewhat outgrown them.

"Chief Wenisa," Atotarho greeted when the man arrived.

Negano studied him. Grisly scars sliced Wenisa's face and his right eye was missing. Whoever had sewn it up had done a poor job. The big irregular stitches had created a shrunken pucker in his repulsive face.

"Chief Atotarho. My messenger says you doubted my word." Wenisa flicked his hand, gesturing to the warriors hauling the unconscious man between them. "Bring him here and drop him."

The warriors dragged the man forward and let his limp body fall on the ground at Atotarho's feet. "Take a good look. This is the dreaded Standing Stone Prophet."

Atotarho scoffed. "It can't be. I sent two warriors to kill him in case one failed." The Chief squinted down at the limp form. The man was unusually tall, broad-shouldered, but his face was so battered it was impossible in the moonlight to identify him. One of his eyes had swollen closed. His jaw bulged, as though several teeth had been knocked out. Atotarho used his walking stick to prod the man, trying to wake him. "What makes you think this is Sky Messenger?"

Wenisa's mouth twisted into a smile that could at best be described as a ghastly grimace. "I saw him before my warriors got to him. It's definitely Sky Messenger."

"Well, I can't verify that claim in this light."

As though to taunt Atotarho, Wenisa lifted both fists into the air and shouted to his warriors, "The great and powerful Standing Stone Prophet who terrifies every warrior on this field lies at my feet with barely the strength to keep breathing. He has *not* called a storm from the sky! None of the Faces of the Forest have slipped from the trees to free him! Elder Brother Sun has not come to his aid! He is a pathetic fool. I could swat him like a fly because my Power is greater than his!" To emphasize his point, Wenisa leveled a bone-breaking kick at Sky Messenger's ribs. The man didn't even groan.

Is he alive?

Whispers of awe and fear ran through both armies. These warriors were clearly terrified of what the Prophet might do to them...as Negano was. Just a few days ago, Negano had seen Sky Messenger lift his hands and call the monstrous whirling blackness that had swept down over the battlefield.

But...as he stared down at the Prophet lying helpless and alone, completely surrounded by his enemies, it seemed somehow unreal, like a made-up dream from another time.

Atotarho's wrinkled face hardened as he watched Wenisa's theatrics. "Why did you bring him to me? As a gift?"

"A *gift?*" Wenisa laughed. "Of course not. He is mine to do with as I please. At dawn, I'm going to drag him—"

A soft voice sounded behind Negano, "War Chief? Forgive me?"

Negano turned to see Yekonis standing with his fists clenched. Negano bowed, said, "Forgive me, I mean no disrespect," and stepped away from Atotarho's circle to grip Yekonis's sleeve and escort him a few paces away where they could speak privately. "What did you find?"

Yekonis's gaze darted around the meadow, as though to reassure himself that they were indeed surrounded. "War Chief, one-hundred-ninety-six blankets are empty."

Negano hissed, "Are you telling me we have only four hundred warriors left?"

Yekonis nodded. "Less. I went to the place of the wounded. Around thirty died in the night."

The hand Negano used to grip the young man's sleeve shook. The ramifications were just beginning to sink into his exhausted souls. "Wenisa will not know the truth until dawn when he can see our forces with his own eyes. I want you to quietly move through our ranks. Inform everyone of this. They'll know soon enough anyway. Tell them to be prepared for the worst."

"But...what does that mean? They're on our side, aren't they?"

Negano hesitated. He didn't want to panic his warriors. The first chance they got they'd run off. He squinted out at his camp and the Mountain army that stood so still around it. From the moment Sindak had betrayed them, this entire effort had been a gigantic failure. He'd already lost more than three-quarters of his forces, and would lose more today, maybe even all of them. Negano would go down in the history of his People as the War Chief who had gutted the nation by destroying his entire army. Stories of his missteps would be told for generations, as warnings to others.

His fatigued eyes returned to Atotarho. *I let a madman ruin my name, my family's name, and taint the legacy of my clan for generations. By obeying his orders, I did this. I killed my friends, my relatives.*

"War Chief?" Yekonis was staring at the man lying curled on his side at Atotarho's feet, and said, "Is that really Sky Messenger? Is the great Prophet dead?"

Negano shook his head. "No, but don't expect him to conjure a miracle to save you from the Mountain army. I don't think he has long to live."

Yekonis swallowed hard. "So...you don't think they're on our side?"

Negano's jaw clenched. He stared at Yekonis, then his gaze shifted to Bur Oak Village. As the darkness brightened, he could start to make out warriors standing on the palisade. He scanned each one until he thought he saw Sindak. He appeared to be speaking with another man, probably trying to decipher the events happening in the meadow.

Strange and treasonous notions slipped around Negano's skull.

It took him a few moments to work up enough courage to face them. He released his grip on Yekonis, and said, "There's something I need you to do."

"Yes, War Chief?"

"As though nothing's wrong, I want you to organize a party of three men, including yourself, to go down to the marsh to fill water bags. Take your time. Three water-bearers shouldn't be a threat to anyone. While you're there, I want you to deliver a message for me."

Yekonis gave him a confused look. "To whom? The only people down by the marsh..." His voice trailed away. As though the devastating truth of their situation was really settling into his souls and he, too, was trying to fathom a way out of the calamity that might well descend upon them shortly after dawn, his eyes scanned the Mountain army that surrounded them on three sides. "What message? To whom?"

Negano began, "After you deliver it, do not return to this army. I'm releasing you. Do you understand?"

Yekonis's eyes had a glazed look, a combination of terror and relief. "No, but...I'm listening."

25

"Who are they?" Sindak asked.

The bottom seemed to have fallen out of Gonda's stomach. He shifted on his oak crutch, wobbling around to survey the positions of the warriors who had just oozed from the trees like dark specters. Breathlessly, he suggested, "Reinforcements from the Hills nation?"

Sindak propped his fist on top of the palisade wall as he scrutinized the scene with narrowed eyes. His lean face and hooked nose shone in the pale blue gleam. "I don't think so."

"Who else could they be?"

Sindak didn't answer for a time while he continued his evaluation. Moans and cries filled the plaza below and seeped from every smoldering longhouse. While they still had two hundred real fighters perched on the catwalks and another three hundred elders and children with bows, their losses yesterday had been staggering: approximately four hundred dead, and five hundred wounded. Jigonsaseh had developed a system. Minor wounds were tended by family and friends in the longhouses. Major wounds that Old Bahna thought would Heal went to the council house. Those who had no chance of getting well were laid in rows at the south end of the plaza...near the growing pile of dead. The worst cries, mostly screams for water, came from the south end of the plaza.

Sindak pointed. "Can you see the headdress worn by the big man in front of Atotarho?"

Gonda peered out into the muted gleam, trying to make out what the man wore. As the image congealed, and he saw the pricked wolf ears, blood seemed to drain from his head. "Blessed gods, that's Chief Wenisa." His heart slammed his ribs so hard he felt sick to his stomach. "They're Mountain People."

"That's what I thought."

Speculations ran up and down the catwalks, creating a low ominous hum.

Gonda's gaze darted over the valley, trying to verify their suspicions. Dawn was coming fast, but not fast enough. He still couldn't see very well. Only the most brilliant campfires of the dead, the big council fires, continued to burn. Flaming points of red and azure, and one lonely fire beaming gold lit the sky.

Wenisa began pacing in front of Atotarho, striding back and forth with his arms waving. From this distance, he was as shadowy and quiet as the wind. Yenda had always been an arrogant fool. Having Chief Wenisa's soul Requickened in his body probably hadn't helped. Wenisa had been known far and wide as the most brutal chief in the land.

In an unnaturally calm voice, Gonda asked, "There must be...what?...two thousand Mountain warriors out there?"

"Two thousand that we can see."

"Then the Mountain People and the Hills nation have created some sort of alliance?"

Sindak examined the irregular line of warriors that surrounded Atotarho's army on three sides, probably wondering what he would do if he were in Negano's place. He frowned. "Do you want the truth, or should I lie to make you feel better?"

Gonda ran his tongue over his chapped lips. They were all desperately thirsty, but there was no water, not even for the wounded children. His souls briefly spun thoughts of hot tea steaming in a cup, warming his hands. Tangy and sweet, it ran warm into his body, easing his rigid joints, and the agony in his broken leg. It was amazing how even dreaming of hot tea helped, especially when a man was staring death in the face. "When have you ever lied to make me feel better?"

"Never, but I thought you might want me to make an exception on this last morning."

Bizarrely, Gonda felt like laughing. "No exceptions, thanks."

Sindak straightened. "Then I suspect they've allied for just this one battle. They're here to take part in the destruction of the Standing Stone nation."

Gonda's voice had an annoyingly desperate ring to it. "What do you think Atotarho promised them in exchange for their help?" *As though it matters...*

Sindak shrugged. "Enough to get them here."

Gonda massaged his brow. It occurred to him that by the end of the day, he would be his old enemy's personal slave...or his body would be lying on top of the pile of corpses. Hopefully, the second.

Sindak said, "There's a man on the ground at Atotarho's feet. I didn't notice him before, but as the light gets better, I'm starting to see more. Who do you think he is?"

"A prisoner delivered to Atotarho? A Hills deserter?"

Softly, he answered, "Possibly." He must be worried that it was one of his own warriors, Saponi, or another trusted friend.

As Elder Brother Sun lifted from the celestial

tree and neared the eastern horizon, the sky took on a pinkish hue. The breeze picked up, sawing through the leafless branches, and sending the musty fragrances of smoke and old leaves sweeping down over them.

"I don't recognize the prisoner's cape, do you?" Gonda asked.

"No, but I can't really make out the designs—just white figures around the bottom."

With an odd fatalistic composure, Gonda said, "Well, I hate to—she's had so little rest—but we should wake Matron Jigonsaseh."

Sindak turned to look at where Matron Jigonsaseh slept on her side on the catwalk. She had no blanket. All blankets had gone to warm the wounded. She had her knees pulled up beneath her woven fox hide cape. Of course, the night had been so warm no one had really needed a blanket. CorpseEye rested limply in her hand. Short, gray-streaked black hair rimmed the furry edges of her hood. She hadn't left the palisade all night. She knew the end was close. Gonda hated to be the one to tell her it was even closer than she'd thought.

"Do you want me to do it?" Sindak said.

Gonda shook his head. "No, I'll do it. I suspect she'd rather hear it from me."

"And why is that?"

"Over the long summers, I've brought her the

news that we're doomed so many times she doesn't really believe me."

"Ah. I see."

As Gonda put his weight on his crutch, his broken left leg shrieked in pain. He clumped down the catwalk, one step at a time, smiling at the warriors he passed, trying to exude a confidence he in no way felt. Each regarded him soberly.

"Who are they, Gonda?" War Chief Wampa hissed as he passed. Red-rimmed eyes and cracked lips dominated her pretty face as she turned to look at him. Her gray cape with brown spirals looked charcoal in the dimness.

"We're not sure yet, but don't worry about it until it gets light. Then we'll know for sure."

"But there are thousands!" She glanced at the warriors nearby, trying to keep her worried voice low. "Are they Hills People?"

"We've been fighting *thousands* for days, Wampa, and managed to hold out. Matron Jigonsaseh isn't going to let you down. She'll figure out something to keep you alive. She *always* does."

Those simple words seemed to affect Wampa like a cool salve on a fevered wound. Her shoulder muscles relaxed. "Yes, I know she will. Thank you, Gonda." She turned back to the wall, taking up her duties again.

As he continued down the catwalk, the warriors who'd heard their conversation stared at him, their gazes flicking back and forth between Gonda and the strange army that had just appeared. Dire whispers eddied.

Despite the noise on the catwalks and the groans and cries in the plaza, when he stood over Jigonsaseh, she still hadn't awakened. Softly, he said, "Jigonsaseh? I'm sorry to wake you." No response. Not even a wiggle. "My former wife, forgive me, but I know you will wish to hear that Chief Wenisa is here with a Mountain—"

She jerked awake as though the name had punctured her dreams like a war lance. "Wenisa? Are you sure?"

"Fairly sure. The man is wearing a wolf hide headdress, which you know Wenisa favors."

As she sat up, she exhaled hard, then leaned back against the palisade and rubbed her eyes on her sleeve. "What does Sindak say about this?"

"He suspects Wenisa joined forces with Atotarho just to destroy the Standing Stone nation."

She inhaled a deep breath and let it out slowly before she dragged herself to her feet. "Then Wenisa is going to be disappointed." Bluish half-moons darkened the skin beneath her eyes. Her narrow nose and full lips bore a fine layer of ash—which had fallen all night from the smoldering village.

"My former wife, it's as bad as can be."

Jigonsaseh tucked CorpseEye into her belt and reached down to grasp her bow and quiver where they stood canted at an angle against the palisade. She slung them over her shoulder and blinked at the warriors on the catwalk. Every eye had turned to her, and she knew it. She squared her shoulders and called, in a voice loud enough for everyone to hear: "Show me where they are."

As she marched toward Sindak, her black eyes blazed, inspiring every warrior with the confidence that once she understood the situation, she'd get them out of this.

Despite the fact that Gonda had known her for more than thirty summers, the sight of her striding down the catwalk even buoyed his spirits.

The whispers along the palisade changed, going from ominous to something more like guarded determination. She was a living prayer, their last prayer, and if it took every breath in their bodies, they would not let her down. They would fight for her until they simply could not lift their hands.

Gonda clumped along behind her, not trying to keep up, just watching the worshipful expressions of the warriors as she passed without a word, gripping shoulders here and there.

When she reached Sindak's side, her gaze carefully scanned the meadow. As Gaha sailed over the catwalk, Jigonsaseh's fox hide hood waffled around her exhausted face.

Sindak didn't say anything for a time, letting her take it in before he softly commented, "With these new forces, I suspect we have a couple hands of time after dawn before the walls are breached."

Jigonsaseh propped her elbows on the palisade beside Sindak, blinking awake, fighting to gain her desperately needed senses. "How many?"

"Maybe two thousand Mountain warriors, but he could have more in reserve in the trees."

"I doubt it. From what I've heard, two thousand is about all they have left in the nation. Which means he's wagering everything on this battle."

Sindak stared at her for a moment. "I hadn't thought of that, but you're right, and it means they're going to fight even harder."

"What's Negano doing?"

"I can't tell, but something is not right out there."

She shifted to face him. "How do you know?"

"It's more of a feeling than anything else." Sindak stared at her and you would have thought they were the only two at the Dance. "Negano's warriors should be on their feet, each one facing the Mountain army. I only count perhaps three hundred fifty to four hundred."

"Yes, but it looks like many are still sleeping. Perhaps he wants to give them—"

Sindak shook his head. "Doubtful. I suspect those rolled blankets are empty."

Jigonsaseh's black eyes moved over the blankets. As the wind picked up and the light brightened, many could be seen napping. "What makes you think so?"

"Earlier, I saw two men kicking over bundles. Blankets flew, but no one stood up."

Gonda lurched forward, his heart thundering, to hiss, "Blessed gods! You mean hundreds deserted during the night?"

"I think it's a strong possibility."

Jigonsaseh stood perfectly still. Only her eyes moved. Studying. "If you're right, and Negano has only around four hundred warriors left, he must know that Wenisa's archers could skewer his forces in a few hundred heartbeats."

Sindak gave her a sober look. "As soon as it's light, Wenisa is going to come to that same conclusion."

Jigonsaseh closed her eyes and rubbed them on her sleeve again. Gonda knew that gesture. She was tired, but she was also thinking, working out what she would do if that turned out to be the case. When she opened her eyes, she said, "Then, within a single hand of time, we may only be fighting a desperate Mountain army. And one greatly diminished. I suspect Negano's warriors will manage to get eight hundred arrows into the air before they fall, and they'll be letting fly from close range. Sindak, how many will Wenisa lose?"

Sindak's brows plunged down over his hooked nose. He blinked out at the warrior-filled meadow as he tried to calculate. "I say...six hundred. Probably three hundred killed outright and another three hundred down with wounds that take them out of the fight."

"Gonda?" she turned to him.

He leaned heavily on his crutch. "I think Sindak doesn't want to get your hopes up, so he's guessing low. I'm going to guess high. If Negano forms his warriors up properly, he'll lose the front line of archers immediately, but it will give his remaining warriors time to loose four or five arrows each. "I say one thousand out of the battle."

She nodded, mulling the information. "So...if they turn on each other first, instead of facing two thousand four hundred, we'll be facing somewhere between one thousand and one thousand two hundred."

Sindak and Gonda nodded simultaneously. A frail tendril of hope twined through Gonda's chest.

"But I don't think that will happen," Sindak said. "Wenisa is an overconfident fool, but not that much a fool. He'll want us to kill as many of Atotarho's warriors as possible to save him the trouble. Which means they won't turn on each other until the middle of the battle, maybe not even until the end."

As she listened, Jigonsaseh continued her examination of the brightening meadow, noting the positions of warriors, trying to see the coming attack before it happened. When she abruptly gripped the palisade, both Gonda and Sindak went rigid. For a time, she seemed to be holding her breath, then almost too soft to hear, she said, "The man on the ground in front of Atotarho—"

"We don't know who he is. Wenisa—"

"That's Sky Messenger."

"What?" Gonda stumbled forward to grab the palisade and stare at the distant figure. He was stirring. He weakly rolled to his back. "That's not Sky Messenger's cape. And if so, where's Gitchi? Gitchi wouldn't leave—"

"They would have killed Gitchi first," Sindak replied.

The man on the ground rolled to his knees and started retching violently. He sounded like he was bringing up his insides. After five heartbeats, he collapsed again as though unconscious.

Gonda whispered to Jigonsaseh, "Don't jump to conclusions. You can't possibly know for certain in this light."

She seemed to realize she'd slumped against the palisade, and her warriors were watching her. She straightened to her full height again, braced her feet and propped her hand on her belted war club. "That's Sky Messenger. Believe me."

Sindak's teeth ground beneath his cheek. He studied her for a long time, before he said, "If you're right, Wenisa is going to use him against us. That's why he's still alive."

None of them said anything for another twenty heartbeats, then Jigonsaseh responded, "Sky Messenger is more valuable to him alive. If Wenisa takes him home and parades him around as proof that he has greater Spirit Power than the renowned Standing Stone Prophet, Wenisa's reputation will soar."

Sindak's head waffled. "Maybe."

As the possibility that it really was Sky Messenger out there began to solidify, Gonda's chest seemed to hollow out and refill with panicked desolation. He blurted, "Then he won't kill Sky Messenger unless we force him to. Is there a way we can get to our son? If there's a break in the battle and we can send out a party to..."

Sindak and Jigonsaseh both stared at him as though his souls had flown away and his body was a senseless piece of useless flesh. *I'm a selfish fool. Any party sent out to rescue Sky Messenger will be slaughtered like dogs at a ritual sacrifice.* Jigonsaseh would never kill twenty in a vain attempt to save one. Not even her son. The suggestion had been ludicrous. He whispered, "I—I wasn't thinking."

A small commotion erupted along the eastern wall overlooking the marsh.

Jigonsaseh ignored it and reached out to put a hand on Gonda's shoulder. "If I could, Gonda, you know that I..."

"War Chief Sindak?" Wampa called as she trotted down the catwalk.

Sindak stepped away from the palisade and walked out to meet her.

Wampa glanced at the warriors nearby and very quietly said, "There's a man in the marsh asking to speak with you. He says War Chief Negano sent him."

"Negano?" Sindak strode down the catwalk briskly, heading for the group of warriors who'd gathered to peer down into the marsh.

Gonda squinted after him. As did Jigonsaseh.

Less than two hundred heartbeats later, Sindak straightened and turned to Wampa. "Get every water pot and canteen you can find and lower them down to Yekonis. Do it now, before it gets light enough that he becomes a perfect target."

Wampa didn't bother responding. She charged down the catwalk, tapping men and women on the shoulders. Her rushed words sent them scurrying down the ladders and toward the longhouses.

As Sindak's stride lengthened on the way back toward Jigonsaseh and Gonda, the news was already spreading around the catwalk like wildfire.

"...Sindak working with Negano...not possible... Atotarho must have thought he could talk Sindak into betraying us...I don't believe."

Sindak didn't bother to respond. He just clenched his jaw and kept his eye on Jigonsaseh.

Gonda saw her turn. By the time Sindak arrived, she stood facing him, her feet braced, a beautiful muscular woman with obsidian-hard eyes that could cut out a man's heart. She'd removed her fox hide cape and slung it over the palisade where the wind softly ruffled the fine red hair. She still had CorpseEye tucked into her belt, but her fingers had tightened around the smooth wooden shaft. She stared at Sindak: a silent question.

"His name is Yekonis, Hawk Clan, from Atotarho Village. He's going to fill as many pots and canteens as he can before full dawn. He's vowed to serve me as a loyal warrior."

Her face showed nothing. "Why?"

"I made no promises. I wouldn't do that without your app—"

"What does Atotarho want?"

Sindak propped his hands on his hips and bowed his head slightly. Gonda watched him. He appeared to be hesitating because he didn't know what to make of the message himself. "It isn't Atotarho who's asking. It's Negano. He suspects Wenisa is going to betray them, and he wants to save as many of his warriors as he can."

The breeze tousled Jigonsaseh's gray-streaked black hair around her still face. "Do you believe this?"

Sindak kept his head bowed, and Gonda suspected he was considering the fact that she hadn't yet asked him "how?" He'd known her a long time. Perhaps Sindak understood that how mattered less to her than his opinion of Negano's trustworthiness.

Sindak looked up. Their gazes held. Finally, he replied, "I don't think we have a choice."

26

As Hiyawento and Towa trotted eastward along the trail to Bur Oak Village, Hiyawento's body entered that timeless void of running where thoughts ceased to exist, and there was nothing except motion and raw heightened sensation. He reveled in the brilliant streamers of orange that spiked up from the eastern horizon. They shot through the hearts of the drifting Cloud People, turning them a sulfurous shade of yellow he had never seen before. Across the forest, balmy air hissed through the trees, setting warm pungent scents loose to wander with the breeze.

When they crested a high point along the rolling trail, he saw smoke rising from Bur Oak Village. Towa momentarily hesitated, as though he wanted to stop, but Hiyawento didn't slow down.

He plunged down the rise, heading for the small creek that crossed the trail ahead.

One hand of time ago, he'd sent a runner ahead with the Truth Belt to let Sky Messenger know they were very close. He'd instructed the runner to come back with information on what was happening there, so they'd have some warning of what they'd be facing. The man had not returned.

Hiyawento feared he'd been killed. Which probably meant a battle raged just head, and they'd arrive in the roaring chaos with a crowd of half-starved women and children at their heels.

Hiyawento wiped his sweating face on his sleeve. It felt like the Moon of Newborn Fawns. All along the periphery of the forest, huge columns of insects spiraled, their membranous wings creating glimmering torrents that spun like tornadoes above the tallest trees.

He and Towa had been moving fast, trying to outrun the weakest followers. They'd lost maybe two hundred of the elders, women, and children, but the heartiest clung to them like boiled pine pitch. They were dedicated, he'd say that for them. Hiyawento cast a glance over his shoulder to see how close they were.

Twenty paces back, Tiyosh ran encircled by fifteen guards, still wearing Sky Messenger's cape with the hood pulled up, despite the heat. He must be roasting alive. Another four hundred paces behind him, the ocean of humanity washed up and spilled over the rolling trail. How many? Three hundred? Four? Laughter drifted through the sea of waving arms as people whirled and clapped their hands in joy, singing their hearts out. They'd been dancing since long before dawn.

To see what Hiyawento was looking at, Towa jerked around, and his straight nose slung sweat. His handsome face ran with it. "I don't know how they have the strength to dance. Most have barely enough flesh left on their bones to walk. It's the most bizarre thing I've ever seen."

"Especially since we're headed into the midst of a battle with Atotarho's army or the Mountain People, or both."

"Exactly! What's there to be happy about? I swear they're demented."

"They're true believers. Their faith is like a Spirit Plant in their veins."

As they plummeted down the slope and through the low spot, Elder Brother Sun slid over the horizon and threw the onyx shadows of the trees across their path. The cool air felt wonderful. The scent of water swelled from the tiny stream that meandered across the trail. Barely one body length across, Hiyawento leaped it easily, and continued on.

Towa leaped, splashed, and cursed before he ran to catch up. "Yes, but Hiyawento, I also believe in Sky Messenger's Dream. The difference is that it scares the heart out of my body." He cast another glance back at the celebration that followed them. "This jubilance is—well, it's unnatural."

"Isn't everything these days?"

"True enough, but do you think they're happy because anything, even death, is better than the life they've been forced to live these past few summers?"

Hiyawento glanced at Towa before he turned his gaze back to the smoke rising into the sky in the distance. "Maybe. I have to admit that I feel a bit of it myself. Anyone who tells me he can end the constant warfare and suffering, which has tormented our Peoples for generations, must be a supernatural Spirit hero. In fact, Towa, I am absolutely certain that Sky Messenger is the human False Face promised in the old stories."

Towa shifted the pack on his back, rebalancing it upon his shoulders. "I am, too, but I still do not understand this raucous euphoria." He paused a moment, then a broad smile came to his face. "I mean within a few days, we'll probably all be in the Land of the Dead, and it doesn't have a single decent Trader. I'm not ready for that."

"How do you know it doesn't have any decent Traders?"

"Oh, come, come, do you know *anyone* who's seen a Spirit wearing an exceptional buffalo wool shirt, or carrying arrows made from extra hard chokecherry from the far west?"

Hiyawento thought about it. "No."

"See? Someone would have noticed. People always notice such things."

"You're trying to take my mind off what's ahead, aren't you?"

Towa chuckled. "Just making conversation."

"Yes, I see." Hiyawento smiled.

In the distance, a man's head appeared, bobbing along the trail. Hiyawento couldn't see his body yet. He ran just below the swell of the trail.

"Runner coming."

"Hmm?" Towa followed Hiyawento's gaze, but apparently didn't see anything. "How far away?"

"I forgot you can't see well at distances. If we maintain our pace, our paths will collide in five hundred heartbeats."

Towa squinted hard at the place he thought the runner must be. "If the runner has any sense, he'll take one look at the crowd behind us and veer off the trail into the forest until we pass."

"Unless he's coming to find us. The Bur Oak scouts should have spotted us one-half hand of time ago. I'd hoped they would give my runner information about what was happening and send him back as I'd asked."

Towa's handsome face tensed. "Maybe the scouts saw the horde following us, and they're still trying to figure out what to do—providing they're not already under attack and too busy to care about us."

"Towa, can you stay here? Slow Tiyosh down while I run ahead to see who he is?"

"Yes, go on."

Hiyawento forced his legs to work harder, trying to get far enough ahead that he'd have at least thirty heartbeats before the masses arrived.

As he pounded down the trail, he saw the man crest the hill. Different cape. Not his messenger. Hiyawento pulled an arrow from his quiver, nocked his bow, and held it aimed at the ground— just in case.

The man shouted, "Hiyawento!" and pounded to meet him, his short black hair flopping over his ears.

"Disu?"

Sindak's man, from Atotarho Village.

Disu's broad face looked like sculpted walnut— tanned and shiny—running sweat. As he trotted up, Hiyawento opened his mouth to speak, and Disu said, "Don't talk, just listen. First, your messenger is safe. He was just exhausted. That's why I came. Second, Tagohsah did not lie to you. Bur Oak is about to be attacked by both Atotarho and Wenisa. And"—he took a deep, halting breath —"Sky Messenger is Wenisa's prisoner. I don't know how it happened, but he—"

"Are you sure?" he asked in panic.

"Yes, absolutely."

"Is he alive?" Hiyawento's mouth had gone dust dry.

"For now, but his head wound looks bad."

"Where's Baji?" He didn't ask about Gitchi because if Sky Messenger had been captured the dog had certainly been killed while trying to protect him.

"Baji? The Flint War Chief? I have no knowledge of her whereabouts. Are you expecting a Flint war party?"

"No. I—"

"Then please listen. We have no time. When your messenger told us you and the crowd would arrive around dawn, we gathered our warriors to discuss—"

"You have warriors?" He gripped Disu's arm. "How many?"

Disu sliced a hand through the air to cut off the discussion. "It's a long story. There are thirty-one of us hiding in the forest to the south of Bur Oak Village. In the spirit of the new alliance, Saponi wishes me to tell you that while he can lead them into battle, he is not a War Chief, and you have led warriors against Wenisa many times. If you will accept command of these warriors, they have each sworn loyalty to you. Including me."

Hiyawento's grip tightened. "Tell me quickly

about the battlefield. How many warriors will we be facing?"

"Around two thousand from the Mountain People and another three to four hundred of Atotarho's warriors."

The numbers stunned Hiyawento. "Atotarho only has three or four hundred? What happened to--"

"Will you command or not?" Disu asked impatiently.

"Yes, I accept. I don't know how much we can do, but thirty good warriors can do something, and we will. Where exactly is Saponi holding his warriors?"

"In the hills just south of where Matron Zateri's forces were camped a few days ago."

Hiyawento swung around to look behind him. Towa and Tiyosh were still twenty paces away. He said, "Wait here," and ran back to them.

Towa's face had gone pale. "Is that Disu?"

"Yes. Bur Oak is surrounded and Sky Messenger has been captured. I must accompany Disu back to evaluate what's going on. Can you lead the crowd to the hills just beyond the old sunflower fields south of Bur Oak Village? Keep them hidden. Even if they will not fight on our side, when the time comes the sight of so many people suddenly appearing will disrupt the battle and give Jigonsaseh a little more time. One last thing." He put a hand on Towa's shoulder. "Before you arrive, make Tiyosh remove that cape. If you and Tiyosh can arrive a few hundred heartbeats before the crowd, it will look like Sky Messenger was just captured by the Mountain People moments ago. There's a slim chance it might rally the Landing warriors to join the Peace Alliance. If it does, we need to get the warriors separated from the rest of the crowd, and ready to fight. Can you do that?"

"Of course I can, I'm a Trader. I can talk people into anything." He slapped Hiyawento's shoulder. "I'll meet you there."

Hiyawento sprinted back to Disu.

If the Faces of the Forest were on Sky Messenger's side, how could everything have gone so wrong?

27

When sunlight finally crept across the meadow, Negano was standing beside Atotarho and Nesi, but his eyes had fixed upon Chief Wenisa, waiting to see the big man's reaction when he finally noticed how few warriors Atotarho possessed. Wenisa's army remained in the same position, surrounding the camp on three sides, but many warriors had squatted down or gathered into small groups to talk. Their strange Mountain People accents lilted through the warm, smoky air.

Chief Wenisa's voice trailed away suddenly, and his jaw slackened as his gaze swept the meadow. After a time, he bent down to whisper something to his War Chief, Powink. Powink subtly nodded. A tall, skinny man, Powink, had a long, sallow face that gave him a perpetually sad expression. Like Wenisa, his clothing was little more than a thin leather sieve. So many tears and rips shredded his knee-length war shirt that from a distance, a man might mistake them for black paintings.

Nesi whispered, "They know."

"Apparently," Negano softly replied.

For the first time, Negano could see that Wenisa had one extraordinary eye. It was dark as coal and filled with a strange wolflike clarity. The cruelty of a predator that feels neither regret nor shame in the act of killing, for it is simply life. His shaggy eyebrows tilted upward and had wild gray hairs curling from their midst.

Negano shifted his weight, trying not to appear uneasy. He'd ordered his three hundred seventy-six warriors to align on the western edge of camp, just out of bowshot of Bur Oak Village, and out of bowshot of most of Wenisa's army. In the open space between the armies, rotting corpses sprawled. Bones, kicked and scattered about in yesterday's attack, lay in tangles, held together by fragments of shirts and pants. Barely fleshed skulls studded the battlefield like half-sunken rocks. Each wore a shrunken rictus that resembled a gleeful smile, as though the souls that remained with the bodies knew they would have company by nightfall. All day yesterday, as his warriors had run back and forth across the meadow, the skulls had rolled and tumbled. At one point, there'd been so many bouncing in the air that the battlefield had resembled a macabre ball game.

Atotarho's gaze slid to Wenisa, and his wrinkled mouth tightened. Gray hair hung over his leathery face, flipping in the light breeze. The rattlesnakes braided into the locks flashed when he repositioned his walking stick to support his crooked body. "There's nothing we can do about it."

Atotarho turned and gave Negano a hateful look, as though it were his fault that so many had deserted in the night.

Negano took the hint. "If you don't mind, Chief, I think I'll walk among our warriors to judge their moods."

"Do so."

Atotarho returned to discussing the strategic situation with Nesi, his former war chief of many summers ago. As Negano started to walk away, Nesi gave him an apologetic look.

Negano needed to speak with Nesi alone...but the opportunity had not yet arisen, and he had to face the fact that it may not.

Negano weaved silently between the tangled corpses, his empty hands clasped behind his back, threatening no one. He wandered, nodded to warriors, and soaked in the fragments of conversations he heard. These were tired men and women, disheartened more than ever. As he'd ordered, they stood with their backs to the Standing Stone nation, and their lowered bows aimed vaguely in the direction of the huge Mountain army facing them across the meadow. Each studied Negano as he passed, ready even now, even after everything he'd done to them, to follow him into the Land of the Dead if that's where he led them. Loyalty lasted too long. It cost too much. Though he thanked the Spirits that warriors had that failing.

Negano slowly made his way to the southern end of the line, and stopped beside a muscular woman warrior named Ohonsta. She had a reputation for humor, but this morning, her smooth triangular face showed nothing—it was empty, inscrutable. Her red-rimmed eyes stared at him as though gazing out across some vast unfamiliar country, which he knew came from utter exhaustion. "It won't be long now. Pass the word down the line that my first order is going to sound like madness, but they must not hesitate to follow it."

Ohonsta blinked. She seemed to be trying to imagine what that order might be. She said, "You're going to order us to slice our own throats? Everybody is ready to do that anyway. It will make perfect sense."

He smiled briefly. "We aren't certain the Mountain People will betray our agreement, but if they do, we've made other arrangements. Be ready."

"I'll pass the word."

Negano continued walking. To his left the charred palisade of Bur Oak Village rose like a hulking forty-hand tall monster. Widely spaced warriors with bows stood upon the exterior catwalk. The two interior catwalks, however, looked vacant, which meant High Matron Kittle no longer had the warriors to guard them. In addition, many of the guards he could see were white-haired elders or children barely tall enough to peer over the top of the palisade. Yesterday, every time a child had fired, he or she had first climbed up, probably onto a wooden block, to aim and let fly. His warriors had, of course, seen the same thing and begun targeting the children before they fully got into position to aim. Negano had no notion how many they'd killed, but the number had surely left parents reeling with grief.

Today, they would fight to their last breaths to justify the sacrifice of their children's lives.

When Negano reached the place in the middle of the line that stood fifty paces from the gates of Bur Oak Village, he stopped and took a long moment to stare up at Sindak who was staring squarely back. The slant of sunlight cast shadows over Sindak's deeply sunken eyes, but his hooked nose and lean face were clearly identifiable.

As Ohonsta's message traveled down the line of warriors, it moved from mouth to mouth past Negano, and his warriors stared questioningly at him...then they turned and followed his gaze to Sindak. Barely a handful of days ago, Sindak had been their War Chief. He had led them to victory after victory, and they loved him for it. Ominous chatter started. Negano made no attempt to still it.

He was walking a tightrope over the abyss. He had to watch his step.

He'd positioned his forces here in the hopes that his words would not get back to Atotarho. If they did, the old chief would suspect treachery and immediately issue an order of his own designed to supercede anything Negano ordered. Would his warriors still obey him if he countermanded their Chief? He didn't know.

He came to the last man in line and stood silently, his hands clasped behind his back, staring not at his warrior, but up at Sindak. The man had been watching Negano, his gaze following him down the line of warriors. Negano knew the kinds of questions Sindak must be asking himself. He also knew that Sindak must have a nest of vipers slithering around in his belly—just as Negano did.

In the end, everything, *everything*, came down to a matter of trust.

28

SKY MESSENGER

I'm not sure where I am. Smoke fills the warm air. My left eye won't open, and all I see through my right eye is a cloudy shifting haze filled with golden twinkles that shoot across my vision like meteors falling to earth. My fingers spastically clench, unclench.

I squint, trying to focus, to make out faces in the haze. All I see are ghostly gray figures spinning like wind-touched mist, without substance or form. Distant voices rush close, then fade to nothingness. I'm not sure they're real.

I faintly remember being struck with a war club. Many times, when warriors are struck in the head, one of their eyes goes milky. I think that's what happened to me.

Somewhere high above me, crows caw, and I hear birds singing. Insects hum in the grass.

Baji? Gitchi? Where are they? Are they right here beside me, guarding me?

Maybe they didn't escape...

Pain too terrible to endure suddenly wrenches me, turning me inside out. I think my arms and legs are flopping, but I'm not sure. When the seizure ends, tears leak from my eyes and trail hotly down my cheeks.

I have the vague sensation that my condition is placing everyone around me in danger, and I have the overwhelming urge to run...but I can't feel my legs.

29

Hiyawento followed Disu, sliding through the dry grass on his belly, heading for Saponi, who wore Hiyawento's Truth Belt around his waist. When the runner had realized Sky Messenger was not here, he'd obviously delivered it to the man in charge. Saponi had wedged himself between two rocks overlooking the battlefield and Bur Oak Village. Even from ten paces away, Hiyawento could see that Saponi's pockmarked face was cold and gray. The scent of fear sweat filled the air. The rest of Saponi's warriors crouched behind the boulders that scattered the hilltop.

Disu shifted to whisper, "Let me tell him you're here."

Hiyawento nodded and wiped his brow while he waited.

A short while ago, Hadui had begun tormenting the hills, thrashing through the forest and hurling old leaves and gravel like weapons. To the north, a black wall of Cloud People was pushing south, and Hiyawento had the feeling the unseasonably warm weather was about to end.

Brittle leaves had blown into every hollow, making the hill look smooth and rounded, though Hiyawento knew from experience, it was not. Dips and rocky holes stippled the ground, making it treacherous footing, especially if a man were running for his life. He'd move these warriors immediately, as soon as he'd talked it over with Saponi.

Disu made it to Saponi and touched his friend's foot, announcing his presence before he crawled up beside Saponi and started talking.

Saponi shoved up on one elbow to search for Hiyawento, then he lifted a hand, waving Hiyawento to join them.

As he crawled forward, the smell of death, of rotting muscles and intestines, drifted through the trees like an invisible miasma, blowing up from the corpses piled against the Bur Oak palisades and the surrounding meadows. It would get worse as the day wore on.

Hiyawento slid forward and Disu moved to the side, yielding his position next to Saponi. Saponi was a burly man with brown eyes and a nose like a flattened beetle. His cape bore the interlocking green and blue rectangles of the Snipe Clan. Hiyawento wedged himself, shoulder-to-shoulder, between Saponi and Disu. Boulders stood twenty hands tall on either side of them.

"We're very glad to see you, War Chief Hiyawento," Saponi said.

"And I to see you. After I heard about the Mountain army, I feared all I would find here was a smoldering pile of rubble."

"Not yet, but we just received word from one of our scouts that there's a Flint war party heading this way."

"They're part of the alliance, Saponi. They—"

"If I knew Chief Cord was still alive, I wouldn't be worried, but he may be dead and the new Chief no friend of ours."

Hiyawento took a breath and through a long exhalation said, "How long until the Flint war party arrives?"

"Nightfall. Even if they're on our side, they won't make it in time to help us."

Hiyawento thought the ramifications through. He didn't have the luxury of worrying about the Flint People right now. He'd consider them later, if he was still alive. "All right. Here's the situation: Towa will arrive shortly, dragging hundreds of Landing People with him. Some are warriors. By the time he reports, he'll have the warriors who wish to fight for us separated out. There may be one hundred. Two if we're very fortunate. The rest are starving women, children, and elders." He vented a breath. "Now, tell me what's happening here?"

Through the narrow crack in the rocks, Hiyawento could see almost the entire battlefield below. He scanned it quickly...Bur Oak Village on the left, along with the useless burned-out husk of Yellowtail Village. Just in front of Bur Oak, in a wavy line, stood around four hundred warriors. Then, out at a distance of perhaps seventy paces, the Mountain army created an enormous crescent. It cupped the meadow on three sides, and was perfectly positioned to close in with crushing force.

"Those are Negano's warriors." Saponi pointed to the four hundred.

Hiyawento grimaced. "Why on earth does Negano have his people sandwiched between the Standing Stone archers and the Mountain warriors? Is he trying to get them killed?"

"We've been wondering the same thing. It is... incomprehensible."

"When the battle starts, the Mountain army will push the Hills warriors right into the range of the Standing Stone archers. They'll be butchered."

Disu added, "Unless they are shot from behind first—as many will be. I don't care what agreement has been made, this is the chance of a lifetime for

Mountain warriors to fulfill blood oaths against the Hills People."

A ghostly wail, high and thin, wavered in the distance and Hiyawento thought for a moment it was mingled cries of unbearable pain, then he saw the Mountain army shaking fists with their heads thrown back. Clan war cries. The army began to move. Like a many-legged beast, it lurched forward with ragged clan flags jerking about in blurs of blue, red, and black.

A wayward arrow thunked into the boulder to Hiyawento's left and splintered into a thousand flying pieces. Disu covered his head and flattened out on the ground. Saponi and Hiyawento just flinched and continued watching the advancing army.

The warriors on the Bur Oak catwalks had their bows fully drawn back, patiently waiting for the enemy to get into range.

Hiyawento shook his head. "Why haven't Negano's warriors already started picking off the people in the open on the catwalk? They're just standing there."

"I don't know how he thinks, but..." Saponi extended a finger toward the far right where the curve of the meadow butted against the rocky eastern hills. Twenty or so people stood in a knot. "You should know that the man lying on the ground before Atotarho is the Prophet, Sky

Messenger." Reverence touched Saponi's voice. He was a believer. He had witnessed the monstrous storm.

Hiyawento examined the body. Sky Messenger appeared to be unconscious. *Blessed Ancestors, please don't let him be dead.* "I can identify Atotarho and Nesi, and Chief Wenisa must be the big man, correct?"

"Yes. The others are the chief's personal guards. They..."

A din of gasps and soft cries erupted from the warriors surrounding them, and Disu said, *"I don't believe it! What are they doing?"*

Hiyawento looked just in time to see the Hills warriors pivot on their heels, swinging full around to face the oncoming Mountain army. They loosed a devastating volley of arrows into the onslaught. Hundreds of Mountain warriors fell, forcing the rushing people behind them to stumble and leap their fallen friends before they could continue their charge. Enraged roars rumbled across the valley. In the stunned moments after the volley, Negano shouted something Hiyawento couldn't hear, but he watched in fascination as Negano's forces turned tail and ran as hard as they could for the Bur Oak Village gates. Screaming Mountain warriors chased after them, loosing arrows on the run. Many of Negano's warriors went down. Just before the survivors hit the gates, they swung open, and his warriors flooded inside to a deafening bellow of outrage from the Mountain People. The gates immediately swung closed, and Wenisa's army hit the walls like a hurricane, shrieking and shouting curses, while Standing Stone arrows rained down upon them.

"Gods," Saponi said. "What just happened?"

Hiyawento shook his head. "I'm not sure."

Disu let out a bizarre cackle, then he threw his head back and laughed. "Don't you see? Negano and his people just joined the Peace Alliance!"

Negano brought up the rear, shoving his warriors through the gates in front of him, shouting, "Move! Get inside! Hurry!"

As he pushed his warriors into the plaza, he heard the guards slam the locking planks on the gates into position behind him, and found himself surrounded by Standing Stone warriors with drawn bows. He shouted to his warriors, "Lay down your weapons! Lift your hands!"

With shocked expressions, his warriors did it. White-faced, they lifted their empty hands, and stared at the circle of bows that had closed like a bristly noose around them.

Negano desperately searched for Sindak but didn't see him anywhere. He was probably still on the catwalk, handling the murderous onslaught outside. Instead, a tall woman, half a head taller than Negano, strode across the plaza. They knew her. Every last one of them. An odd hush came over his warriors. They shoved each other aside to create a path for her to reach Negano, and she walked through the press alone, her stony black eyes fixed on Negano's.

He held his hands higher in the air. She had just allowed around three hundred enemy warriors into her village, into the midst of vulnerable women, children, and elders—warriors who had been murdering her people yesterday. He didn't know what to expect, and nothing on her expressionless face told him.

Blessed Spirits, she had a presence. She looked completely unafraid, or maybe she'd just given herself up for dead days ago. When she stood before him, her black eyes glistened with deadly intent.

Negano said, "Matron Jigonsaseh, thank you for helping us, we—"

"Get your people up on the catwalk immediately. We're going to be short on arrows. I want one dead Mountain warrior for every arrow loosed. Move!"

"Y-Yes, Matron," he stammered. He half-bowed, hesitated for only a heartbeat, then marched into the middle of his warriors to shout,

"Pick up your bows and get to the catwalk now! Careful shots. One arrow for one kill. Go!"

She watched him with stone-cold eyes as Negano led his people to the closest ladders, and they charged up to join the battle...

30

N esi stood gaping, momentarily frozen at the sight of Hills warriors flooding across the Bur Oak catwalks. Heartbeats later, they fired a coordinated, decimating volley of arrows into the Mountain warriors at the base of the palisades, warriors who'd been scrambling on top of the corpses, shooting straight up into the faces of anyone who leaned over to aim at them. Hundreds went down. Then more, as Negano's archers launched arrows into the fleeing horde whose senseless rage had led them way too close to the village.

Yesterday, most of the people standing on the catwalk had been elders and children with poor aims. As of this moment, the Standing Stone nation had three hundred of the finest warriors in the land.

Nesi's fists ached as he clenched them tight and turned to face Chief Wenisa. Nesi was a big man, but Wenisa was bigger, his shoulders wider, his upper arms more massive. Though a cacophony of threats and curses had erupted from Wenisa's personal guards as they stalked about in fury... Wenisa stood eerily quiet. Just calmly watching the battle with his bulging muscles about to burst through his shirt.

Nesi's gaze slid to Chief Atotarho. The old man hunched over his walking stick, gripping the head with knobby parchment-like hands. His crooked body quaked with repressed violence. Muscle spasms twitched across his wrinkled face with such ferocity that Nesi thought he might be about to collapse in convulsions. Negano's move had left the Chief with five personal guards in the midst of a swarm of deadly Mountain warriors.

Nesi met the gazes of Atotarho's other guards. Terrified and stunned, they looked like they didn't know what to do. Each one who silently glanced down at his weapons belt, or shifted his shoulder to indicate his slung bow, received a subtle shake of Nesi's head. Gods, that was the last thing...

A wild-eyed youth came careening across the battlefield, leaping corpses in a heedless charge to reach Chief Wenisa. Shoulder-length black hair flew around his face. "Chief! Chief! I saw her first!"

Nesi studied the youth of perhaps fifteen summers. He had misshapen eyes and spoke like a simpleton. Tears streamed down his bucktoothed face to stain the front of his ragged deer hide shirt. His eyes glistened as though he'd seen Sky Woman herself descending from the clouds.

Wenisa sneered as though the youth was a well-known imbecile. "Get him away from me."

As two of Wenisa's personal guards grabbed the young warrior, he shouted, "She's coming! *She's coming!* Listen to me. I saw her in the forest. I was the first one!"

"Shut the fool up!" Wenisa shouted.

One of the guards clamped a hand over the warrior's mouth and dragged him off.

Someone must have called retreat. Mountain warriors fell back from the village, out of bowshot, and a curious sound—like eels coiling in mud—moved across the battlefield. It started slowly. As a mass, warriors turned to the north, then came bursts of low questions erupted.

Nesi followed their gazes.

Where trees disturbed the path of Hadui, a lilting symphony of whistles and shrieks answered back: the music of the windswept forest.

Only slowly did he become aware of her. She appeared standing in the deepest forest shadows. A tall figure, broad-shouldered for a woman, wearing a simple doe hide war shirt. Long black hair whipped around her beautiful face. Strangely eerie, the locks resembled black serpents striking at the air.

"Blessed Faces of the Forest," someone whispered.

As she started walking down the slope and across the meadow, her skin had an alabaster radiance. A huge wolf strode close at her side. Where they stepped, butterflies flitted from the warm grass and danced around them. The woman carried no bow or quiver, but her weapons belt glistened with light, the bone stilettos casting slender iridescent flashes.

Nesi shook his head, jimmied the images, the odd shadows. Her movements were so graceful she seemed to be floating, not tethered to the ground. It had to be a trick of light, that or he was dead and didn't know it. Perhaps he'd stepped out of his body into the world of the corpses that surrounded him.

Wenisa shifted to stare at her through his one good eye. "Who is that?"

One of his guards replied, "I...I think that's War Chief Baji from the People of the Flint. We fought against her two moons ago. She led the defense of Wild River Village."

No one loosed an arrow at her or the wolf. Her sudden appearance—or perhaps her beauty—had stilled every fighter on the field of battle.

She walked straight to the unconscious

Standing Stone Prophet and spread her feet as though ready to fight the world to defend him. Her expression was granite hard, her dark eyes brilliant with challenge. When the wolf lay down on the ground and began licking the Prophet's swollen cheek, murmurs passed through the guards. The animal whimpered softly.

As though the woman could have cared less that she was surrounded by enemies, she kneeled beside the Prophet.

"It's me," she softly said, then she sat down in the dry grass and gently drew his wounded head into her lap.

31

Baji smoothed the tear-soaked black hair from Dekanawida's cheeks. His purpled misshapen face was almost unrecognizable. His left eye had swollen closed, and his right eye was filled with milky fluid. Dried blood covered his shirt.

"Dekanawida?"

No answer.

Thunder rumbled in the distance, bringing the storm closer. Trees battered one another, and everything loose on the battlefield tumbled across the ground as though hurled by gigantic fists. Broken arrows and torn quivers cartwheeled by her.

"Dekanawida? Can you hear me?"

He roused slightly, then seemed to sink back into the oblivion that had swallowed him.

She stroked his short black hair. "I'm here. I'm right here beside you."

Barely audible, he said, "Baji?"

"Yes. I'm here. I'm not leaving you."

His lips twitched in what might have been an attempt at a smile.

Baji bent down to examine Dekanawida's milky eye. "Can you see anything? Can you see me?"

He whispered, "Clouds...just clouds."

She lightly pressed her lips to his. As she lifted her head, the whirling columns of insects that had, moments before, glistened at the edge of the trees, evaporated, and the birdsong faded away until it lay stone dead upon the forest.

The Thunderers rumbled again, and a brilliant flash of lightning lashed outward from the leading Cloud People to crackle white fire across the sky. The afterimage burned into her eyes was of a gigantic tree of light.

"Wr-wrass?" Dekanawida asked.

"He'll be here. You know he will."

"...Yes."

As the storm approached the air cooled, and the light shifted, flickering across the meadow in curious stripes. At first she thought it was just the leading edge of the clouds blotting Elder Brother Sun, then she noticed the butterflies in the grass, hiding themselves as though afraid.

Her heart started to pound. She murmured, "Dekanawida?"

As though Great Grandmother Earth had exhaled her last breath, the wind stopped. Just stopped. Conversations hummed as warriors turned to each other in confusion.

Baji's gaze darted around. *"Dekanawida? I think..."*

His fingers flexed, and he shifted in her lap as though feeling was coming back to his limbs. Upon his swollen face, she saw the sunlight turn from amber to an unearthly blue, and she lifted her eyes to the sky.

In the strange shadow-bands of light, Elder Brother Sun seemed to tremble, then a midnight abyss opened beside him, and slid forward, cutting a black hole in the universe.

Gasps and cries swept the meadow.

"It's the Dream!"

"Dear gods, it's happening...I told you it was true. I knew it!"

Every warrior lifted his face to the sky, and a low moan quavered on the air.

A sliver of Elder Brother Sun's face disappeared, then more, his light and warmth being sucked away into eternal darkness.

Gasps rose, followed by shrieks.

"Run...Run before it's too late!"

Mountain warriors started to throw down their

weapons. The clatter of a thousand quivers hitting the ground at once sounded like the sky splitting.

"I'm leaving!" One of Wenisa's guards pounded away.

Wenisa took a step backward, then another. Finally, he whirled and ran as hard as he could for the cover of the trees.

Atotarho and his guards stood gaping, as though too shocked to move as Elder Brother Sun fled the world.

Finally Nesi shouted, "Come on!" He grabbed Chief Atotarho, threw him over his shoulder, and sprinted away with his men behind him.

As soon as they entered the forest, a surprised roar went up, and Baji saw hundreds of warriors surrounding them. Their clan symbols were from both the Hills and Landing nations. Wenisa roared in outrage, and she saw him fighting the strong hands that held him.

Hiyawento appeared at the crest of the hill. Tall, his eyes blazing, he briefly studied the situation, then charged toward her, his long legs pumping.

With a stunningly brilliant flash, Elder Brother Sun vanished and white fire, *white feathers*, sprouted from his shoulders. His newborn wings fluttered wildly. He was flying away into the darkness...

"Baji?" Dekanawida weakly rolled to his knees. "Help me up."

As she carefully pulled his arm over her shoulder, she said, "Hiyawento's coming."

Dekanawida heaved a deep sigh, as though all was now as it should be.

Hiyawento tossed his bow to the ground, and said, "Let me help you."

Together, Baji and Hiyawento lifted Dekanawida onto his feet. "I can stand."

"No. No, you need me—"

"Back away, Baji," Hiyawento said. "He has to stand alone."

Reluctantly, she stepped back, leaving Dekanawida wobbling in the bizarre fluttering light. Gitchi leaped in front of Dekanawida with his fangs bared, daring anyone to try to hurt him.

On the verge of collapsing, Dekanawida stumbled and righted himself. When he'd managed to stiffen his knees, he sucked in a breath, and slowly lifted his arms as though to embrace the vanishing heavens themselves.

32
SKY MESSENGER

I fight to clear my vision. Images are jumbled. Like thin sheets of ice struck with a rock, everything appears shattered. Warriors are splintered shards of colors. Hiyawento could be made of fire-cracked quartz. Each angle of his face reflects the unnatural gleam differently. At my feet, Gitchi stands like a melting ice-sculpture dog, his shoulder blades sharp as knives.

The only thing whole in the entire world is Baji. To my right, she stands as a coherent woman-shaped shadow, a living shadow, moving, breathing. I long to reach out and touch her, but dare not move. My legs are shaking too badly. I don't know how long I can stand.

I let my head drop forward long enough to get a full breath into my lungs. Sounds and scents seem exaggerated. The cries on the battlefield surround me like soaring birds, flying about, puncturing the air. And the tears! The scent of tears claws at the back of my throat like a stone hand trying to find a way into my heart—a way to die a meaningful death.

I exhale hard before I tilt my face up to the sky.

In the center of the eerie blue background, a single black eye wavers, watching me. Huge and velvet.

"Please, Elder Brother, I beg you..."

My knees are about to buckle. I fight to keep them rigid as I stretch out my hands, and in a deep agonized voice, cry, *"No more! No more war!"*

In the distance, a deafening roar booms and rolls across the sky. The ground beneath my feet trembles. Then the blast comes. Blinding flashes sear my eyes as gigantic white roots split the Skyworld and crackle outward to the four directions.

Hundreds of warriors throw down their weapons and flee, abandoning the field of battle. The sound of frantic feet tripping over corpses strikes like fists.

...And I wait.

I wait for a voice. For a child to cry out. I have heard that suffocating little boy's voice so many times in my nightmares.

Hoarse breath tears my lungs.

It's growing darker as Elder Brother Sun flies farther and farther away, but I can't hold my arms up any longer. As I lower them to my sides, tears trickle from my wounded eyes and flow down my face.

Hiyawento suddenly shouts, *"Look!"*

My heart seems to stop when a blinding crescent of Elder Brother Sun's face reappears. As he steps from the abyss, white veils flutter, pouring down from the heavens. A man yells, *"Elder Brother Sun is turning his face back to the world!"*

I see it. The light in the darkness shines.

Something cold strikes my face.

Snow. Snow drifting down. Spinning flakes flash and dance around me like tumbling petals of pure light.

"Odion?" Hiyawento points.

The gates of Bur Oak Village are thrown open. People rush out carrying clan flags. As the carriers weave across the meadow, cheering at the tops of their lungs, their lines furl and unfurl like dark tines raking through a sea of white.

Hiyawento reverently whispers, "I finally understand. Gods, Odion, I understand."

From the southern hills beyond the old sunflower fields, women, children, and elders flood down the slopes and onto the battlefield. Sobs of joy and cheers shred the cold air. I know that accent. They are Landing People.

As my knees shudder, and give way, my vision sparkles.

Both Baji and Hiyawento lunge to grab me, but I fall...and fall...landing without a word in the glistening blanket of new-fallen snow.

33

That night, Baji sat around a campfire to the east of Bur Oak Village, listening to the stunningly beautiful cries echoing across the moonlit hills. It was as though the very fabric of the air was woven of long drawn-out howls, melodic hooting, and the shrill calls of plummeting eagles. For the first time since Atotarho's ambush on her war party, the cries were unbearable. They created an ache of longing in her soul like nothing she had ever known, and she knew at last that such beauty could not possibly exist in this world.

She looked around the fire. The most important people in her life were here—except for Cord, Jigonsaseh, and Zateri. As they talked, her heart thumped painfully. To her right, next to the warm flames, Dekanawida lay on a litter beneath a pile of hides. Jigonsaseh had ordered that he be taken to one of the warm longhouses, but he had refused, saying he had to be out among the people where they could see him and know that he had not been killed.

For many hands of time, the line of awestruck people had passed by him, reverently looking down, whispering gratefully to him, then moving on to allow others to see.

Finally, at dusk, they'd gathered in the meadow below, where they danced around dozens of great fires, singing and laughing with joy.

Scents of roasting venison and acorn bread wafted on the cold breeze. It was as though not a single person doubted the war was over, and with the burden gone, their happiness overflowed. Most of their songs were about the Creator and Sky Woman. Rumors had already begun to filter across the camps that Dekanawida was the returned soul of Sapling, and Jigonsaseh was Sky Woman herself. Within a moon, Baji suspected everyone south of Skanodario Lake would believe it...and even unknown peoples far beyond.

She looked down at Dekanawida's swollen face. In the firelight, the purple bruises had a bluish-orange tint. It comforted her to see him. He was still here. Still alive...after all the horrors they had lived through together. If only she could lie at his side with her arms around him, watching his breath rise and fall, absorbing every small movement of his body, while the long summers etched the lines deeper into his face, her life would be perfect. During the long periods when they had not seen each other—she had lived in fear that he would vanish as her parents and sisters had vanished. The terror had tormented her dreams.

And now...now...

She reached beneath his hides to squeeze his warm hand and sighed.

Across the fire, Towa and Sindak carried on a quiet conversation with Gonda and Hiyawento. To Gonda's left, Tutelo listened. Occasionally, Tutelo's young daughters asked her some question. Baji barely noticed when a messenger arrived from the darkness requesting to speak with Sindak, and he rose and walked away.

She concentrated on stroking Dekanawida's hand. He'd been drifting from consciousness to unconsciousness throughout the night. Each time he opened his milky eye, he gave her a faint smile, and glanced down to make certain that Gitchi still slept on the soft blanket at the bottom of his litter. The old wolf always wagged his tail when Dekanawida woke and looked at him. As Dekanawida sank into sleep again, Gitchi's luminous gaze returned to Baji, and his heart shone out of his eyes, as hers did when she looked at him.

Sindak returned to the fire, and said, "That messenger was from the Ruling Council of the reunited Hills nation. They ordered Negano to use his forces to help us. He was so thankful I thought he was going to faint. His warriors now consider him a great hero."

Gonda replied, "I'm sure he thought he was going to be executed as a traitor...along with you."

"He wasn't the only one who thought that," Sindak replied. "Gods, I hope the Landing People join us."

Towa's long braid sawed across his cape as he turned to stare at Sindak in disbelief. "Are you joking? Of course, they will join us. Look at the Landing People below! Once Sky Messenger's followers return to Shookas Village and tell their stories of what happened today, how can they refuse?"

Sindak paused as though wondering. "Do you think the same will be true of the Mountain People?"

There was a moment of rustling shirts and shifting feet as they all turned to look northward to where Chief Atotarho and Chief Wenisa were being held in a heavily guarded camp. A small spruce-bough structure had been thrown up beside a campfire. Guards passed back and forth in front of the flames.

Gonda said, "I know Sky Messenger ordered that we release both chiefs, but I plan to spend some time talking to them before we do that."

Towa added, "I'm no longer worried about Atotarho. High Matron Zateri and the Ruling Council will tend to him. But Wenisa is another question, I—"

"He won't be a problem," Hiyawento said. His eyes still glistened. A strange peace had come over him. "It will be the same thing as with the Landing People. By the time he gets back to his village, his warriors will have been there for a full day telling their stories. The Mountain People's Ruling Council will have already made up its mind."

They all went silent, staring at the fire. Tutelo's youngest daughter, perhaps five summers, whispered something to her, and Tutelo kissed the little girl's head and hugged her.

"Baji?" Dekanawida breathed her name, and exhaled a shallow breath.

"I'm right here. I've been here all along." Baji laced her fingers with his, and a sensation of contentment filtered through her. He weakly squeezed her hand back.

"...I know."

Hiyawento saw them speaking, and said, "Baji,

ask Sky Messenger if he's hungry or thirsty. We have plenty..."

A commotion suddenly rose from below. People ran across the meadow, and the singing stopped. Curious voices rose to replace it. Someone shouted. From the east, a large party, perhaps five hundred warriors, trotted into the firelight. Near the front, four warriors carried a man on a litter.

"Is that Chief Cord?" Hiyawento asked.

Baji's gaze longingly clung to her father as he was carried toward Bur Oak Village.

Gonda said, "Yes, it's the Flint war party. Let's go greet them. The Ruling Council is going to ask Cord to address the entire village."

He'll tell the story of the ambush at Rocky Meadows.

Baji's hands trembled.

Out in the trees the lonesome howls and the drumming of partridge wings were growing stronger, getting closer. Somewhere very near, just beyond the circle of firelight, deer hooves crackled through piles of old leaves, kneading the ground as though anxious to be on their way.

Dekanawida seemed to sense her tension. He opened his right eye, and peered up at her through the milky haze. As she leaned over him, making sure he could see her, her long black hair tumbled around his face. In the firelight, his eyes had a sheen like tears. "Not yet...please...stay?"

She blinked down through suddenly blurry eyes. "Do you hear them?"

"I've heard them...off and on...all day."

Baji's throat ached as she bent down to press her lips to his.

Across the fire, Sindak and Towa rose to their feet. Through her hazy vision, they seemed to swim in the firelight. Gonda, Tutelo, and her daughters rose as well. Their gazes remained on the Flint war party, studying it as it wound through the camps. Cord's litter bearers carried him through the Bur Oak gates, where he disappeared.

"We'll meet you there," Gonda said. He and Tutelo, with children trailing behind them, started down the hill toward the village.

Sindak said, "Towa, why don't you take the bottom of Sky Messenger's litter. I'll grab the top."

They walked forward, and Baji backed away. They carefully lifted the litter and started to carry it down to the village.

"Wait...wait!" Dekanawida's hand extended from beneath the hides, blindly reaching for Baji.

Hiyawento came around the fire, frowning. "What's wrong?"

Sindak and Towa had confused looks on their faces, but they stopped. Baji walked forward, grasped his hand between both of her palms, and squeezed hard. "I'm still here."

He forced his left eye open a slit to look at her

with both eyes. She'd seen that same look the night they'd been rescued outside of Bog Willow Village. Koracoo had told Odion that Wrass would not be meeting them at Fire Cherry Camp, as he'd promised, because he'd been recaptured by Ganna-jero. Odion's high-pitched little boy scream of "*No!*" still rang in Baji's ears.

He whispered, "I'm sorry...I'm sorry."

"You have nothing to be sorry for. You saved me so many times."

"...kept you...too long."

"No, no, you didn't."

Hiyawento walked around the litter to stand beside Baji and gaze into her eyes. "What's he talking about?"

"He's delirious. That's all. His fever is very high."

Sindak shifted the weight of the litter, indicating they were ready to head back to the village.

Baji squeezed Dekanawida's hand one last time and bent to whisper in his ear, "I'll see you soon," then she kissed him and forced herself to back away from the litter.

Hiyawento gave her a strange look. "Coming, Baji?"

"I'll be along shortly. Tell my father not to worry about me. Tell him I'm all right."

Hiyawento nodded and followed several paces

behind Sindak and Towa as they started down the slope.

In ten heartbeats, Baji was alone. She watched Dekanawida's litter travel through the middle of the celebration. As he passed, people gently ran their hands down the side-rails, or reverently touched his blankets. Several fell into line behind the litter and followed it through the Bur Oak gates into the village.

She didn't realize until he nosed her hand that Gitchi had remained at her side. Baji looked down and found the old wolf gazing up at her with hurt yellow eyes. As she scratched his ears, Gitchi sat on his haunches and leaned heavily against her leg, as though he would never leave her.

"Want to run with me for a little way?"

Gitchi stood up, hesitantly turned to look at the village, at the place where Dekanawida had been taken, then whined.

They started out at a slow pace, trotting through the camps until they hit the trail that led westward. In swift silence they wound through the snowy woods, their footsteps barely audible. Shining owl eyes watched them, and wolves yipped when they glimpsed them passing through the striped moon-shadows.

Every step increased the mysterious euphoria that possessed her.

On the opposite side of the valley, the forest

grew thicker, the trees taller, and frozen acorns scattered the trail like small rocks. She was wildly happy, running with Gitchi faithfully loping at her side.

When she crested the hill, a herd of four deer, all bucks, came into view idly grazing in the silvered gleam. Their antlers shone when they lifted their heads to look up at Baji and Gitchi.

She studied them, only mildly afraid, then knelt beside Gitchi to stare into his beautiful old face. Rings of white hair encircled his worried eyes. She hugged his big body against her chest, and held him for a long time, stroking his back. "I suspect I'll see you first. I'll be waiting for you at the bridge, old friend."

When she released him and rose, she pointed to Bur Oak Village. "Now. Go find Dekanawida."

Gitchi cocked his head, as though trying to understand why she didn't want him.

"You have to guard him for me, Gitchi. He needs you."

Gitchi whimpered and backed up, but refused to leave her.

"Go on now," she said gently. "You have to go home. Please, go home."

Finally, he loped down the hillside, but he kept glancing back at her. Several times he looked like he might disobey her and charge back to her side.

She waited until he disappeared over the crest of the hill, then she slowly turned back to the deer.

They'd started frolicking, kicking up their heels, playfully tossing their antlers.

She clenched her fists and walked toward them.

From somewhere behind her, Gitchi let out a soul-rending howl that echoed through the stillness...but his agonized voice grew fainter and fainter, until it blended with the many-voiced cry that serenaded the brilliant darkness.

34

So many people had crowded in front of Hiyawento that he'd fallen far behind Sindak and Towa. But he was in no hurry. It seemed that everyone wished to hear Chief Cord. The gathering in the plaza had spilled outside the gates and flowed around the palisade. Cord was being bombarded with questions. In another one or two hands of time, things would settle down, and Hiyawento would get his chance to speak with Cord personally.

Hiyawento turned and walked out away from the camps into the moonlight that streamed across the forest. He could faintly hear Cord's voice rising over the Bur Oak palisade, and warmth spread through him. Every man had heroes in his life, and so many of his were here tonight, Cord among them.

He tilted his head back to look up at the night sky. The Path of Souls had dimmed with Grand-mother Moon's rising, but he could make out its shape. His gaze unconsciously fixed on the fork in the Path where it was said that all the animals a man had ever known in his life waited at the bridge that led from this life to the next. He wondered...

A hushed roar went up in the village. What had Cord said? He was probably telling the story of how he and Baji were ambushed after they left Bur Oak Village. It must have been exciting. The roar grew louder before it faded, and Cord's voice rang out again.

Hiyawento bowed his head, just standing in the darkness, trying not to think or feel. The day had drained him of both abilities.

From the corner of his eye, he saw Gitchi come out of the trees to the west. The old wolf walked through the moonlight with his head down, his muzzle hanging so low it almost touched the snow-covered ground. His shoulders rolled as though every step hurt.

Hiyawento walked out across the field to meet the wolf. When Gitchi spied Hiyawento, he looked up at him with sad eyes.

"Gitchi? Are you all right? Where's Baji?"

Gitchi's ears pricked at her name, then he walked forward and slumped down at Hiyawento's feet with a deep sigh.

Hiyawento frowned. "What's wrong?" He sat down beside Gitchi and ruffled the thick fur on the wolf's neck. "Everything's all right."

Gitchi lifted his gray muzzle, whimpered, and stretched his neck across Hiyawento's lap. The wolf's luminous eyes seemed to be staring mournfully up at the night sky where the Path of Souls shimmered.

As he petted Gitchi's side, Hiyawento thought about Zateri and Kahn-Tineta. He missed them desperately. In a few days, once they'd collected their dead and helped the Standing Stone nation Sing their relatives to the Land of the Dead, he would accompany the war party that carried Atotarho home to face the Ruling Council. Before they entered the village, Hiyawento would comb the snakes from the old chief's hair. Symbols of war were no longer...

"*I don't believe it,*" Taya shouted as she exited the village with Sindak. "Everyone saw her. People touched her!"

Hiyawento frowned. She sounded distraught.

Sindak touched Taya's arm, then swiftly strode out across the meadow, vaguely heading toward Hiyawento.

When he got closer, he called, "Hiyawento? Is that you?"

"Yes, I'm over here."

Sindak stopped two paces away, and shifted

uncomfortably. "I don't know how to...how to tell you...I...please, you have to come. Cord needs to speak with you."

"I thought he was busy telling stories. I was going to wait—"

"He wants to speak with you *now*. We've all told him our stories, but he wishes to hear it from you. You have to come."

Gitchi heaved a sigh, and shoved to his feet with a groan. He knew the word "come."

Hiyawento rose and dusted the snow from his pants. "Wishes to hear what from me?" Gitchi took a few moments to lovingly lick his hand and lean against his leg. Hiyawento petted his head.

Sindak said, "Just...come with me."

"Lead the way. We'll need to go slow, though. Gitchi's bones really hurt tonight."

35

SKY MESSENGER
MOON OF NEW FAWNS

Dogwood blossoms tumble through the fragrant late afternoon air, whirling around Wrass where he stands beside me on the hilltop to the south of Bur Oak Village. Brilliant green maples surround us, filtering the sunlight that falls through the canopy. Wavering yellow diamonds flutter across the forest floor at our feet. I wonder if he has the same aching hollow inside him that I do. It's been a long day, one that has been long in coming.

Thousands fill the meadow below, commemorating the last great battle in a war that almost destroyed our Peoples. Far to my right, just at the crest of the hills, Shagoniyoh stands with one hand braced upon a boulder. He hasn't spoken to me, and I fear that he thinks, as of today, I no longer need him.

A shout goes up from below.

As the clans parade across the lush wildflower-strewn meadow toward the deep hole we've dug beneath the old pine tree, Hiyawento says, "I can't believe that all five nations joined the Peace Alliance. I swear it's the greatest miracle in the history of our Peoples."

My eyes tighten. I do not answer, because I can't find any words that have meaning. For thirteen summers, he has stood behind me like a stone wall in the bitter campaign for survival—always there, always fighting for me with blind loyalty. But...after today, there will be no more fighting. I suspect part of my emptiness comes from the fact that I don't know how to face a world without war. I have never seen one. Nor has anyone in the meadow below.

I squint at the gathering.

The last representatives come forward. They wear their best clothing, heavily painted with bright clan symbols. When it is his or her turn, the chosen one reverently places weapons in the hole, submerging them in the river of Great Grandmother Earth's blood that rushes beneath the ground, cleansing them of the taint of death.

I heave a sigh and unconsciously reach down to pat Gitchi's head. The old wolf stands beside me with his ears pricked, listening attentively.

Mother is the final representative. She stands at the head of the Bear Clan, beside her new husband,

Cord, wearing a white ritual cape painted with black bear tracks. When she walks forward and places CorpseEye on top of the cache of weapons, I wonder what she must be thinking. CorpseEye has saved her life many times...he is an old and dear friend. The war club has been a part of her family, handed down from warrior to warrior, for generations. But she understands the symbolism.

No more war...

As he straightens, Shagoniyoh's black cape catches my attention. I turn in time to see him stride away into the trees where he melts with the shadows.

Have I done something? Has he forsaken me? Perhaps it's just that others need him more now. I pray that someday he will show me where his bones lie so that I can collect them and Sing his soul to the next world. He deserves to be released from this earth. His loved ones in the Land of the Dead have been waiting for him too long.

When the ceremony below is over, Gitchi rises to his feet and silently trots away up the trail that leads westward, and I realize it's time. Elder Brother Sun sits just above the western horizon.

"Where's Gitchi going?" Hiyawento asks.

"To his special place. I usually run with him. Do you want to come along?"

"I do."

We trot side by side, following Gitchi, who lopes

in front with his tongue hanging out. The forest scents strike me like blows today, moss and deadfall warmed in the dappled sunlight, dogwood and wildflower blossoms. Ferns sway as Gaha silently creeps beneath the trees.

"Today is a day of great joy, yet you look sad, my friend."

I smile faintly and study the ground passing beneath my feet. When I turn to look at him, he's frowning at me in concern. His shoulder-length black hair jerks with the beat of his feet, and sweat shines on his eagle face. I have not seen Hiyawento without a weapons belt, bow or quiver, since we were eleven summers. It must feel odd not to have the weight around his waist. My gaze drops to his hands and lingers on the missing tip of his finger—sawn off by Gannajero long ago.

"Not sad, Wrass. I think it's just…loneliness."

We wind through the growing shadows, our moccasins quiet on the trail. Ahead, Gitchi enters a grove of ancient oaks that cast gigantic wavering shadows. The old wolf slows to a walk, as though the cool air feels good on his gray coat, and he wants to absorb it before he enters the small clearing where sunlight sheathes every blade of grass and nodding wildflower.

"He comes here every day," I explain.

Hiyawento frowns. "Why?"

We follow Gitchi out into the center of the

meadow where he lies down and braces his white muzzle on his forepaws, watching. Just watching the meadow.

"I first noticed he was doing this right after my head wound began to heal. Every afternoon, he was gone. Finally, I followed him. He came here, stretched out, and watched the meadow until darkness fell. Then he came home."

"What's he doing?"

"I'm not sure. I think...I think this is the last place he saw her. I think he's waiting for her to come back to him."

As I am.

Hiyawento puts a companionable hand on my shoulder. Only Hiyawento, who knew her and loved her, can understand that this one single act of an old grieving wolf rends my heart like nothing else.

"I believe there is a bridge, Odion. I believe Gitchi will be waiting for you on this side, to help you across, and she will run to meet you on the other side."

As evening slowly descends around us, the trees drip dampness. A soft pattering fills the forest.

I listen to it and watch Gitchi. He hasn't moved. His shining yellow eyes monitor the meadow.

"I'm going to sit with him until he's ready to go," I say. "You don't have to stay. I know Zateri and Kahn-Tineta are waiting for you back in the village. Everyone will be feasting. The Songs and storytelling have probably already begun."

Hiyawento grips my shoulder hard. "I want to sit with him, too."

Together, we walk out across the meadow, and sit down on either side of the old wolf who waits so patiently, his eyes filled with unbearable longing.

AUTHORS' NOTE

Some of the Peacemaker stories say that in the end, Atotarho submitted to Hiyawento and let him comb the snakes from his hair. When Hiyawento had finished, the evil cannibal-sorcerer transformed before his eyes. The Chief's lost soul returned, his crooked body straightened out, and his heart turned toward reason and compassion. For the rest of his life, Atotarho was a good and just leader who dedicated himself to implementing Dekanawida's message of peace. The Great Council Fire of the League of the Haudenosaunee is still safely kept in the land of the Onondaga.

A LOOK AT: PEOPLE OF THE OWL
THE EARLIEST AMERICANS
BOOK ONE

New York Times bestselling authors W. Michael Gear and Kathleen O'Neal Gear masterfully bring to life an ancient America, long forgotten in the mists of time, yet strikingly relevant in today's world.

Four Thousand years ago, in the lower Mississippi Valley, a civilization thrived that would lay the foundations of the great Indian Nations. In a long-lost land of forests, swamps, and hidden waterways, A boy is thrust into leadership of America's first city, forced to become a man before his time.

Salamander, only fifteen winters old, would rather chase crickets and marvel at blue herons than navigate the treacherous politics of his clan. But when his revered brother is slain, Salamander is thrust into the role of leader in what will one day be known as the American South's first city.

Burdened with the legacy of his brother's two wives—who despise him—and a marriage to the daughter of his mortal enemy, Salamander must forge alliances to secure the trade goods his people need to survive. Yet, in a world where enemies lurk in every shadow, and assassins strike without warning, Salamander must grow from boy to man, and from a reluctant leader to a formidable one.

Can Salamander navigate the brutal landscape of ancient politics and emerge as the leader his people need? Or will the passions of the human heart devour him before he can claim his destiny?

AVAILABLE NOVEMBER 2024

ABOUT W. MICHAEL GEAR

W. Michael Gear is a *New York Times, USA Today,* and international bestselling author of sixty novels. With close to eighteen million copies of his books in print worldwide, his work has been translated into twenty-nine languages.

Gear has been inducted into the Western Writers Hall of Fame and the Colorado Authors' Hall of Fame—as well as won the Owen Wister Award, the Golden Spur Award, and the International Book Award for both Science Fiction and Action Suspense Fiction. He is also the recipient of the Frank Waters Award for lifetime contributions to Western writing.

Gear's work, inspired by anthropology and archaeology, is multilayered and has been called compelling, insidiously realistic, and masterful. Currently, he lives in northwestern Wyoming with his award-winning wife and co-author, Kathleen O'Neal Gear, and a charming sheltie named, Jake.

ABOUT KATHLEEN
O'NEAL GEAR

Kathleen O'Neal Gear is a *New York Times* bestselling author of fifty-seven books and a national award-winning archaeologist. The U.S. Department of the Interior has awarded her two Special Achievement awards for outstanding management of America's cultural resources.

In 2015 the United States Congress honored her with a Certificate of Special Congressional Recognition, and the California State Legislature passed Joint Member Resolution #117 saying, "The contributions of Kathleen O'Neal Gear to the fields of history, archaeology, and writing have been invaluable..."

In 2021 she received the Owen Wister Award for lifetime contributions to western literature, and in 2023 received the Frank Waters Award for "a body of work representing excellence in writing and storytelling that embodies the spirit of the American West."

GLOSSARY

Flying Heads—Just heads with no bodies that thrash wildly through the forests. These fearsome creatures have long trailing hair and great paws like a bear's.

Gaha—The soft wind. She is spoken of as Elder Sister Gaha.

Gahai—Spectral lights that guide sorcerers as they fly through the air on their evil journeys. Sometimes gahai lead their masters to victims, other times to places where they can find charms.

Hadui—A violent wind.

Hanehwa—Skin-beings. Witches sometimes skin their victims, enchant their skins, and force them to do their bidding. Hanehwa warn witches of danger by giving three shouts.

Hatho—The Frost Spirit.

Haudenosaunee—The People of the Longhouse, called "Iroquois" by the French.

Ohwachira—The basic family unit. An ohwachira is a kinship group that traces its descent from a common female ancestor. The ohwachira bestows chieftainship titles, and holds the names of the great people of the past. It bestows those names by raising up the souls of the dead and requickening them in the bodies of newly elected chiefs, adoptees, or other people. In the same way, if a new chief disappoints the ohwachira, after consultation with the clan, it can take back the name, remove the soul, and depose the chief. It is also the sisterhood of ohwachiras that decides when to go to war and when to make peace.

Otkon—One of the two halves of Spirit Power that inhabit the world. The other is Uki. Don't think of these as good and evil, however. Both powers share equally in light and dark. Otkon and Uki form a unified spiritual universe that must be kept in balance. Otkon has a trickster-like character. It's unpredictable and can be either beneficial or harmful to human beings. It's half of the day lasts from noon to midnight. Otkon is often associated with the Evil-Minded One, the hero twin also known as Flint.

People of the Flint—The Mohawk nation. However, the word *Mohawk* is an Algonquian term meaning "flesh eaters." They call themselves the Kanienkahaka, or Ganienkeh, meaning "People of the Flint."

People of the Hills—The Onondaga nation. The word *Onondaga* is an anglicized version of their name for themselves, *Onundagaono*, which means "People of the Hills."

People of the Landing—The Cayuga nation. Including People of the Landing, several other possible derivations have been offered for the word *Cayuga*, including "People of the Place Where Locusts Were Taken Out," "People of the Mucky Land," and "People of the Place Where Boats Are Taken Out."

People of the Mountain—The Seneca nation. They call themselves the *Onondowahgah*. Their name can also be translated as "People of the Great Hill."

People of the Standing Stone—The Oneida nation. The word *Oneida* may be a rather poor Anglicization of their name for themselves, *Onayotekaono*, meaning "Granite People," or "People of the Standing Stone."

Requickening Ceremony—The raising up of souls for the purpose of placing them in other bodies, such as those of adoptees. This concept does not exactly correspond to the eastern religions' concept of reincarnation. For example, there's no idea of karma to be accounted for. Being reborn is neither punishment, nor reward. Instead, there is a strong concept of duty to the People. Only strong souls were requickened, usually within the same maternal lineage. The ceremony was performed in the hopes of easing grief and restoring the spiritual strength of the clans, but a returning soul also had an obligation to help the People in times of crises. Many "Keepings" of the Peacemaker story say that Dekanawida was the returned soul of Tarenyawagon—also Tarachiawagon, the culture hero also known as Sapling, the Good-Minded One, who served as the Creator. Those same traditions identify Atotarho as Sapling's troublesome younger brother, Flint—Tawiscaro/Tawiscaron—who was called the Evil-Minded One. Jigonsaseh, similarly, was sometimes identified as the returned soul of Sky Woman's daughter, the Lynx.

Uki—One of the two halves of Spirit Power that inhabit the world—see *Otkon*. Uki is never harmful to human beings. It's half of the day lasts from midnight to noon. Uki is often associated with the Good-Minded One, the hero twin also known as Sapling, or Tarenyawagon.

SELECTED BIBLIOGRAPHY

Bruchac, Joseph. *Iroquois Stories: Heroes and Heroines, Monsters and Magic*. Freedom, CA: The Crossing Press, 1985.

Calloway, Colin G. *The Western Abenakis of Vermont, 1600-1800*. Norman: University of Oklahoma Press, 1990.

Converse, Harriet Maxwell. "Origin of the Wampum Belt" and "The Legendary Origin of Wampum." In *Myths and Legends of New York State Iroquois*, New York State Museum Bulletin 125, edited by Arthur Caswell Parker, 138-145 and 187-190. Albany: University of the State of New York, 1908.

Custer, Jay F. *Delaware Prehistoric Archaeology: An Ecological Approach*. Cranberry, NJ: Associated University Presses, 1984.

Dye, David H. *War Paths, Peace Paths: An Archaeology of Cooperation and Conflict in Native Eastern North America*. Lanham, MD: Altamira Press, 2009.

Ellis, Chris J., and Neal Ferris, eds. *The Archaeology of Southern Ontario to A.D. 1650*. London, Ontario, Canada: Occasional Papers of the London Chapter, OAS Number 5, 1990.

Elm, Demus, and Harvey Antone. *The Oneida Creation Story*. Lincoln: University of Nebraska, 2000.

Engelbrecht, William E. *Iroquoia: The Development of a Native World*. Syracuse University Press, 2003.

Fagan, Brian M. *Ancient North America: The Archaeology of a Continent*. 4th ed. London: Thames and Hudson Press, 2005.

Fenton, William N. *The False Faces of the Iroquois*. Norman: University of Oklahoma Press, 1987.

--. *The Iroquois Eagle Dance: An Offshoot of the Calumet Dance.* Syracuse: Syracuse University Press, 1991.

--. *The Roll Call of the Iroquois Chiefs. A Study of a Pneumonic Cane from the Six Nations Reserve.* Cranbook Institute of Science, Bulletin No. 30, 1950.

Foster, Steven, and James A. Duke. *Eastern/Central Medicinal Plants.* The Peterson Guides Series. Boston: Houghton Mifflin Company, 1990.

Hart, John P., and Christina B. Rieth, eds. *Northeast Subsistence-Settlement Change: A.D. 700-1300,* New York State Museum Bulletin 496. Albany: University of the State of New York, 2002.

Heckewelder, John. *History, Manners, and Customs of the Indian Nations Who Once Inhabited Pennsylvania and the Neighboring States.* New York: Arno Press, 1971.

Herrick, James W. *Iroquois Medical Botany.* Syracuse: Syracuse University Press, 1995.

Hewitt, J. N. B. "The Iroquoian Concept of the Soul." *Journal of American Folklore,* 8 (1895): 107-116.

--. "Orenda and a Definition of Religion." *American Anthropologist,* N.S., 4 (1902): 33-46.

--. "Status of Woman in Iroquois Polity before 1784." In *Annual Report of the Board of Regents,* 475-488. Washington, D.C.: Smithsonian Institution, 1933.

--. Wampum." In *Handbook of North American Indians North of Mexico,* 904-909. New York: Rowman and Littlefield, 1965.

Jemison, Pete. "Mother of Nations: The Peace Queen, a Neglected Tradition." *Akwe:kon* 5 (1988): 68-70.

Jennings, Francis. *The Ambiguous Iroquois Empire.* New York: W. W. Norton, 1984.

Jennings, Francis, ed. *The History and Culture of Iroquois Diplomacy.* Syracuse University Press, 1995.

Johansen, Bruce Elliot, and Barbara Alice Mann. *Encyclopedia of the Haudenosaunee (Iroquois Confederacy).* Westport, CT: Greenwood Press, 2000.

Kapches, Mima. "Intra-Longhouse Spatial Analysis." *Pennsylvania Archaeologist*, 49, No. 4 (December 1979): 24-29.

Kurath, Gertrude P. *Iroquois Music and Dance: Ceremonial Arts of Two Seneca Longhouses.* Smithsonian Institution, Bureau of American Ethnology, Bulletin 187. Washington, D.C.: U.S. Government Printing Office, 1964.

Levine, Mary Ann, Kenneth E. Sassaman, and Michael S. Nassaney, eds. *The Archaeological Northeast.* Westport, CT: Bergin and Garvey, 1999.

Mann, Barbara A., and Jerry L. Fields. "The Fire at Onondaga: Wampum as Proto-writing." *Akwesasne Notes* (1995): 40-48.

--. *Iroquoian Women: Gantowisas of the Haudenosaunee League.* New York: Peter Lang, 2000.

--. "A Sign in the Sky: Dating the League of the Haudenosaunee." The Wampum Chronicles, www.wampumchronicles.com/signinthesky.html.

Martin, Calvin. *Keepers of the Game: Indian-Animal Relationships and the Fur Trade.* Berkeley: University of California Press, 1978.

Mensforth, Robert P. "Human Trophy Taking in Eastern North America During the Archaic Period: The Relationship to Warfare and Social Complexity." Chap. 9 in *The Taking and Displaying of Human Body Parts as Trophies by Amerindians,* edited by Richard J. Chacon and David Dye. New York: Springer, 2007.

Miroff, Laurie E., and Timothy D. Knapp. *Iroquoian Archaeology and Analytic Scale.* Knoxville: University of Tennessee Press, 2009.

Morgan, Lewis Henry. *League of the Iroquois.* New York: Corinth Books, 1962.

Mullen, Grant J., and Robert D. Hoppa. "Rogers Ossuary (AgHb-131): An Early Ontario Iroquois Burial Feature from Brantford Township." *The Canadian Journal of Archaeology/ Journal Canadien d'Archeologie* 16, (1992).

Murray, David. *Forked Tongues: Speech, Writing, and Representation in North American Indian Texts.* Bloomington: Indiana University Press, 1991.

O'Callaghan, E. B., ed. *The Documentary History of the State of New York.* 4 vols. Albany: Weed, Parsons and Co., 1849-1851.

Parker, Arthur C. *Iroquois Uses of Maize and Other Food Plants,* New York State Museum Bulletin 144. Albany: University of the State of New York, 1910.

--. *Seneca Myths and Folk Tales.* Lincoln: University of Nebraska Press, 1989.

--, writing as Gawasco Wanneh. *An Analytical History of the Seneca Indians,* 1926. Researches and Transactions of the New York State Archeological Association, Lewis H. Morgan Chapter. New York: Kraus Reprint Co., 1970.

Parker, Arthur C. ed. *Myths and Legends of the New York State Iroquois,* New York State Museum Bulletin 125, 138-145 and 187-190. Albany: University of the State of New York, 1908.

Richter, Daniel. *The Ordeal of the Longhouse: The People of the Iroquois League in the Era of European Colonization.* Chapel Hill: University of North Carolina Press, 1992.

Scheiber, Laura L., and Mark D. Mitchell, eds. *Across a Great Divide: Continuity and Change in Native North American Societies, 1400-1900.* Tucson: University of Arizona Press, 2010.

Slotkin, J. S., and Karl Schmitt. "Studies of Wampum." *American Anthropologist* 51 (1949): 223-236.

Snow, Dean. *The Archaeology of New England.* New York: Academic Press, 1980.

--. *The Iroquois.* Oxford: Blackwell, 1996.

Snyderman, George S. "The Function of Wampum in Iroquois

Religion." *Proceedings of the American Philosophical Society* (1961): 571-608.

Spittal, W. G. *Iroquois Women: An Anthology.* Ohsweken, ON: Iroqrafts, Ltd., 1990.

Talbot, Francis Xavier. *Saint Among the Hurons: The Life of Jean De Brebeuf.* New York: Harper and Brothers, 1949.

Tehanetorens. *Wampum Belts of the Iroquois.* Summertown, TN: Book Publishing Company, 1999.

Tooker, Elizabeth, ed. *Iroquois Culture, History, and Prehistory.* Albany: University of the State of New York, 1967.

Trigger, Bruce. *The Children of Aataentsic: A History of the Huron People to 1660.* Montreal: McGill-Queen's University Press, 1987.

Trigger, Bruce, ed. *Handbook of North American Indians, Vol. 15: Northeast.* Washington, D.C.: Smithsonian Institution Press, 1978.

Tuck, James A. *Onondaga Iroquois Prehistory: A Study in Settlement Archaeology.* Syracuse: Syracuse University Press, 1971.

Wallace, Anthony F. C. *The Death and Rebirth of the Seneca.* New York: Vintage Books, 1972.

Walthall, John A., and Thomas E. Emerson, eds. *Calumet and Fleur-de-Lys: Archaeology of the Indian and French Contact in the Midcontinent.* Washington, D.C.: Smithsonian Institution Press, 1992.

Weer, Paul. *Preliminary Notes on the Iroquoian Family.* Prehistory Research Series. Indianapolis: Indiana Historical Society, 1937.

Whitehead, Ruth Holmes. *Stories from the Six Worlds: Micmac Legends.* Halifax: Nimbus Publishing, 1988. Williamson, Ronald F., and Susan Pfeiffer. *Bones of the Ancestors: The Archaeology and Osteobiography of the Moatfield Ossuary.* Gatineau, Quebec: Canadian Museum of Civilization, 2003.

www.ingramcontent.com/pod-product-compliance
Lightning Source LLC
Chambersburg PA
CBHW011026260626
47153CB00020B/2926